the Belonging

Someone of Substance

BOOK THREE

PD JANZEN

THE BELONGING

Printed in Canada

ISBN: 978-1-4866-2188-0
eBook ISBN: 978-1-4866-2189-7

Word Alive Press
119 De Baets Street Winnipeg, MB R2J 3R9
www.wordalivepress.ca

Cataloguing in Publication information can be obtained from Library and Archives Canada.

I lovingly dedicate this book to my mother, Doris Peters. As she will admit, she's not a perfect person, but in the middle of her often-difficult circumstances, she taught me about the unwavering love of a heavenly Father who has been my great joy and strength. Because of this I owe her a deep and heartfelt thank you.

I love you, Mom.

Prologue

SEPTEMBER 1979

HELEN HAD ESCAPED YOUTH GROUP AGAIN TO SECRETLY MEET UP WITH JACK. She had almost reached the corner of the street where they'd agreed to meet when she spotted his sister walking alone beside the road. The little girl didn't look worried, and Helen suspected this had happened many times before. Jack was at the local greasy spoon in town where he worked part-time. Helen wondered if he'd be mad that they wouldn't be able to be alone, since his sister was there. Helen had never seen Jack get mad before, but she had only known him for a few months.

"You like my brother, don't you?" asked Annie, looking up at Helen from where they sat waiting on the curb at the side of the road.

Helen smiled down at Jack's little sister. "I do," she admitted, her face flushing.

"I knew it," smiled Annie, clearly proud of her young knowledge. "He likes you too, you know," she added, as if sharing a deep secret.

Helen's blush deepened as she looked away from the little girl beside her.

"I'm glad he does," Annie stated with the simple honesty children aren't shy to voice. "You're nice and ... not everyone is."

Annie's countenance changed then, and Helen suddenly felt an ache where her heart was. She wondered what Annie had seen or experienced to make her sound so knowledgeable about such things.

"How old are you, Annie?" asked Helen, wondering if Jack had ever told her.

"I'm nine," replied the girl, before adding proudly, "and almost a half."

Helen nodded.

"How old are you?" returned the girl. "As old as my big brother?"

Helen shook her head. "I'm fifteen."

Annie laughed. "That's still pretty old."

Helen smiled. She had been pretty sheltered by her strict, religious upbringing, and although she was much older than this child, she felt, strangely, that she was the younger of the two of them. From what Jack was like—street-smart and worldly—Helen wondered even more about his and Annie's history.

"My mom is out with her boyfriend." Annie broke the silence. "He says he loves me, but he doesn't, and I hate him."

Helen wasn't sure if any of this was her business, but since she was curious and Annie didn't seem to mind talking about it, she asked, "Why?"

Annie peered up at her and her face reddened, as if suddenly embarrassed. She didn't answer right away, and Helen waited, wondering. Annie finally shrugged with a sad expression on her face and looked away from Helen before she quietly replied, "I just do."

Helen didn't know what she meant, but she suddenly suspected something bad had happened between Annie and her mom's boyfriend, and all she wanted to do was make this child feel better.

"Well," began Helen, smiling, "I like you. In fact, I like you a lot. I think you're great."

Annie looked up at her again, and the tear on her cheek didn't escape Helen's notice. She didn't mention it as Annie quickly brushed it away.

Helen had planned to give the other half of the necklace to her friend at school the next day, but instead she reached into the pocket of her dress and lifted out a small, gold chain.

Annie watched as Helen held on to the treasure's clasp but let the rest fall into her palm. The small bauble in the middle of the chain was half of a broken heart. The tiny writing simply declared "friend," and Annie smiled, reading it softly out loud.

"That's so pretty, Helen," she breathed, looking up at her again.

"Well," said Helen tenderly, "I'm going to give this to you because I consider you my friend."

Annie held her breath as Helen put the necklace around her small neck. It was too long for her, but that didn't matter to Annie. As soon as the chain was clasped securely, she grasped the trinket gently and didn't let go.

Helen smiled as she showed Annie the chain around her own neck. "See? I have the other half of the heart."

Annie looked closely at the other side of the gold heart, which lay just below Helen's throat, and gasped. "Yours says 'best!'" she exclaimed.

Helen nodded, moved by Annie's enthusiasm. "I have the 'best,' and you have the 'friend.' That means we're best friends, and whenever we see each other, and even when we don't, we'll always know that and have part of each other's heart."

Annie's expression told Helen that the girl had very rarely, if ever, received a gift, and she was suddenly even more glad that she'd given Annie the necklace.

When Jack pulled up, Annie ran to the Mustang and told him all about her new best friend, showing him the precious gift she'd received.

Jack smiled at Helen, and she couldn't help but wonder if he'd ever received a gift.

They just drove around that night, not parking like they usually did, but that didn't bother either Helen or Jack. They glanced at each other and smiled as Annie's enthusiastic chatter rang out from the back seat.

Later, when they knew youth group would be ending, Jack dropped Helen off, not far from the church but far enough that they wouldn't be seen. Annie had just dozed off, and Jack glanced back at her. He turned to Helen before she could climb out of the car and gently grabbed her arm. "Hey," he said, motioning sheepishly to the back seat, "thanks for that."

Helen felt another wave of sadness infuse her heart, but instead of speaking, she nodded once and leaned in to give him a kiss.

Before she left the car, he whispered, "You won't forget to meet me here tomorrow, will you?"

Helen shook her head and looked up into his eyes, a small smile still on her lips. "No. I'll be here."

Jack watched her leave and then looked back again at his little sister. When he looked up, an even bigger ache filled his own chest before he drove away toward their home and whatever he and Annie would find there.

Chapter One

FEBRUARY 2017

THE PRAYER THAT ECHOED FROM THE FRONT OF THE CHURCH WAS LENGTHY, and although well thought out and meaningful, I must admit that I wasn't really hearing it. I reached for Grant's hand on one side and my mother's on the other. I wanted to be strong for my mom, but at the same time I wanted to melt into my husband's arms and weep like a small child. The man who had meant the most to me for the majority of my life was gone … at least, he was gone from me.

It had only been a week since my father, Ted Holmes, had died, but the days had gone by in such a blur, I wondered if I'd even started to grieve. I was in shock. That was clear. I glanced sideways at my mother, Helen. She sat, her posture straight, as at most times, but her eyes were red and puffy from crying. My heart ached for her and all she'd lost. It hadn't been that long since my parents' lives together had blossomed and their love had grown into something deeper than it had ever been before. At least she wouldn't live with regret—other than, perhaps, the regret of time wasted.

I felt Grant's hand leave mine and his arm move to come around my shoulders. "You okay, Trish?" he whispered so softly I hardly heard it.

I nodded my head, almost imperceptibly, and shrugged my shoulders ever so slightly. He moved quickly to hold my hand again, knowing I'd fall apart completely if he hugged me. I was tired of crying, especially ugly crying, in front of everyone in the congregation. I cast a sidelong glance Grant's way and saw his smile of encouragement. I smiled back and felt so thankful to have him beside me.

The pastor continued, now speaking to those of us in the family. I would've paid attention if I hadn't had to concentrate on my will not to break apart, but I'm sure it was all very nice.

What do you say of a person who is gone from you? It must be easy if the person wasn't loved, but maybe that's even worse. I loved my father fiercely, and I would miss him more than anyone who had ever been taken from me before. I clung to the knowledge that he had an eternity in heaven to look forward to, and it was the only thought that kept me from letting my grief loose as I sat, waiting.

As usual, my attention wandered … this time to thoughts of heaven. The more people I knew who died, the more I looked forward to going there. I'm not impressed by thoughts of golden streets but with seeing my Saviour and all the people I've known who've gone before me. Heaven is so real in my mind, and I'm honestly starting to think of it more and more as "home." Earth is just a steppingstone to something so much greater, if you believe.

My father believed, and he is there now. I have no doubt about that. I like to think he's waiting for me and that when I send messages up there, he somehow gets them. Maybe I still make him smile from way down here. If I were in heaven and thought of my family back on earth, though, I'd cry. So I imagine my father no longer thinks about us or knows what we're doing. Being a doctor, I like to think of him helping others, even in heaven, but since there's no pain or sadness or suffering, I don't know what he's doing. I imagine he wouldn't know what to do with himself if he couldn't use his skills. Thinking of these things, I smiled.

Grant glanced down at me and squeezed my hand. I looked up at him and noticed a question in his eyes. I don't know if I'd accidentally said something out loud or if it was just my smile, but he smiled back, catching me in one of those stares that makes my heart still skip a beat.

"Are you going up?" he whispered.

"Oh!" I said, suddenly aware that everyone close to us was looking in my direction.

It was my turn. I was, after all, Ted's only daughter and, as my mother said, it would only be appropriate. So feeling thus obligated to read the eulogy, I had agreed.

"Do you want me to go with you?" Grant added as I tried to rise.

I paused before fully standing. "No." I smiled a little, shaking my head. "I've got this."

I walked carefully up to the front of the church and was relieved to have a full-length wooden podium in front of me as I started. I couldn't seem to get control of my shaky knees, but since no one in the crowd could see them, I wasn't too worried.

"Ted Holmes was my father," I started, quite strongly actually. "He was born on ..." I stopped to look up and my voice trailed off. I saw the hundreds of people who had come to pay their respects and say goodbye to my father. He'd not only been my dad but a husband to my mother, a grandfather to Kylie, a relative to many, a physician to even more, and a friend and colleague to many, many others.

Everyone stared as I looked at so many familiar faces, and others I didn't know at all.

I took a deep breath before I spoke again. "I'm not going to read this eulogy actually. It's all written there, on the card in your hands. I'm sure you can read it for yourselves. You probably already have. Instead, I'm going to tell you about my father and how much he meant to me."

I hadn't written any notes because I had planned to simply read out loud what was typed in the inside of the bulletin. But when I saw the many faces of the people who were there to honour my father, I just had to tell them, from my heart, what I'd loved about him and how much I'd miss him. I told all those people about how my dad wanted me to be a doctor but I'd decided on nursing because I felt like nurses did most of the patient care, and I wanted to be beside the patient. I told them how he had laughed at that and then told me in a secretive tone that doctors knew the nurses did most of the work. I told them about how my dad would laugh and had such an optimistic attitude, no matter what seemed to be happening. I told them how loved I felt and how encouraging he'd been to me. I told them about how wonderful a grandpa he'd been to Kylie and how much she adored him. Finally, I told them, as I looked at my mother, how he had treasured her. I didn't cry, which surprised not only me but Grant as well. When I finished, I hoped that if my father could have heard it, he would have laughed, hugged me hard, and told me he was proud of me.

My mother enveloped me in a huge hug when I sat back down on the front bench beside her, and after the service was over, many people expressed how much they'd appreciated what I had said. I don't remember all the details, but I suppose that's what happens when you're in the middle of the shock of grief.

• • •

"That was a beautiful funeral, I suppose," said my mom, sitting across from me in their living room later that night.

We both looked at each other and smiled. We'd discussed this before. How can people really consider funerals nice or beautiful or anything as happy as those words? I don't care what people say—when you've just lowered someone into a grave, there is little nice or beautiful about it. And it doesn't matter where the person was expected to end up either. It doesn't change the fact that he or she is gone from you. The hole in your heart is huge, no matter how good the lunch was after the service.

"I'm glad we had the interment before the service," I said. "At least only close family was at that. I think that was as good as it could be. At least I knew everyone there. Did you even know half the people today, Mom?"

She smiled at me then. "Of course not, Trish. Your dad knew everybody."

"It sure looked that way," I agreed. "I think the whole town was there, and many more besides."

Grant came from the kitchen then. "I just talked to Melissa. Kylie's being good for them. She and Trent say we can leave her there until we're ready to go back home."

I smiled at him as he crossed the room to sit next to me on the couch.

"You two feel free to stay as long as you like, but I'm fine with you going home too. Life goes on, and you have to carry on with yours. I'll be fine," said my mom.

As much as I wanted to believe her, I knew my mother's history. Although I'd never brought up her previous suicide attempt, I was nervous for her in her grief.

"I'll stay for a while, Mom. Stephanie said she'd be willing to stay with you as well, until things get easier," I offered, looking up at my husband. "If that's okay with you, Grant, since you're her boss."

He nodded, giving my shoulder a squeeze. "Of course."

My mother nodded too and then yawned. "I'll think about it, but now, I'll excuse myself. It's been a long day, and I'm going to turn in early," she said as she stood and looked at me. "But you and my granddaughter need to get on with your lives, Trish." She paused before adding what had always just seemed like tradition, but tonight, somehow, it felt that much sweeter. "Can I get anything for either of you before I go to bed?"

"Of course not, Mom," I said, getting up too quickly and then sitting back down.

"What's wrong?" Grant and my mother asked me, with concern.

"I'm fine." I shook my head, feeling the room spin. "I just got up too fast. I'm good. Just tired."

Grant put his arm around me and smiled up at my mom. "Helen, thank you for everything. We're fine. Please feel free to go and rest, and if you need anything, you know we're here for you."

"Thank you, Grant," she said, leaning down to hug me. "Trish, you've been such a blessing to me during all of this."

Suddenly I felt like crying, more than I had all day, so instead of saying anything, I hugged her harder.

As she left the room, Grant pulled me over to rest my head in the crook of his arm. It was peaceful and quiet, as it often had been in my parents' home. Even though my father, before his short retirement, had often been gone for long stretches of time with work, his absence now was a much greater void.

I felt Grant's even breathing, and I would've fallen asleep if he hadn't spoken then.

"C'mon," he said quietly. "Out with it."

"With what?" I whispered, my head starting to feel better and the nausea passing. I hadn't told him, but I'd wanted to so many times over the last weeks. Something had always stopped me, though. Somehow it didn't seem fair to the grief if happy news were spoken.

It had only been a few days between Grant's mother's, Sandy's, marriage to Jack and my father's heart attack, so it never seemed quite the right moment. Now, only two weeks after that beautiful celebration, our family had this one—a celebration of a life gone. If only we had "celebrated" my father when he was still alive.

"Remember," Grant said just as quietly, interrupting my dozing thoughts again, "I was married to someone who was pregnant twice. I think I know at least some of the signs."

That woke me up. "How long have you known?" I asked, sitting up straighter and looking at him. Why was I so surprised? He'd been married to my half-sister, Stacy. They'd lost one child, and she'd given birth to our Kylie. Of course he would know the signs.

He smiled right up into his eyes, which I love. "A week or so?" He shrugged. "I suspected, anyway," he grinned.

"Well," I said, almost shyly as he held my gaze, "are you happy about it?"

He thought about his answer before he took my hands. "I know this probably isn't the right time, since we just said our goodbyes to your dad, but … I'm so happy, Trish. Another baby, a brother or sister for Kylie! That's the best news you could've ever given me."

He kissed me then, and a thrill ran up and down my spine.

"You need some rest," he said as he pulled away from the kiss to stand and help me slowly to my feet.

"You're probably right," I agreed. "It's been a tough day."

We walked to the guest room and got changed for bed.

"Have you talked to Stephanie?" Grant asked suddenly.

"Yes," I answered, nodding. "Today. She really wanted to come to Dad's funeral, but with seeing Abigail at the wedding, she said she needed some time alone. I don't think she wanted to see her daughter again if Trent and Melissa brought her to the funeral."

"I can't imagine how difficult this is for her," Grant said, going into the bathroom that was adjacent to the guest room.

"Well, Steph is still adamant that she's not sorry she gave Abby up for adoption, and she's really happy that Trent and Melissa are Abigail's parents, but it's still hard for her. I don't blame Stephanie for not coming today. She talked to Mom this morning and said she was sorry, but Mom understands," I said, grabbing my toothbrush too. "Steph said she'd be okay to come and stay with Mom if that's okay with you. It might be good for her to spend some time with her grandmother."

"That's fine. Whatever your mom needs right now, we'll make it work, and when Stephanie gets back to the office, she'll be busy. That should help her."

"Stephanie does like to keep busy, and she loves working for you, so maybe that'll be good," I agreed. "She'll talk more to me yet, I'm sure. It's just been so crazy lately."

Grant left the bathroom as I finished brushing my teeth. In a few minutes, I turned off the lights and joined him in bed. Staring into the darkness, I didn't feel as tired as I had earlier. I tried to look at my husband, but his back was to me, and his breathing had already slowed. "Do you think she'll tell Joe that Abigail is their baby?" I whispered.

"Course she will," answered Grant in a mutter. "When she's ready."

I could hear him yawn, and as I turned my back to his, I yawned as well. Grant is such a patient person—something I am not. He has a deep faith, not only in the goodness of God but in His unconditional love for us as well.

My father, although we hadn't spoken about it very often, had held those same beliefs. His life's focus had been helping others and, more recently, focussing on his marriage to my mother. They'd gone through some tough things in the last year, but his love for my mom, his family, and all of those around him had become his legacy. As I stared into the dark, I thought of my dad, imagining his body in the cold ground, and I had to remind myself that it wasn't him we had buried today but rather just his shell. My father was alive and well and had no more worries in the beautiful place in heaven prepared for him.

I thought Grant had fallen asleep, but when I started to cry, I felt him move and his arm encompass me in a gentle hug. Nothing more was said, but before we succumbed to an exhausted sleep, I felt his hand come to rest over my lower abdomen, where the miracle of life stirred.

Chapter Two

STEPHANIE FELT AMBIVALENT ABOUT LEAVING GR-JO HOLDINGS TO VISIT HER Grandma Helen. She had a few accounts that needed attention, but Grant had told her he was okay taking them over for the short while she'd be gone. She'd made sure to send him the marketing files for two accounts and told him that if he needed anything, she'd be a text or phone call away.

"Now you're sounding like the boss," Grant grinned as Stephanie stared, over his shoulder, at the computer screen. She had just pointed to something she thought important to show him and that he shouldn't forget to tell the client.

"Oh!" replied Stephanie, straightening, her face turning pink. "I'm sorry if I overstepped. I just—"

Grant laughed. "I know, Steph. You just don't want me to forget anything. I've said it before, and I'll repeat myself again … you're better at the marketing piece. My stronger suit is the accounting."

They were in his office, and as Grant ran his hand through his dark hair, Stephanie smiled down at her boss. He'd always been such a huge encouragement to her, and after the many months she'd worked for him, it seemed as though they were more like partners sometimes rather than employer and employee.

"Really … show me everything you need to and then go spend some time with your grandmother. Trish thinks Helen needs you right now, and

I think she's right. It might be great for both of you to spend some quality time together, but …" He paused, looking directly up at Stephanie. "Do you want to go?"

"I do," replied Stephanie quickly before hesitating. "Although … I'm a little nervous, to be honest."

Grant sat back in his chair, ready to listen. Stephanie turned her eyes away from him and the computer screen, walking the short distance to sit in the chair across from her boss's desk. "I don't know what to expect, Grant," she began. "I mean … can I be totally honest with you?"

"Sure." Grant leaned forward and placed his elbows on his desk, suspecting what she'd say next.

"In a way I'd just like to stay here and keep working. Don't get me wrong—I love Grandma Helen, but Grandpa Ted was always easier to talk to. I guess I've always felt a little nervous around Grandma because of her … history."

Grant nodded. Stephanie hadn't been around when his mother-in-law had attempted suicide, but of course she'd heard about it. Although it was in the past for Helen, things like that didn't simply disappear from people's conversations or memories.

Grant smiled encouragingly at Stephanie. "I hear you, Steph," he began. "I get it, but Helen has asked forgiveness for that, and although no one will ever forget, she's a different person now. I think knowing you—her daughter's child—has helped her tremendously to deal with losing Stacy before she ever got to know her. Helen loves you like crazy, and you yourself have said that you've become closer to her than you were before. Maybe you both need some time together."

Stephanie smiled at Grant. Since she'd joined this family, he had always seemed to know how to make her feel more at ease, and today was no different.

"But," he said, glancing at the computer screen again and then back at Stephanie, "if you really don't want to go, it's not like I can't use you here."

"Nice try," she replied as she tucked a few strands of her long, red hair behind her ear. "You used to do all of that without me, so I'm sure you'll be fine."

Grant laughed again and told Stephanie to stay safe on her two-hour drive to her grandma's house.

When she was finished doing a few final things in her office, Stephanie turned to be sure she'd left everything as tidy as she liked it. Then she glanced at the list she'd jotted on the small piece of paper in her hand. After she stroked a few more things off, she'd be on her way.

• • •

Trish's plea that Helen have someone with her during the time her grief would be more intense had made sense to Stephanie, and now, after only a short time with her grandmother, Stephanie was incredibly glad she'd come. Within hours she felt completely at ease with her, and over the next days they became much closer. Although Ted hadn't been Stephanie's biological relative, she enjoyed talking about him with her grandmother and listening as her grandma shared many stories and memories of him.

Another thing that bonded Stephanie to her Grandma Helen was Stacy—Stephanie's mother—the daughter her grandmother had given up for adoption after giving birth to her at fifteen years old. Stacy had been married to Grant but had died after delivering Kylie. Unfortunately, Helen and the rest of the family had known nothing about Stacy until after her death.

They spoke minimally about the little they both knew of Stacy because Helen suspected that any memories Stephanie had were not pleasant ones. She had been adopted by a lovely couple after she'd been taken away from Stacy for reasons of neglect. Although Stacy had given her life to God after meeting Grant, it didn't take the sting out of what Stephanie knew had been her life before the age of six. Fortunately, Stephanie didn't remember much of that time, but when Helen shared about her own harsh upbringing, she felt a bond with her grandma that only two people having suffered can share. Although she'd nodded when her grandma talked about Stacy's later positive life change, Stephanie still couldn't understand how all of that could be forgiven when her mother hadn't just hurt herself but others as well. After that night, they hadn't spoken about Stacy again.

"Are you going to be okay?" Stephanie asked, hugging her Grandma Helen before leaving to return to the city.

"You know," replied Helen, "I need to carry on, Stephanie. Melissa just can't do all the event planning by herself. She's so busy with Abigail, and she really needs my help in her business. It's gotten much busier than either of us thought it could be, which is good. So ... in answer to your question, sweetheart, yes. I'm going to be okay. I have doubted it a few times, but, like I told you, it's not as if I've never been alone before. When Trish and Grant left, I hated the quiet in the house, but then you came and brought along such a bright light of happiness and hope. I honestly think I'm going to do just fine. I'll just remember the wonderful time we've had together."

Stephanie's eyes teared then. If she was honest with herself, she'd have to admit that when she had first met her grandmother, she feared her a little. She seemed so strait-laced and proper in everything she did and said, but now after their time together, Stephanie knew what a unique and loving person her grandmother really was. She'd also learned things that she would never have known if not for her grandmother's honesty. She'd gone through some similar things as Stephanie, and that had brought them even closer. Her grandmother told her about the years she'd spent basically alone. Although she loved Ted, he had been pretty absent for most of their years together. She didn't blame him, however, but said she knew it was the plight of many doctors' families. It had only been recently, when Ted had retired, that their relationship changed after Helen had been honest with him. Stephanie listened, and they'd both cried when her grandma told her about her suicide attempt. After that admission, her grandma worried that Stephanie would think less of her, but to Stephanie, it had only increased the respect she had for Helen. Being able to admit so many things, and being real with her granddaughter, had made Stephanie feel special. The conversation had turned even more intimate when they talked about having babies and giving them to other people to raise. Then they'd talked about the men who hadn't known about the consequences of their actions.

"Can I ask you a really personal question, Grandma?" Stephanie asked tentatively a few nights before she left.

"Anything, sweetheart," replied Helen.

"Do you ever think of Jack?" Stephanie left the question hanging but immediately regretted asking her grandma about something so personal.

What was she thinking? Her grandma's husband had just died, and now she was asking something so inappropriate.

Helen, however, looked at Stephanie and answered honestly. "I wish I could say I didn't, but in all honesty, I guess I do." She paused, thinking. "Different people touch our lives in different ways, Stephanie. That summer with Jack was so short, and although he was Stacy's father, that was so long ago. Almost a lifetime has passed. I don't know Jack now, but I believe he's had a rough life, and all I want for him is happiness. I'm really glad he's found it with Grant's mother, but I do think about him sometimes and what might've been. I think on some level, even as a young girl, I loved him, but my love for Ted was so much stronger and deeper because it was worked for." Helen's eyes had filled with tears before she glanced up at Stephanie again and added, "But I don't think anyone forgets their first love."

Stephanie nodded.

"Do you think of Joe?" asked Helen softly.

"Oh Grandma," Stephanie breathed, "it wasn't the same as you and grandpa. We just had a one-night stand." Stephanie blushed and looked down at her hands. "But ... I do. I think of him all the time."

"Have you told him that you know where your baby is?"

Stephanie looked up with tears in her eyes. "No," she replied. "Not yet."

Helen smiled but felt her granddaughter's pain.

"You've been through so much for your young years, Stephanie, but you've weathered everything extremely well. Just think of all the people who have come into your life recently who you weren't even aware of just months ago. We're all so glad we found you, Stephanie." Helen took a quick breath before continuing. "I think that if you believe what you did was best for Abigail, he will understand too."

Stephanie shook her head. "I don't know, Grandma," she started. "When I told Joe about giving the baby up, he really wanted to know more details, and I'm scared he'll want to take Abby away from Trent and Melissa when he finds out she's with them, but that wouldn't be right. I *know* I made the right decision for her ... and for me, but I don't know about Joe."

Helen sat back and stared at her beautiful red-headed granddaughter. Stephanie had been through so much—first with finding out about being neglected and abandoned at the young age of six by her birth mother, and later with some of her own poor life choices. Perhaps Stephanie couldn't see it, but God had kept her in His hand, even in the worst of it. She had only to accept His promise of faithfulness as her own and she would see it too. Helen was sure it would happen, as she and others in the family were praying. Now Helen prayed for wisdom before she spoke again.

"Can I give you one suggestion?" asked Helen seriously.

"Of course, Grandma," agreed Stephanie eagerly.

"Maybe I have no right to give you advice, knowing that some of my own life choices have been ... well, less than wise, but before you spend too much time and energy worrying about what Joe thinks, try to come to terms with what *you* believe, Stephanie. I think it's really important to know what you believe and what God means to you in your own life ... you know, before you worry about everyone else around you. It's too easy to slip up and make bad decisions if you're not sure of what you believe. And I think you'll know when to tell Joe about Abigail."

Stephanie nodded and thought again about what the pastor had asked the congregation in the last church service she had attended with her grandmother. "What do you believe?" That question had haunted her ever since.

It was late when Stephanie left her grandmother's place that night, and their many conversations looped through her mind. She had a lot to think about on her long drive home.

Chapter Three

HELEN WAS NERVOUS TO PICK UP THE PHONE BUT DID IT ANYWAY. "HELLO."

"Hi," hesitated the voice on the other end. "This is Annie—Jack's sister. I saw you a few weeks ago ... at his wedding. I ... I thought I'd call you, but ... I hope that's all right."

Helen heard the exhale of breath on the other end of the phone and silently had her own before saying, "I was really glad to see you again, Annie. It's been a long time."

This time the woman on the other end let out a nervous laugh. "More like a lifetime," she said quickly.

"Yes," Helen agreed.

"I'm sorry to hear about your husband, Helen."

Helen couldn't imagine how Annie would know about anything involving her, but before she could wonder for long, Annie spoke up again.

"Jack told me," Annie said, as if she'd read her mind.

"Oh," stated Helen, wondering why she and Ted would be the topic of conversation.

"He feels very bad as well," offered Annie.

"He and Sandy sent a card and flowers ..." Helen trailed off, wondering why she'd thought it important to mention that to Jack's sister.

"Well, anyway," offered Annie after a short pause, "it can't be easy for you right now, Helen, so I probably should have waited, but ... I hope it's okay." She waited for a response, but when Helen remained silent, she continued. "I know it's been a long time, but when I saw you at their wedding, something came back to me."

Helen nodded, but then realizing she couldn't be seen, she quickly said, "Yes. You told me that when I saw you. I'm sorry I couldn't talk then. My husband was waiting for me, and—"

"It's okay. That's why I'm calling now," interrupted Annie. "I just want you to know that, although this may seem silly now, I really … I mean … the necklace you gave me when I was a kid, well … that really meant something to me back then and … geez. Now it just sounds stupid even mentioning it."

"No!" gasped Helen, not realizing she'd been holding her breath. "I mean … no. It's not stupid. I wanted you to have it."

"Well, we were kids, right?" added Annie. "Stuff like that means a lot when you're a kid, and I hadn't … well, what I mean to say is … I hadn't received a lot of presents up until then, and I want you to know that it meant something to me. It really did, and I'm actually really sorry that …"

The silence stretched on.

"Sorry?" urged Helen quietly.

"I lost it." Annie's voice broke a little before she quickly cleared it. "I know it's dumb. Really. I don't know why I even called. I'm such a stupid woman, but it did mean a lot to me, and for some reason when I saw you again, I thought about that and, well, I wish I still had it. I do remember exactly what it looked like, Helen. I didn't want to lose it."

Helen's eyes teared as Annie spoke. After she'd found the necklace lying between the cracks of the wooden porch that night, Helen had let the chain fall between her fingers. She'd stared at it then, wondering how the chain's clasp had become broken. She knew it meant something to Annie when she'd given it to her, so it hadn't made sense that she'd lost it. Then, before Helen left the hospital that night, a nurse had handed it to her, telling her they'd found it grasped in her palm and that she wouldn't let it go until they'd persuaded her to. Fortunately, her mother hadn't seen it, but the nurse had noticed Helen's own necklace and asked her who she'd planned to give the other side to. Helen hadn't answered. As she'd gazed down at the broken heart in her hand, she wondered if Annie had thrown it away, much like she'd thought Jack had done with her.

"What happened to it?" Helen asked now, wondering why it mattered but knowing it did.

Silence from Annie's end made Helen inwardly berate herself. It was none of her business, and Annie had said she'd lost it. Of course she wouldn't know what happened to it.

"My mother's boyfriend took it from me before we left," Annie said softly. "I think I told you how much I hated him. Well ... he hated me too, I guess."

Helen swallowed, wishing she could rewind the conversation. "I'm so sorry," she managed.

"Yes," agreed Annie, taking a deep breath. "Well ... that part of my life is over and done with, Helen. It's no big deal, but I wanted to say thanks anyway. You ... made a big difference in a little girl's life that day."

She paused, and Helen couldn't breathe. The silence stretched for a while between them before Helen heard another deep breath on the end of the phone.

"You know, this may sound really silly, but I still kind of wish I could go back to just those few moments of the summer when you gave it to me and then we drove around with Jack that evening. I think it was the last day we spent in your town, but it's really one of the best memories I have, and I really wanted to tell you that," ended Annie, as if relieved.

"I found it," blurted Helen, suddenly knowing she needed this as well.

"What?" asked Annie, so softly Helen doubted she'd heard it.

Helen nodded again, as if Annie could see her. "I did. I found it on the porch when I came to look for Jack. I was going to go away with him ... with you ... but I found your necklace instead."

A moment of silence stretched again before Helen added, "And I still have it."

• • •

Helen had debated taking the two halves of the broken heart to the jeweller she knew in town. Normally she would have done that without giving it much thought, but then she decided against it. Although they'd cost Helen a fair amount of her limited allowance money those many years before, she now assumed it was pretty cheap jewellery, and the jeweller might think she was crazy to even try restoring them. Then there would probably be questions that she didn't feel like answering either.

She hadn't seen them for a while, so she had to hunt a little in some old storage bins before she found them. As she lifted both from the small box she'd placed them in, she couldn't help but smile. They didn't appear to be as tarnished as she expected.

She googled "restoring jewellery," and after a few videos and reading the step-by-step instructions, both charms glistened. Maybe, she suspected, cheap jewellery wasn't as cheap back then as it is today. They weren't quite as shiny as she remembered them being, but they were close, and she felt great satisfaction in what she'd accomplished. She would've tried to save the chains as well, but as she stared at the broken clasp on Annie's, Helen shuddered. She wondered how the necklace had been taken from her and thought it might have been torn off her small neck. She quickly discarded both chains and went to her jeweller to purchase thin gold ones of longer lengths. Helen then packaged up Annie's and mailed it to her.

A week later, Annie phoned Helen to thank her profusely for the small treasure she remembered so well.

"Helen, I think it's even more beautiful than it was back then," breathed Annie.

Helen laughed at that and enjoyed telling Annie how she'd googled a site to get instructions on how to bring old jewellery back to life. Annie laughed and Helen wondered if she'd sounded unintelligent by being so excited about googling something successfully. After all, Annie was a professor of some kind. She probably used the internet all the time. Helen had learned more as she planned more events with Melissa, but her younger counterpart did most of the computer-related things.

Helen felt better, though, when Annie said, "I google things all the time. It seems to be the only way people nowadays want to learn, but you clearly found a good site. Good work."

After a few more minutes of everyday chatter, Annie fell quiet.

"Really, Helen," she finally said, and Helen could hear a catch in her throat, "thank you. I mean … I just can't stop staring at this necklace. This meant so much to me back then and almost does as much now."

Helen's throat constricted in the way it does when you're moved by another's sincerest words. "Annie," she started, taking a deep breath, "you don't have to thank me. I wanted to give it to you then, and I'm really glad I kept these. It's such a small thing, but I'm glad it means something to you. It means something to me too. I hope we'll stay friends for a long time."

"I hope so too, Helen. I really do," agreed Annie.

They both paused before they pressed END on their phones, but both women sincerely meant those words with all of their hearts.

Chapter Four

JOE GRUNTED, LIFTING THE BALE AND TOSSING IT OVER THE FENCE TO WHERE a few of the ranch's cattle stood. He was in a hurry to get his work done today. He was interviewing at a shop in the city for a job involving woodworking, and he needed to get done and cleaned up. He couldn't be late. Although nervous, he was excited as well. He'd take a few small items with him that he'd made, and maybe that would help them see that he wasn't bad at working with his hands.

As soon as he finished with the chores in the barn, he ran to the bunk house to clean up. He'd been staying in their small, rustic cabin while working for his Uncle Joey and Aunt Sue as a ranch hand for over a half a year. He was just finishing up and taking one last look in the mirror to fix a patch of wavy, dark blond hair that wouldn't stay in place, when his Uncle Joey knocked at the door.

"This is from your Aunt Sue," said his uncle after closing the door behind him and handing Joe a packed lunch. "I guess she doesn't know that you're a grown man who probably could get himself lunch, especially since you'll be in the city n' all."

Joe smiled. "She still thinks I'm a kid. Maybe she'll always think of me that way."

Joe's uncle looked at him and adjusted his cowboy hat but didn't remove it. With a serious expression, he replied, "Well, it's time you make the women in this family see that you're not a kid anymore."

Joe looked at his uncle's demeanour, and his smile left him. He felt a bit surprised. He knew his uncle as a soft-spoken man who didn't usually talk very much either.

"Don't get me wrong," said Joey. "You're a fun guy and that's fine, but it's time to grow up, Joe, and I think this interview is a great way to start. You have a talent for this kinda thing," he added, running his hand over the back of the rocking chair Joe had just finished making.

He continued to admire the workmanship his nephew clearly had a bent for. Joey cleared his throat a few times before continuing. He was uncomfortable with conversations such as these, but he knew his nephew had been struggling. Since Joe didn't have a dad around, Joey sometimes felt that he should have tried harder to step into that role. Maybe it wasn't too late to at least encourage the guy. "I'm really glad you came to help out on the ranch, Joe. It's been much appreciated," Joey continued.

Joe nodded. "Yeah ... it's been good for me too."

Both men looked at each other, and when the threat of an uncomfortable silence filled the room, Joe quickly said, "It helped me lay off the drinking too, and I guess I should thank you for that."

Joey looked at his nephew's reddening face and adjusted his cowboy hat again. "Yeah ... well ... that's good too," he managed, looking down at the toe of the boot he was now scraping on the bunkhouse's rough wood floor. More silence ensued until Joey looked up and sighed. "I guess I just wanted to say thanks for all the help, Joe. And it's okay that you're not a whole lot like Grant."

Joe's suddenly confused look made Joey pause. Now it was his turn to blush. "I mean ... don't get me wrong. I think your brother's great, and he's really good with our books and all the stuff he does for the ranch, but ... well ... it's just that ..." Joey shook his head before quickly saying, "I like workin' with ya, man. You're a good ranch hand, and if you ever wanna come back, feel free to, anytime. But like your Aunt Sue says, you have a greater gift to be shared, so as sorry as I am to see you go, I'm glad you're going for this interview. We're both pretty sure you'll get the job."

Joe opened his mouth but quickly closed it again as he stared at Joey. He hadn't expected anything like this from his quiet uncle.

"Now go and use the gift God gave ya—the way He wants you to," stated Joey.

Joe couldn't help but smile as he nodded once at his uncle. Joey looked at his nephew and nodded back.

Joe didn't know why everyone in the family always seemed to mention God in what seemed to him to be every conversation, but coming from his uncle just then, it didn't seem to bother him as much.

His uncle opened the door, but before leaving, he turned to Joe again. "Don't blow it," he added, looking at his nephew before abruptly leaving the bunkhouse.

Joe's brow furrowed a little as he stared at the closing door. He turned back to the mirror and glanced at the face in it. He brushed his dirty blond hair back, noting that the piece of hair he'd tried to tame before seemed to be staying in its correct place. Satisfied with what he saw this time, he took a deep breath. "Don't blow it," he told his reflection.

Chapter Five

AFTER RETURNING HOME FROM HER GRANDMA HELEN'S, STEPHANIE SPENT the weekend with Doug and Vi, the parents she'd known for most of her life. She and her father had gone to see a condominium that Stephanie had immediately fallen in love with, and soon they were moving her very few belongings into the cute place she would now rent. It was close to GR-Jo Holdings, and on summer days she'd be able to bike there easily.

After seeing Abigail at her Grandpa Jack and Sandy's wedding, staying with her parents and seeing again how much they loved her was just what Stephanie needed, and she learned to appreciate them even more.

When she'd noticed the heart-shaped birthmark on Abby's cheek, Stephanie knew this was the baby she'd given up for adoption two years before. She hadn't told anyone about her pregnancy then, and no one had found out about it until she had recently divulged the information. Although she'd kept her pregnancy hidden, the decision to give the baby up for adoption was made out of pure love. Stephanie was pretty sure she would have been a capable single mother, but she was convinced that the decision she'd made was better for her baby. She wanted her child to have two parents who would love her unconditionally. Trent and Melissa were crazy about Abigail, and because Trent was a nurse, Stephanie was even more convinced that Abby had gone to the perfect couple. She had learned recently that Abigail had a syndrome of some sort, which made Stephanie even more grateful for who her parents were now.

"God always knows the bigger picture," reiterated her mother as she stared at a picture of the smiling toddler on Stephanie's phone. "Clearly Abigail is in the right family."

"Yes, she is," nodded Stephanie, sitting beside her mom on the couch.

"Do you think it's more difficult for you now, Steph—knowing where she is and who she's with?" asked her mom, handing back Stephanie's phone. Vi hated to see her daughter hurting but wanted Stephanie to know that she could talk openly and honestly with her about it all.

"No, actually," Stephanie said. "I was so shocked when I saw her at the wedding, and I just wanted to hold on to her forever, but then I looked at them. It was hard, but when I saw how Trent and Melissa were with her, I just felt … calm. It's hard to explain."

"Oh honey," said the only mother Stephanie had known, "that's God giving you the peace that you made the right decision."

Vi didn't want to preach at her daughter, so she said nothing more. She knew Stephanie had been having a spiritual struggle, and Vi had been praying vigilantly for her. God would have to do the work in her daughter's heart.

"I'm glad Trish told Trent and Melissa about it all after the wedding. They were really great about it. They've been sending me pictures of Abigail ever since. I think I might run out of phone space for all of them," smiled Stephanie, scrolling through the pictures and showing even more to her mom.

Although Vi and Doug wished they could meet Stephanie's daughter—their granddaughter—neither one had suggested it to Stephanie yet. They would wait and see what happened as time went on. They'd heard that Abigail had a condition that gave her seizures, so they were praying about that too.

"I better get to work," said Stephanie, closing her phone case. "I want to get in early because I'm sure I'll have stuff to catch up on, and I want to get a head start on my day."

Vi laughed. "I'm sure you do," she smiled at her daughter. "I think you're a good employee."

"I hope so." Stephanie grinned as she caught her mom's hug.

"Would you like to come for supper tonight? I'm not making anything special, but we'd love for you to join us," suggested Vi.

Stephanie thought about it, and although tempted by her mom's good cooking, which was always great, she shook her head. "I better not, Mom. I want to get more settled at my place, and I need to start doing more for myself again. But thanks for the great offer!"

Stephanie watched as her mom's smile faded. "Soon though, okay?" She knew that since she'd moved out it was harder for her mom to let her go again.

Vi brightened and added, "I'll hold you to that, dear daughter."

Stephanie laughed as she walked to her car.

As Vi watched Stephanie pull away, her brow wrinkled. She was glad that Stephanie wanted to be independent. She knew it was best for her daughter, but she couldn't help but worry a little as well. From what Steph had told her about this Joe person, Vi was unsure about a few things, and she suspected that her daughter still had a soft spot for him. Vi couldn't understand that. Stephanie knew she would have to tell him about who was raising her baby, but from other things her daughter had told her about Joe, Vi wasn't impressed. The only thing she clung to was that Grant was Joe's big brother, and she and Doug had great respect for him. Maybe his brother wasn't so bad, but then she'd think of him—drunk and taking advantage of her Stephanie—and all her anxiety would return. Although Stephanie had told both her parents that their one-night stand had been just as much her fault as Joe's, he sounded like a piece of work to Vi, and she couldn't help but be very concerned for her daughter.

Stephanie was long gone before Vi turned from the window. It was time to get something done around the house, and her list wouldn't complete itself. She sighed as she walked into the kitchen. Like her husband said, better to be busy than fretting about stuff she had no control over. And there was a lot to pray for—it seemed like more every day.

Chapter Six

"WHAT BROUGHT YOU IN SO EARLY TODAY, STEPH?" ASKED GRANT, TAKING OFF his coat and hanging it on the stand in the entrance of GR-Jo Holdings.

Stephanie was putting a file on Alicia's desk. The secretary wouldn't be in for another hour or so.

"Oh!" jumped Stephanie, startling a little as she turned toward Grant.

"I'm sorry," apologized her boss. "I didn't mean to scare you."

Stephanie shook her head and laughed. "No. It's fine. I was just concentrating." She paused before answering his first question. "I couldn't sleep, and I'm still playing catch-up from being away, so I just thought I'd get another early start."

"Well," smiled Grant, "I've been really glad since you've been back. We noticed your absence, Steph."

Stephanie smiled up at her Aunt Trish's husband. He was a good boss and always made her feel important and at ease.

"Thanks, Grant," she said appreciatively. "I missed work too."

Stephanie continued smiling as Grant grabbed himself some coffee she'd just made.

"You've been in a good mood," he observed as he took his first sip. "We haven't had much time to talk. Did you have a good visit with Helen?"

"Oh yes," she nodded. "It was really good, actually. She's great and … I think she gets me." Stephanie looked at her feet, and Grant wondered what had changed.

Visiting with someone who was grieving so deeply might've brought her mood down, but when she looked back up, her expression held a look of contentment.

"We talked a lot about a lot of … stuff," she said, looking at Grant with the half-smile that showed off the slight asymmetry that Grant loved about a lot of the women in his life.

As he watched her, Grant couldn't help but think of Stacy. If only she had told him about the baby she'd had before they'd met. She would have loved her fiery red-headed daughter.

Grant gave his head a shake and smiled again at Stephanie. "Well, I should get started," he said, starting the short walk to his office.

As he sat in the chair across from his computer, he looked up. Stephanie had followed him into his office and stood, looking troubled, in the doorway. He saw that her eyes had teared a little, and he leaned further back in his chair as he waited.

"I … I …" stammered Stephanie. She opened her mouth and closed it again.

"It's okay, Steph," Grant encouraged. "You can tell me anything."

"I know," she whispered. "You've always been so nice to me. I just want you to know that I'll talk to him … I'm … I'm just—"

"You're not ready," Grant said softly.

Joe had been on Grant's mind a lot lately too, and he'd suspected that Stephanie hadn't stopped thinking about his brother either—and for the same reason. After all, he did deserve to know that Abigail was his daughter, but it wasn't Grant's news to give.

"Stephanie," he said, praying for wisdom, "Joe deserves to know, and you know how it is. He will find out, somehow, eventually. But I'm praying that God will give you wisdom in the timing."

Stephanie nodded, looking more relieved and a little confused. "I will tell him, Grant. I promise. I'm just … really nervous about how he'll react."

"Well," smiled Grant without humour, "he does have a temper, but I don't think he'll do anything crazy." He paused then before offering, "I can be there with you."

Stephanie considered that and nodded before looking at the floor.

"Bottom line, Steph," Grant encouraged, "you'll tell him when you're ready, and we'll all be there for both of you."

Stephanie's face came up, and she smiled at Grant. "Thanks," she managed. "I appreciate that."

Grant settled further back in his chair as Stephanie turned on her heel to walk to her office. He stared up at the ceiling as he silently prayed that when Stephanie did tell Joe, the news wouldn't completely shatter his brother and change all the good that had happened since Stephanie had come into their lives.

Chapter Seven

SANDY AND JACK SAT ACROSS FROM ONE ANOTHER IN THE BOOTH, LOOKING around the western-themed saloon in the little town they'd chosen for their honeymoon. Jack had always been interested in the "wild west," so when they'd finished their research, they decided this little town would be the one they would explore in the Rocky Mountains.

Sandy took a deep breath and sighed as she looked back at Jack, who was trying to read the small print on a framed old newspaper article that hung near him. As he squinted, Sandy smiled.

"What are you smiling about?" Jack said when he glanced back at her.

"Nothing," she said innocently, trying not to laugh.

"Oh," he observed softly, "there's something."

Sandy laughed then. "I'm thinking that maybe you might need … uh … glasses?" she ventured.

Jack's forehead wrinkled as he immediately denied what he felt was an accusation.

Sandy continued smiling as she reasoned, "You know, my optometrist told me when I turned only forty-five that I needed reading glasses. I was shocked, but she told me that it's pretty normal. In fact, I could use a new prescription too, I think. I get fuzzy sometimes. We could go together when we get back home." Her smile didn't leave her face as she observed his look of distaste. "It's not a bad thing to admit, Jack. After all … you're already in—"

"I know how old I am, Sandy," smiled Jack, putting his hand up to stop her. "But I'm not as old as—"

"Hey!" It was her turn to stop him. "You promised me you wouldn't throw my age in my face. Wasn't that even in your marriage vows?"

It was his turn to laugh as he gazed at his beautiful wife. "No, it wasn't in my vows, and it's only a few years. Doesn't count anyway," he said, reaching across the table to take her hand. "Besides, you should be older than me because you're a lot wiser, and God knows I need that."

Sandy looked down at Jack's large hand, which covered hers completely. She loved his hands. They were so muscular, like the rest of him, and as she gazed up his tattooed arm to his handsome face, she smiled again. The long scar on his cheek deepened as he returned her smile, and he reached up with his free hand to adjust his blue bandanna.

"I love you, woman," he whispered, making Sandy blush a little. "I'm so glad we decided to stay here for a couple of months. That was a good call."

Sandy's smile left her then as she looked down at the table. "I'm really glad we've had time alone, Jack," she began, "but I'm still sorry that we didn't go back for Ted's funeral."

Jack looked at the top of Sandy's blonde head and pondered. He knew she felt bad about not being there for her son and daughter-in-law. After all, from what Jack had observed, Sandy was often everyone's caregiver. She loved her family fiercely, and although she appreciated their independence, whenever they needed her, she'd been right there, often forgetting her own needs and putting everyone else's first. But if Jack were honest with himself, he was relieved when she'd agreed not to return for the funeral. Although he was in love with his new wife—more deeply than he'd ever imagined he could ever love someone—Jack couldn't help but wonder what would've happened if he'd had to see Helen grieve.

"Well," he ventured now, "it's over, and I really think Trish and Grant understood."

Sandy looked up at him again, smiling. "Of course they understood, and I would've felt the same if it would've been me, but—"

"You just have to be everything for everyone, Sandy."

Sandy thought about that as she looked at Jack. "Look who's talking," she smiled.

Jack looked at his wife and chuckled a little in a low vibration Sandy felt. He shook his head before speaking. "Annie just thinks I saved her because I finally stepped in and stuck up for her. That was a long time ago."

"A long time ago doesn't matter, Jack. When she called you her saviour, that's because, in so many ways, you were. That's really how she saw it, and she still does," said Sandy.

"Well," he admitted sadly, "I saved her from one jerk that night, but I wonder if a lot more went on before I knew about it—maybe for a lot longer than I thought."

"You were a teenager, honey," said Sandy gently.

Jack nodded, knowing she was right. As they'd discussed before, and Jack had agreed, it hadn't been his responsibility to care for Annie, but whereas his mother had failed both of them, Jack still felt he could have done a better job trying to protect his sister. Before leaving for their honeymoon, Annie had spoken to Jack at length about a few things. Although she hadn't told him everything she'd suffered, she had thanked Jack over and over for being her saviour the night they had left that small town. Jack had tried to tell her that he was no saviour, but he could tell her about the One who had saved him. Suddenly, she hadn't wanted to continue the conversation and ended it shortly after.

"At least you and your sister have connected again, Jack," smiled Sandy. "You've got a great opportunity to get to know each other again. We'll pray for her, and God will do the rest. I'm sure of it."

Jack gazed at Sandy with an intensity that took her breath away. He nodded slightly and then said, "I'm so glad I married you."

Sandy blushed again and looked deeply into his eyes as she whispered, "Sometimes I wish I would've married you even sooner, Jack."

Hearing his name whispered by his new wife like that made Jack feel a rush of excitement, and he smiled back at her, lifting his eyebrows. Sometimes he felt so much younger when he was with her.

The food service worker came to take their order, and although Jack wasn't hungry for food any longer, he ordered the appetizer platter they'd agreed on. The waiter was just taking their menus from them when Jack glanced back at Sandy. "What's wrong, honey?" he demanded, as he took in her sudden pallor and blank stare.

Before she could answer, Jack watched as his new bride suddenly fell to her side on the bench across from him.

• • •

"Sandy!" were the next words she heard, as if coming from far away. "Sandy!"

As she felt herself being shaken, her eyes slowly opened, and she blinked as she tried to focus. As her eyesight cleared, she stared into the worried eyes of her husband.

"Wha ..." she started, grabbing a fistful of Jack's long hair that had fallen around him as he looked down at her. "What am I doing on the floor?"

"You must've fainted ... or something," Jack said, worry etched in his low voice. "I put you on the floor."

Sandy looked at the many people standing around her, and others left sitting but still staring from their seats.

"I'm okay," she said, trying to rise.

"Hey," commanded Jack, "slow down. Don't move so fast."

Sandy's embarrassment overtook her logic as she tried to ignore him, but Jack held her and made sure, as he helped her to sit, that it was done very slowly and to his satisfaction.

The sound of nearing sirens compelled Sandy to say, "Tell me you didn't call an ambulance, Jack."

"Of course we called for help," replied her husband. "No one here knows anything about medicine. Believe me ... I asked."

The restaurant employees moved aside as a paramedic and another ambulance attendant quickly entered the restaurant. After examining Sandy, the paramedic told both her and Jack that, although they thought it probably was a simple fainting episode, she should be assessed more thoroughly at a hospital. When they told her that her vital signs were within the normal ranges, Sandy became adamant that she would not be going to any hospital. Since she hadn't eaten in a while, she was sure it was caused by her own foolhardiness.

After the ambulance attendants left, it still took a lot of convincing on Sandy's part, but eventually Jack gave in and didn't insist on driving to the nearest clinic or hospital. He did tell Sandy, however, that if it happened again, or if she felt unwell at all, she would have no choice but to go. They ate and Sandy told him she felt fine the entire time. It was, however, only long after their meal was finished that Jack started to relax again.

Later, much to Jack's distress, they went for a short walk to a waterfall nearby. Sandy had insisted on it, and Jack suspected she was more driven to do so, if only to prove to herself and him that she was perfectly all right. It would have been a longer hike, but Jack was adamant that they return to their hotel suite and relax. He suggested they watch a movie, but Sandy hadn't seemed keen about that. She enjoyed the occasional show, but as she told Jack, she hadn't come on her honeymoon to watch TV.

"Woman," he told her, "you're going to be the end of me if you keep this up, and we've only been married a few weeks."

Sandy smiled as she gazed at him from across the hot tub she'd convinced him to get into. He was so strong and handsome. She always felt safe and incredibly loved when she was with him. "I'm fine," she breathed. "I feel great, actually. Just like … I have the perfect life."

Jack knew the struggles Sandy had gone through. Losing her husband at such a young age and raising two boys on her own couldn't have been easy, but as she always told him, God had been her rock.

As Jack watched Sandy's eyes close, he smiled. She was a beautiful lady who had shown him a love he never thought someone like him could receive. Through her, he'd learned of even a greater love he'd never been able to imagine. His life with God was so real to him now, and God loved *him*—a man with so much bad in his history.

As Jack closed his eyes, he remembered a little of what he'd read on the wall of the saloon—interesting characters with sullied histories. He wondered if any of those notorious legends had given their lives to Jesus before they died. He hoped so, because it would be interesting to meet them in heaven someday.

Jack felt himself almost dozing off when he felt her move beside him.

"Hey," Sandy whispered. "Time for bed? If you fall asleep in here, I won't be able to get you out."

Jack said nothing but stood up, taking her hand as they both got out of the hot tub. It hadn't been busy in the pool, but a few older kids had just entered the area. As they walked back to their room, Sandy yawned.

"Maybe early to sleep tonight?" suggested Jack, still concerned over what had happened in the restaurant.

"Are you kidding?" replied Sandy as Jack opened the door of the small cabin they were renting. "I'm on my honeymoon, mister, and I'm not about to waste all my time sleeping."

When the door closed behind them, Jack gave his wife a promising kiss and slowly moved her toward the bed.

"Hmm ..." sighed Sandy. "A lot more of this would be nice, but I've got to shower first. Join me?"

"You feeling okay?" Jack asked, after breaking from another kiss.

"I'm fine," encouraged Sandy. "I've been thinking about that, and I'm wondering if it happened because of *my* eyes? I'll make us both an appointment when we get back home."

"You won't let that go?" asked Jack, grinning as he ran his hands gently up her arms to surround her delicate face.

After he kissed her again, she whispered mischievously, "Nope."

As Jack moved his fingers to slowly undo the swimsuit tie at the back of her neck, he hoped that a simple trip to the optometrist would be all they both needed.

Chapter Eight

MELISSA HAD BEEN UNCHARACTERISTICALLY QUIET FOR TOO LONG, AND AS Trent watched his wife, his heart ached for her. She had tried to be optimistic and look happy through all of the latest reveals in their life, but even Trent knew she'd need to vent at some point.

Trent had been watching her for the last hour or so from their living room. Melissa was standing by the kitchen table with her hot glue gun, busy making what he knew would be more decorations for an upcoming wedding or some such happy event. Trent didn't know all the details about his wife's business, but he knew she'd become successful at planning large or small parties, and she seemed increasingly busy organizing from their small home. Unbeknown to her, Trent had been putting away money, with plans to surprise her by having an additional room added to their home. Not only would it serve as a badly needed space for her plethora of event decorations, but she'd have an area for all the administrative work she did as well. Thankfully, Trish's mother, Helen, had stepped in to help, but still the materials needed for the business remained, strewn everywhere around their moderate home, and seemingly growing with every event. Trent was getting tired of their entire house being full of the many things that were apparently needed for all the events being planned. It would be nice for them all to move, perhaps, out of the living room, kitchen, and sometimes even their bedroom.

Trent smiled now as he looked at his wife and her deep concentration as she placed a flower in the perfect place on top of a frothy white something-or-other. She did seem happy, surrounded with bolts of various material, something called tulle, and all kinds of flowers.

"Can I help?" he asked, knowing the answer.

"No, I'm good," she said, not turning from her chore at hand.

Trent had been working long hours too and had just gotten off shift that morning after working a long string of night shifts at their town's hospital. Now as he looked at Melissa, he was determined to talk things out and get back to their previous, stronger connection. He got up and walked to stand behind his wife, wrapping his hands around her waist.

"You smell good," he whispered as he nuzzled her neck, blowing gently at a strand of her brunette hair. He could feel her smile and hugged her more firmly.

As she turned her head she said, "So do you, Trent."

He doubted that. Although he'd showered immediately when he got off shift at the hospital, he often wondered if the sometimes less-than-appealing smells of the ER followed him home. Right before shift change, a patient with a bad case of gangrene in one of his lower limbs had come in with a cardiac arrest. Perhaps Melissa didn't smell it, but Trent had caught faint traces of the odour even after he'd showered.

"I'm glad," he answered. "I was hoping to take you out tonight, but you're busy. Maybe tomorrow?"

Melissa turned her head again to stare at the bow she'd just finished and, happy with the result, put it and her glue gun down. She turned around to face her handsome, blond husband. "Trent Bellamy, you know I can't. The Hanson wedding is tomorrow."

Trent couldn't help but groan. "Is that tomorrow?"

Melissa kissed him quickly and turned again to her crafting. "This is the first event that Helen is helping with since Ted passed away, and she's really excited about it. She'll be here any minute."

Although Trent was sincerely glad for his wife's enthusiasm, he had to admit that with their often-conflicting schedules, at times it was a challenge to get enough time together.

Trent sighed as he turned to walk back to the living room. He went to check on Abigail, whom they'd put to bed shortly after dinner. He stared at their sleeping child and softly ran his fingers through some of her auburn curls. What a blessing she was to them. As Trent gazed at his daughter, he couldn't imagine life without her. Trent's mind skipped back to Jack and Sandy's wedding and the moment his closest friend, Trish, had told them that Stephanie was Abigail's birth mother. He hadn't been able to breathe. He'd actually felt dizzy before purposely taking deep, almost gulping, breaths. Melissa had stood beside him—unable to speak as well. But then they'd felt such relief later when Stephanie told them, face to face, that she didn't plan to ever take Abigail from them. As soon as they were alone again, both he and Melissa had cried in each other's arms from the sheer joy of that revelation.

Their happiness in that promise was short-lived, however, when they found out that their Abigail had been fathered by Melissa's cousin, Joe, after he and Stephanie had partied together one night. Since Stephanie still hadn't told Joe, Trent had been left with a constant feeling of foreboding, and he suspected his wife had too, but she hadn't verbalized it. This worried Trent. Although it didn't seem so, he didn't want his wife to slip into the depression she'd experienced after their miscarriage.

Now Trent gazed at his daughter, and his eyes teared. She had Sturge-Weber-Syndrome, associated with the port wine stain birthmark on her cheek. Calcifications of some of the blood vessels in her brain on the side of the birthmark caused her to have seizures. Her medication had, once again, been increased, and thankfully the seizures had lessened again. The muscle tone on the opposite side of her body, however, was becoming weaker, and although both he and Melissa worked with Abby doing the physiotherapy exercises they'd been taught, she had shown little improvement. Abigail tripped often, but it didn't seem to bother her all that much. Most times she'd quickly get up, smiling, and Trent and Melissa would laugh too so that she'd know it was no big deal. If she did hurt herself, they were ready with kisses, hugs, and brightly coloured and cartoon-themed bandages that seemed to work best to abate her tears quickly.

Trent sighed as he turned and walked out of his daughter's room. Maybe he'd turn in early. He knew Abigail would be up at the crack of dawn and he'd be caring for her all day since Melissa was busy. He smiled thinking of it and started making plans.

"Hey," Trent said after his call had been answered. "Wanna do something with the kids tomorrow?"

• • •

Melissa looked at her reflection in the mirror. At least she just looked more wrecked than she felt. She could fix this. As she began dabbing foundation on her face, she sighed. She would rather just order a pizza and get into her comfortable pyjama pants, but she knew she needed time with Trent. He'd been quiet after she'd turned down his invitation for dinner a couple of nights ago, but she hadn't had time to worry about him then. He'd always understood before, and she was sure he did now, but they hadn't had any quality alone-time for weeks, and soon he'd be back on shift. Tonight she needed to make him a priority. She sighed, satisfied enough with what looked back at her in the mirror. But when she left the bathroom, she gazed around at their messy home. She almost regretted turning down Helen's invitation to take everything to her house. Melissa knew it made perfect sense, and Helen's house was huge compared to theirs, but something had stopped her. Maybe she was too controlling, but it was her business, after all. She'd started it and, in part, it was what had helped her to climb out of the depression she'd fallen into after finding out that she'd not only lost a baby but would never have a successful pregnancy.

Melissa took a deep breath and looked at the time on her phone. She probably still had a few minutes before Trent would be home from the park with Abby.

• • •

Abigail had gone to sleep like a dream, which wasn't typical for their daughter, but as Melissa tip-toed from her bedroom, her smile couldn't have been larger.

"She's fast asleep," she announced quietly. "She should stay that way for you, Tess," Melissa added, smiling at the nurse who would care for their daughter when they were out for dinner.

Trent and Melissa found it difficult to leave Abigail with anyone but close family or someone familiar with what to do if she should have a seizure. They were hard to find, but some of Trent's colleagues had offered to help if they could, and he and Melissa had appreciated them beyond words. They didn't go out often without their daughter, but sometimes it was necessary.

"Thanks again for doing this," said Trent, nodding at their friend.

"No problem at all," began Tess, smiling. "I actually was wishing she'd be up. I haven't seen her for a while."

"She was getting cranky," answered Melissa. "You wouldn't have wished that for long."

"Well," Tess smiled, "I brought some studying to do. I'll never be a nurse practitioner if I don't get busy and get this done."

Trent looked at Tess. He'd worked with her for a while and knew she was a dedicated nurse. Other than the fact that she was single, he didn't know a lot about her personal life. Unlike a lot of other nurses he worked with, she hadn't shared much of her private life, but she was a great nurse who put her patients' wellbeing first, and he enjoyed working with her.

"I hope you're not too sad about Abby being asleep," he said, wondering if Tess felt lonely at all.

She smiled up at him again and said sarcastically, "What's sad is that I don't have a date or anything better to do than babysit for you on a Sunday night, Trent. Now go and have fun."

Melissa laughed and thanked her again for babysitting, assuring Tess that they wouldn't be out for long.

The restaurant was full, but Melissa had made a reservation, so Trent was thankful when they were seated almost immediately. He hadn't had much for lunch, and he could feel his stomach growl. They ordered their drinks and smiled at each other.

"I've been missing you," Trent said, taking a gulp.

"I know," Melissa agreed, stirring hers with the straw before taking a sip. "It's ridiculous, sometimes, how our schedules almost seem to work against each other, Trent. But at least Abigail usually has her mom or dad taking care of her."

Trent watched his wife's smile. He didn't want to change her happy mood, but he hoped they could have a real conversation. He needed to know that she was genuinely all right. Sometimes, he'd learned, she would cover her real feelings behind her brilliant smile, and he didn't want what could happen to—well—happen. He thought about the money he'd put aside for a new space in their home. Although he hadn't planned to tell her yet, he suddenly felt compelled to share it with her.

"I have some news," he ventured, a small smile playing on his lips as he looked down at his drink.

"Really?" Melissa asked, continuing to stir her drink as she looked at him.

As he continued to smile but avoid her eyes, she looked at him more seriously and asked, "What?"

His grin grew as he looked up at her.

"C'mon, Trent," she laughed, her curiosity piqued. "You can't sit there with that smile and not tell me."

He cleared his throat before he began. "Well, I've had an opportunity to save a bit of money, and I have some plans for it, but I need to know you'll be okay with this."

Melissa didn't know what to think. He'd hidden money away? Since they both had their own bank accounts, she figured it was fine, but it still seemed like a strange admission.

"What plans?" she asked, looking at him seriously.

Trent looked at the expression on his wife's face and almost felt sorry he'd started the conversation. Maybe she'd be upset that he hadn't included her in the decision right from the beginning.

"I was just thinking," he started in a rush, "you're getting really busy with all the events you plan, and I know our place isn't the biggest. Since we have a fairly big yard, maybe you'd be okay with us building an additional space. It won't be huge, but you'll have enough room to store all your stuff. I was looking at some plans, and I think we can make it big enough so you can have all the administration stuff in there too, or maybe we can even afford two rooms. I don't know." Trent rammed his hand through his hair and almost looked to be pleading with Melissa by the time he stopped to take a breath.

"You don't know?" Melissa's voice trailed off. "What don't you know, Trent?" Her heart was so full she found herself at a sudden loss for words.

"Wh … wh …" he stammered. "What do you think?" Before she could answer, he added, "I'm sorry I didn't tell you I was planning this. I probably should have."

Melissa couldn't speak, but she got up from her side of the table and walked over to throw her arms around her husband. She didn't care that the other patrons in the restaurant looked at them with concern or curiosity. She didn't care when the hug didn't end quickly and Trent had pushed back his chair so she could continue her grasp, sitting on his lap.

"Hey," laughed Trent, relieved to take her hug and more than glad to give it back.

"Thank you," her muffled voice kept saying into his neck. "Thanks so much, Trent."

When she pulled away from him, he saw her tears and smiled at her.

"I know the house has been a bigger and bigger mess lately. I just don't have any room left," explained Melissa. "It's been getting to me too, Trent."

Trent laughed, hugging his wife again. "That's not the reason I'm building on, Mel. You need the space—your place—to keep that important part of your life. I figure this way, we can just be us in the main part of the house." He looked at her again and gently pushed a few strands of dark brown hair away from her face. "Maybe you can leave the work in the other room."

Melissa smiled back at him, touching his cheek. "I think that's a great idea."

They didn't care where they were as they kissed each other like they hadn't in a while. Their appetizer came then, and Melissa was suddenly sorry to have to sit away from him again.

As they ate their meals, Trent showed Melissa pictures on his phone of some ideas he'd found on the internet for the new space.

When they were offered dessert, they both declined, wanting to move the rest of their "date" back home.

As they drove up to their house, all looked quiet, and Trent sighed as he parked the car but left it running. "We're okay, right?" he ventured, turning a little in the driver's seat to look directly at Melissa.

"So okay," smiled Melissa, looking into his gaze.

"You too?" he asked tentatively.

Melissa knew what he meant, and her smile left her. "I think so," she said softly.

"A lot's happening for everybody," he stated, never taking his eyes from hers.

Melissa nodded as she bit the side of her lower lip.

"You and Trish talk yet?" he asked.

Melissa nodded. "Yeah ... a few times."

Trent gave her a small, pensive nod back, waiting.

"I think she doesn't like to talk about her pregnancy with me. She's so sad for us, and I think she's worried I won't be happy for her, but it hurts that she doesn't want to talk about it with me. I am happy for her and Grant, Trent. I really am."

"Did you tell her that?" Trent asked gently.

"I don't know how to talk about it. Honest, I don't," she admitted. "I guess if I'm truthful, I am a bit jealous ... maybe I'll always feel that way around anyone who's pregnant. I mean ... I really wanted your baby, Trent."

Trent reached over and grabbed Melissa's hand. "I know."

"But we have Abby, and I couldn't love her more," she continued, as if needing to explain it to him.

As sad as he was for his wife and her anxious thoughts surrounding all things pregnancy-related, he felt relieved that she was talking to him about it now. This was the work people talked about when speaking of marriage, and Trent had always been up for the work. As he watched his wife, he couldn't help but smile a little.

"I want to be happy for my friend, Trent," Melissa continued. "I mean, Trish and Grant are our closest friends, and it's like I can't share one of the best things in Trish's life with her because she's so scared of how I'll feel. I get that, and I appreciate it, but even if I cry sometimes, I'm still happy for her."

Trent didn't know what to say, so he gripped Melissa's hand a little more tightly.

"That's not my biggest worry, though," she sighed.

"I know," replied Trent, now feeling his anxiety increase.

It was Melissa's turn to wait and watch her husband, but she didn't have to wait long.

"When Stephanie tells Joe that Abigail's his biological daughter, I want you to know that I'm not giving her up without a fight, Mel," stated Trent loudly. There! He'd said it! Suddenly Trent realized that it hadn't only been Melissa who needed to vent. He'd had this thing hanging over him since the night of Jack and Sandy's wedding. Now as he took some deep breaths, he felt a little dizzy with the enormity of it all.

This time Melissa grabbed Trent's other hand and held them both in hers, boring her gaze even more directly into his.

"Trent, no matter what happens, we will always be a huge part of Abigail's life, but we have to be prepared for anything. I'm glad we're finally talking about this. I mean, if Joe suddenly wants to keep Abby ... well, that might happen, Trent. Fathers often get custody of their children, and if he insists ..." She swallowed, trying not to cry. "He is her biological dad, and he's my cousin, Trent. It could be a real mess. We don't want to fight over Abby. Ever. I only want the best for her, and even if Joe doesn't seem to have his act together right now, he's starting to try." She looked at the unreadable expression on her husband's face before continuing, but she had to make him understand. "I think we're really the best choice for parenting her, Trent, but if it comes down to a fight, I can't put Abby through anything like that. We have to wrap our heads around anything that could happen here."

Trent couldn't name every emotion he felt at that moment, but he knew his respect for his wife had just grown in leaps and bounds. He'd expected her to ready for a fight to keep their daughter, but instead, she was only thinking of Abigail and what would be easiest for her. Trent couldn't speak, but his eyes teared as he reached over the console in their car and tightly hugged the woman he loved.

Melissa hugged him back for a long while before she pulled away and looked at him. "We'll get through this, Trent. We will. We'll keep praying, and we won't stop until we know what's what." With that, she nodded once and turned to open the door to the cool air outside the car.

When they quietly entered their home, they saw Tess asleep on the couch. Trent woke her up by calling her name, and after she apologized for falling asleep, she left for home.

"Too many night shifts for Tess," Trent whispered as he came up behind Melissa, who was gazing at their daughter, safely asleep in her toddler bed.

"She's fine," assured Melissa to Trent and herself.

"Of course she is," he whispered.

As they got ready for bed, they both fell into a comfortable silence, each a little lost in their own thoughts.

When Melissa climbed into bed beside him, Trent grabbed her hand as she laid her head on his chest. Then, before making love, they prayed together for everyone in their circle, but especially for Joe.

Chapter Nine

"WELL, WHAT ARE YOU THINKING? SAY SOMETHING, PLEASE," GRANT SAID WITH sudden concern in his voice.

He was right. There weren't many times in my life that I'd been lost for words, but today was one of those rare moments when I just ... was.

I took a deep breath before sighing.

"You're overwhelmed?" he guessed.

Of course I was overwhelmed. He should be too. I looked at him and tried to smile, but this was an occasion when a bit of knowledge was not a good thing, and I had more than just a bit of it. Too many things could go wrong, and my mind sped back to the many complications I'd seen in my years of being an obstetrical nurse. As exciting as this should be, and would be for many, I couldn't think past the troubles I'd seen.

"Trish," Grant urged, now looking increasingly concerned. "This is exciting news, babe. Please say something."

I turned my head to stare at him and got just a little lost in his blue stare, but that didn't change my feelings of anxiety. "Are they fraternal or identical?" I asked the ultrasound technician, turning my face back to her and hoping she wouldn't say what she did.

"Identical twins," she said cheerfully. "I can't tell if they're both boys or both girls yet, but we should be able to tell at your next ultrasound. You're just about thirteen weeks now."

I wanted to feel excited. I did. "Is there a membrane between them?" I asked, hoping for good news.

The technician looked at me questioningly as I shrugged. "I'm a labour and delivery nurse."

She smiled then and nodded at me. "Yes. See here?" she answered, putting her cursor to an area on the screen that showed a white membrane between the two babies. At least that was a positive thing.

Although I thought I'd felt flutters in the last few days, I had told myself it was way too early, but now it made sense. Of course I'd feel something earlier if there were two babies.

Grant was squeezing my hand and smiling, clearly excited about the news of two more children.

I smiled, trying my best to feel the same, if only for his sake.

"Everything looks nice, Trish," assured the technician. "There isn't a huge difference in their sizes—just a couple of millimetres. They're both moving a lot, and the placenta is away from the cervix. The early anatomy looks good for both babies too, from what I'm seeing, but that will be in the report." She was clearly trying to allay my fears and probably was saying more than she should.

"Babies," I whispered. I felt Grant's excitement again as he smiled at the technician and squeezed my hand.

When the ultrasound was over, we saw the obstetrician, Lisa, a friend of mine who had delivered many babies, twins among them.

"Trish," Lisa said as Grant and I sat across from her in the examining room, "quit worrying. You know too much. That's the problem. I want you to enjoy this time. This is exciting!" Seeing my continued expression of concern, she spoke in the quiet way she had with all her patients. "Try to let the worrying go. Tell yourself this: on this day, at this moment, everything looks good."

I nodded again, trying to smile.

"That's what I told her," Grant agreed with Lisa. "Apparently, sometimes ignorance is bliss. Take me, for example. I'm totally up for this because I really don't know all the stuff that can go wrong, and I'm glad. We've got to give this to God, Trish."

Lisa and I looked at him. Lisa laughed and nodded, placing the blood pressure cuff around my arm. "Listen to him," she said, motioning toward Grant with her head. As she took my BP, Grant squeezed my other hand, still unable to stop grinning.

As I felt the pressure of the cuff lessen and glanced at the machine, which displayed a normal blood pressure reading, Lisa continued. "You've been through a lot with your dad dying recently. If you want to talk to someone, Trish, or need anything, please let me know, okay?" Lisa took the cuff off and keyed my blood pressure into my electronic chart on the computer in the exam room. She printed out the requisitions for the routine prenatal blood work I would need as well. I learned that I'd need ultrasounds about every two weeks for the remainder of the pregnancy. I wondered then if I'd ever noticed exactly how many ultrasounds my labour patients with twins normally had during their pregnancies. Had I ever read all those reports? If they were printed out, that would be a lot of trees.

I suddenly realized that both Grant and Lisa had become very quiet while I'd been daydreaming, and they were both staring at me now.

"I'm okay," I stated suddenly, as I shook myself out of my reverie.

If there was ever a time I would have loved to talk to my dad, it was now, but I knew he'd probably say the same things Lisa and Grant were telling me.

When Grant and I were in the truck and on our way home, I couldn't help myself. I regained my speech and began listing, while counting on my fingers, all the things that I knew could go horribly wrong when carrying identical twins. As Grant became quieter, I kept counting. It was just after I'd tried to explain Twin-to-Twin-Transfusion Syndrome, which could end with pregnancy failure, that I realized the change in Grant's demeanour. Every muscle in his back and arms appeared tense, and his hands clenched the steering wheel while his eyes stared straight ahead. I stopped then. Although I knew about all the worst-case scenarios, and had seen them, he'd lived some of those, and I immediately felt tides of guilt and sorrow for the man I loved. I took a breath, my mind reaching to figure out how to reverse my rant.

As he remained silent, I ventured, "What do you think? Boys or girls? Or do you even want to find out?"

When he didn't answer, I stopped talking, wondering what could possibly be going through his mind. He'd lost a son at term from an irreparable heart anomaly, and he'd lost his wife, after she'd given birth, from a postpartum hemorrhage. And now I wouldn't shut up about all the things that could go wrong in our pregnancy. How could I have been so thoughtless?

An uncomfortable silence filled the small space of the truck cab. Thankfully, before I could continue speaking, Grant sighed and pulled the truck over to park on the side of the street a few blocks away from our home. He then turned to face me after throwing the truck into park.

"Trish," he said as he reached over the console to take my hand in his right one. He cleared his throat as he threaded his fingers through mine. "I can't see how this is going to work if you're going to be scared the whole time you're pregnant. I'm going to pray that you'll get a peace about this right now."

I immediately bowed my head, waiting for him to start, but I peeked up at him when I heard nothing. He was staring at me, and as I looked at him, he almost whispered, "If you think I'm not at all worried, you'd be wrong."

Even more reams of guilt poured over my head, but I couldn't respond.

Grant looked at me with an intensity I'd never before seen in his eyes, and my heart sped up. "I love you, and I love these babies," he said quietly. "Could something go wrong? Yes. Could we lose them? Yes. Could I … I lose you?" His eyes teared as his voice caught, and I felt his grip tighten. "Yes, I know that can all happen, but …" He closed his eyes and took a deep breath. My eyes had filled with tears and now one plopped, none too quietly, on my lap.

Grant started to pray then. It was as powerful a prayer as I'd ever heard. He prayed for peace and for ongoing health for me and our precious twins. When he finished with the "amen" that often ended our prayers, we looked at each other and saw each other's tears. He reached to wipe mine away as I wiped his.

"It's all good, Trish, and even if it's not, we *will* leave this with God. After all, He made these children, and He made you to carry them, so I have to believe that He'll hold on to all three of you."

Again, all I could do was cry and thank God for giving me Grant and his total and complete faith in his Lord and Saviour.

When we got home, Sandy and Jack welcomed us back. They'd returned from their honeymoon and had been excited to see Kylie, so they'd been more than happy to babysit while we went for the ultrasound. They were excited about the news that there were two blessings coming along, and I, again, was overwhelmed by everyone else's happiness.

"Babies?" said Kylie later that night, patting my stomach.

I laughed and said, "Yes, Kylie. Two babies." I tried to show her how to hold up two fingers. "Just like your age."

She smiled and threw herself at me with a huge hug.

"I better get as many of these in as I can now, before my lap gets too big to hold you, young lady," I laughed, feeling better about all of it.

Sandy and Jack left early because Sandy had a headache.

"It's just a migraine, Trish," she said, smiling, after I offered her an analgesic.

"Are you sure, Sandy?" I had just recently learned about the more frequent headaches she'd been having, but she always seemed to have an excuse for them. I had agreed that perhaps they had been from all the stress and busyness of the wedding preparations, but I thought they should have gotten better over their honeymoon.

"Maybe you should get checked out," I suggested. "You seem to get a lot of those. How were they when you were away?"

Sandy smiled, but her eyes evaded mine. "I'm fine, Trish. Really. I had a doctor see me right before our wedding. He said not to worry, so I'm not. Things will settle down now, and they'll pass. You just concentrate on growing those grandchildren for us. If they're anything like Kylie, Jack and I are going to have such fun with them. You just made our day."

I watched as Jack put his arm protectively around his new wife before leaving, but his slight frown didn't escape me. Had there been something else?

I didn't have time to wonder about it or ask anything more because Kylie was having a tough time letting her grandparents leave, and Grant was looking at me with the unspoken expression I'd learned was his cry for help.

Later, as I reflected on our busy day, I thought of my in-laws. What a wonderful couple they made.

As I placed my hand on the lower part of my belly, I managed a genuine smile. I thanked God not only for the two new members of our family, who I would have the privilege to bear, but for the wonderful family they would get to be a part of.

Chapter Ten

IT TRULY IS EXCITING TO TELL THE PEOPLE YOU LOVE ABOUT A PREGNANCY. AS much as one baby would have been enough, two seemed to be ridiculously exciting news to give—especially for Grant. He was ecstatic and couldn't wait to tell, what seemed to me, the whole world. As much of a novelty as it was for me at times, I knew it was definitely more so for the people around me ... you know, the ones not carrying two children.

Shortly after the ultrasound, we went out for ice cream one evening with Trent and Melissa to break the news of the twins. Spring was in the air, and although early, the weather was uncharacteristically warm, so we bundled Kylie a little and met them at a park.

"They'll be so pumped for us, Trish," Grant said, not understanding my hesitancy. "I don't know why you wouldn't let me call them right away. We tell them just about everything, and they're our closest friends."

"Yeah, well," I began, "our 'everything' has never included telling them about a pregnancy with twins, Grant. It might be tough for them."

Pregnancy news was something Trent and Melissa would never have the privilege to share with us, and I needed Grant to understand that perhaps this might be a sensitive subject to broach with our dear friends.

Nothing, however, could abate Grant's exuberance. "They'll be fine," he assured me. "They'll be happy for us, Trish."

I gave him a side-long glance, not feeling convinced at all. It would be better if they heard it from us, however, and not someone else in the family, so it best be done sooner rather than later.

As our two girls played with, more than ate, their small ice cream cones, Grant couldn't wait any longer.

"Enough small talk," he suddenly announced. "You know we're pregnant, but we're having identical twins!"

I would've spewed my mouth full of milkshake everywhere if I hadn't instead swallowed the wrong way at that exact moment, which started a choking fit instead. As Grant gently pounded me on my back, he laughed. "She's still in shock."

Another side-long glance of disapproval from me to him, and Grant said nothing more.

As my choking resolved, I peered across the picnic table. Although at this particular moment it could've been debated, I stared with concern at the two people I loved almost as much as my husband.

To my relief and admiration for the best friends I have, and will ever have in this world, they both broke out in the hugest smiles, which I hadn't expected. I was so moved that I immediately did the only thing I could. I started to cry.

As Grant put his arm around me, Melissa crooned. "No, Trish. What's wrong? Is something wrong?" She looked at Grant. "What's wrong?"

I don't know exactly what broke the damn this time. Perhaps it was the stress of what I really did see as a daunting pregnancy ahead, or maybe it was how guilty I felt about feeling anything but thankful as I stared into the eyes of two people who would've probably given up a limb to be in my situation. I'd also spoken to Stephanie that afternoon, and she still hadn't told Joe about fathering Abigail, which also could be detrimental to our closest friends. For whatever reason, I cried as everyone watched and waited until I could join in any semblance of conversation.

Melissa was so relieved that there was nothing wrong with me—physically, anyway—that she laughed. She and Trent were so gracious and appeared to be genuinely happy, but Trent, knowing me like he had for the entirety of our lives, must have picked up on my doubt. Before leaving that evening, as Grant and his cousin Melissa wiped up the sticky messes our girls had become, Trent pulled me over to the side.

"I hope you're not going to stop sharing everything about this with me and Mel. She'd be heartbroken."

When I looked questioningly at him, his gaze bore into mine as he firmly told me, "Trish, Melissa feels bad enough. She can't seem to tell you this, so I will. She feels like you've been sort of avoiding her since you found out about your pregnancy. She doesn't want you to feel sorry for her, and neither do I. She really wants to be happy for you and share this with you. You have to let her."

I suddenly felt great chagrin for what I thought had been me being sensitive to my friend's feelings. It didn't help when, before walking away from me, Trent added, "Be a better person, Trish."

As I stood, unmoving, and watched him walk back to our families, my mouth gaped open. Better? I thought I'd only been thinking of them. How dare he speak to me like that! My hormones threatened to send me into a rage on top of Trent's head, but thankfully it ebbed in the minute I was given to regroup. As I stared over at Grant and my two best friends laughing at our two toddlers who were running around wildly from the sugar high their ice cream had induced, my heart softened.

I walked over to Melissa and grabbed her in a hug that couldn't have been more sincere. She had been nothing but gracious and loving toward me, and here I was holding her at arm's length.

"I love you, my friend," I told her. "I feel so bad that you can't have this experience, but I'll share mine with you, if you want that."

Melissa's eyes teared as she broke into a smile. "Of course I want that, Trish. Of course."

We hugged again, but soon after, when we were saying our goodbyes and the girls were both crying because they didn't want to leave one another, I chose not to hug Trent. That didn't seem to faze him, however, as he climbed into their vehicle. As I stealthily glanced his way before we drove away, I saw his smile. He threw a direct look my way and mouthed "better" with an approving nod of his head. I looked away then because I couldn't let him see the smile that betrayed me on my own lips.

Chapter Eleven

OVER THE NEXT FEW MONTHS, AS THE ROUTINE OF FURTHER ULTRASOUNDS and pregnancy blood work continued, I began to relax a little more. Things seemed to be going along quite well, and both babies were growing, with their difference in weight, or discordancy, within normal limits. It was in the middle of the pregnancy, after both babies' anatomy scans were reported as normal, that Grant appeared even more excited about our coming children. I couldn't blame him. I too found much relief in words like "normal" written on the many reports involving our babies. Due to the loss of his firstborn from a heart anomaly, I suspected his thankfulness probably far exceeded mine. He even thought it necessary to throw a spontaneous family gathering one evening, without informing me, and ordered in pizza and salad for dinner. Unfortunately, my eight-hour day at work had turned into twelve, and I'd had no choice but to extend my shift. Too many labouring women needed the too-few tired nurses that day, and it was after 7:00 p.m. when I drove up to our house.

When I saw the vehicles parked outside our home, I sighed, knowing what was happening. Strangely, I felt less than gracious about it. I may have had a better attitude if my shift had been less busy, but all I'd planned to do before leaving work was to enjoy some peace and quiet with a warm bath and immediate bedtime. Now I'd have a houseful of company to entertain before any of that could happen.

I took a deep breath and tried to quietly open the front door without being noticed. I knew it was unlikely that no one would be in the living room, but as I cracked open the door and peeked inside, my hopes soared. Perhaps I could at least sneak upstairs for a quick bath before anyone noticed me. I closed the door as softly as possible behind me as I heard happy voices coming from the kitchen, which I figured would help cover any noise I might make. With any luck …

"Momma!" squealed Kylie, running around the corner after spotting me tiptoe to the stairs. Shoot! So close! Oh well … I didn't believe in luck anyway.

"Kylie," I tried to say excitedly, without much success. I felt a bit of guilt as I looked at my gleeful girl. I had hoped she would've been put to bed, actually, and wondered if any other mother in the world was as pathetic as I was in that moment. Wouldn't a normal mom crave to see their child after working all day and being away from them?

"Trish," said Grant, coming from the kitchen after her. "C'mon. Take a load off and I'll feed you pizza. Everyone's here and …"

He stopped when he saw the expression on my face. As guilty as I was feeling about my unimpressive maternal instincts, I was just as unimpressed that he hadn't warned me of what was happening in our own home.

"I'm guessing I should've let you know?" he asked, still smiling, which irked me a little more.

"Ya think?" I said sarcastically.

Grant must have thought I wasn't serious, but then, as I stared him down, it began to dawn on him.

"Listen, Trish," he started, coming over to hug me, "it's the only night that worked for mostly everyone, and I didn't know you'd stay late. I knew you weren't scheduled to work tomorrow, so I thought it would be nice to have the family in. I'm sorry now that I didn't tell you, though, but everyone was excited to come and celebrate with us. I thought I'd surprise you."

I looked at this man who had always put me first, and I wanted to be gracious, but instead, my sore feet won out as I simply said, "I'm going for a bath first, if that's okay." I knew I needed to adjust my attitude, and maybe after a quick soak and a few moments of quiet I'd feel better. Then, I expected, I'd apologize for my apparent narcissism, like I often had to.

Grant looked a little hurt before I kissed him quickly and ran up the stairs, but I could hear him laugh as he told the others that I'd be right down after getting cleaned up.

As I sunk into the warm tub of water I'd hurriedly poured, I made the mistake of closing my eyes and concentrating on my breathing. My mind looped back, re-evaluating my busy day. It seemed there had been too many complications for such a short twelve hours. Although I didn't want to, my mind fixated on one young couple who had come into the hospital, excitedly awaiting the arrival of their first baby boy. Perhaps it should have been seen on ultrasound during his gestation, but it happened. The baby had been born with a unilateral cleft lip and palate. It was difficult to tell the young parents, who had readied their phones for pictures of their precious newborn, but after seeing their sweet boy, they hadn't taken one photograph. I thought of how the abnormalities blatantly seen sometimes seemed harder to bear, even when not life-threatening. This baby's anomaly would be surgically repaired, and their baby boy would go on to live a normal life. I thought of Trevor then and thanked God that our twins' hearts both appeared to be normal. Of course Grant would want to celebrate that. It deserved this celebration and many more.

I went to get up from the warm bath, but then promising myself only another five minutes, I settled back in. The next thing I felt was something soft against my cheek, almost like a whisper. I groaned softly before becoming fully conscious, and when my eyes opened, I stared into the deep blue eyes I'd fallen in love with.

"Oh!" I startled then. "I'm so sorry, Grant!" I said sincerely. "I'll be right down. Just grab me my towel please."

His face remained close to mine as he broke into a smile. "Too late," he breathed, kissing me lightly before moving back to stare at me as he settled himself to sit on the edge of the tub.

"Wh ...what do you mean?" I asked, confused. I couldn't have been in the bathtub that long, although as I felt the temperature of the water around me, I wondered.

"No worries, babe," Grant shrugged. "It was late, and we'd already eaten by the time you came in anyway. Everybody understood, Trish. You had a long day. Your mom put Kylie to bed and decided to stay over, so you can see her in the morning."

More guilt washed over me as I reached for the towel Grant was blocking me from. He grabbed both my hands and threaded his fingers through mine as he pushed me gently to sit back in the tub again. He turned the hot water on to warm the bath and started getting undressed.

"Really, Grant ... what time is it?" I asked, still surprised that I'd slept that long in a bath.

"Not that late, milady," he answered, trying for silly and making me smile.

"Oh my gosh!" I exclaimed, grabbing over the edge of the tub for my phone and realizing that it was, indeed, late enough. "How did I not drown sleeping in a tub of water for that long?" I continued.

"Well, I didn't just leave you here," Grant said, stepping into the tub and sitting across from me, displacing the water that now threatened to spill over the edges.

He smiled suggestively as he watched my face. His expression changed and he laughed. "Trish, I came in and saw you fast asleep. You clearly need to rest, and I saw that you weren't about to drown, so I just couldn't bring myself to wake you up."

I relaxed again in my end of the tub and smiled my thanks to him. Although I still felt bad about ignoring our guests, I was more than thankful for the needed rest and the now warmer water.

"So ..." I paused before flicking some water his way with my fingers. "If you know I need to sleep, why are you in my bathtub, Grant Evans?"

His stare deepened, and I couldn't look away. I tried a different approach. "I feel this is wildly inappropriate with my mother still in the house, Grant."

My guilt and anxiety vanished as he moved toward me with more of a grin on his face, and his eyebrows suggesting a promise we both needed fulfilled.

"You owe me for leaving me alone with all of them tonight," his soft whisper growled.

"Hey ... you did that to yourse ..." I started before he kissed the rest of the word from me.

I decided then that I would gladly apologize to our guests, and to my mother, but not until the next day. Right now I was just glad to pay him back.

Chapter Twelve

"THAT REALLY IS BEAUTIFUL WORK, JOE," SAID HIS BOSS, LOOKING DOWN AT THE rocking chair Joe had just finished. "Really nice work." Glenn nodded again.

He showed Joe one small thing he could improve and then asked him to come into his office. When they were both seated, he got right to the point. "I want to move you up to other things. You've quickly mastered the basics and even more over the months you've been here, and I need someone to make the bigger items that are so in demand lately. You okay with that?" asked Glenn.

Joe shrugged. "Sure," he agreed, trying not to smile. He honestly didn't care what he was asked to make. He just loved working with his hands, and he liked the sense of pride he felt in what he made and what he could design. He may need to follow a pattern here, but he had already added a few embellishments to some of the projects, and Glenn had appreciated most of them.

"You keep doing this well, and I'll send you on to school after you get in the hours you need. It'll take some time, but I can see you becoming a journeyman carpenter … if that's what you want," Glenn said, looking serious.

"That would be great, sir." Joe looked down momentarily, feeling a bit surprised, but when he looked at his boss again, he stood up and stuck out his hand. "I'd really appreciate that."

Glenn nodded as he stood to shake hands with Joe. They left the office and walked to the large workshop near one side of the property. Glenn began showing Joe some of the projects he wanted him to begin working on and then left him with some of the other employees.

Joe could hardly believe it. Maybe he would be good at this. It felt right, and he hadn't made too many mistakes. Maybe he had finally found his niche.

After work, Joe was just about to climb into his truck when he heard a voice from behind him.

"Hey," asked Marty, one of the guys who worked with him, "you wanna meet at the bar? Mike and I are gonna celebrate his new baby. Some of the other guys are going too. You're welcome to come."

Joe thought about it. He hadn't been to a bar for a while, and the thought tempted him. It would be a chance to get to know the guys he worked with and become part of something again, but to celebrate a baby? He shook his head. "Maybe another time," he answered. He wasn't sure, since he'd been sober for not even a year yet, if he could go to a bar and not drink. "Thanks for asking, though."

"Oh, come on, man," Marty chided. "We only do this once in a while. Don't be like that."

Joe smiled but shook his head again. "Sorry, I made other plans, but maybe another time," he lied.

"Okay," accepted Marty, "but I'm holding you to that, Joe. Next time."

Joe gave him a nod and waved as Marty drove away.

Their boss, Glenn, had overheard the conversation and walked over to Joe after locking up the shop. "Not into the bar scene?" asked the older man, suddenly even more interested in his newest employee. Glenn hadn't learned a lot about Joe. He'd kept pretty much to himself, and he did really good work, but that was all he knew.

Joe had always enjoyed being in a crowd, but since living on the ranch, he'd become quite content keeping more to himself, and now he almost preferred it that way. Maybe it was his true self when he wasn't drinking. "Just not tonight," answered Joe with a small smile.

"Hmm ..." Glenn observed. "That's not my scene either ... anymore. I've gotta get home to my missus anyway."

When Joe only nodded, Glenn continued. "Any special someone in your life, Joe? Someone to go home to?"

Joe laughed then. "Nah. Not my own woman. I'm staying with my brother and his wife right now. My sister-in-law is enough to contend with if I get outta line."

It was Glenn's turn to laugh then. "Holds you accountable, eh?" he asked.

Joe stopped laughing and a look of confusion came over him as he looked at Glenn. He considered his answer before saying, "Sort of ... I guess." Joe didn't know exactly what Glenn was talking about, but he knew he didn't want Trish to ever see him at his worst. Truth be told, she scared him a little sometimes. She wasn't afraid to tell him what she thought either, and sometimes what she said put him in an uncomfortable place. Of course he could, on occasion, give back what she dealt out, but more recently some of the things she'd said had hit too close to home.

Glenn continued, ignoring Joe's serious expression. "Take my advice, man. Find a good woman of your own who holds you accountable for your actions and you'll have a happy life. My lady keeps me out of trouble, I'll tell you. She's a force to reckon with, but I wouldn't have it any other way."

Joe nodded, thinking immediately of Stephanie and not really knowing why. Hadn't he'd just mentioned Trish? He shook his head and smiled. "Thanks for everything, Glenn. I appreciate everything you've done for me. I really like it here."

Glenn looked at Joe like he wanted to say more but nodded once instead. "Good. I'm glad. See ya tomorrow, Joe."

As the two men drove away, Joe thought more about Stephanie. He'd seen her at Grant and Trish's last night, but they hadn't really talked. He was so incredibly attracted to her, but she seemed like a dream that could never be fulfilled, even more so after their last phone conversation. They'd talked a few times over the last while, and each time Joe couldn't help but think that she wanted to say more. He didn't know what exactly ... just more. He had even asked her that night, after she had finished telling him about an account she'd worked on. Even though he no longer worked with his brother at GR-Jo Holdings, he understood the work. He found himself enjoying her enthusiasm when she told him about a few accounts he himself had worked on, albeit a long time ago. When she had paused to take a breath, he had tried. "Is there something you need to tell me, Steph?"

She'd told him recently that he could call her by the shortened form of her name. She had told him long ago that she only allowed friends to call her by that name. It meant more to Joe than he thought it would when she'd changed her mind about that. Maybe now she considered him at least some sort of friend.

"What do you mean?" she had immediately asked, almost accusatorially.

Joe hadn't expected that so decided to avoid it. "Nothing," he laughed. "I'm just raggin' on ya."

Stephanie had soon begged off the phone, and although Joe thought it strange, he'd let it go. He guessed that if there was something she needed to tell him, she'd do so when she was ready. Now as Joe drove to Grant and Trish's, he still thought something was gnawing at her but had no idea what.

He picked something up for dinner on the way and ate in his truck before going inside. When he did arrive, he went straight to the basement, where he spent his nights. He didn't feel like visiting with anyone tonight, not even his niece, Kylie. Besides, maybe Trish was getting tired of having him there. She hadn't even had dinner with the family yesterday when she'd gotten home from work.

Joe sighed as he turned on the TV across from his bed in the basement. He loved the space down here and the fact that no one really ever came downstairs but just left him alone. He scrolled through some ads for rental apartments and condos but saw nothing that looked promising, so he threw down his phone to watch an episode of some detective show. His mind turned to the things he had learned, even in the short time he'd worked for Glenn. He was a great teacher, and Joe had learned a lot already.

"A good woman," Glenn had said. "Someone to hold you accountable."

Joe wasn't even sure he knew what that meant, exactly, but it sounded intimidating. As he went off to sleep, Joe dreamed of a girl with red hair, excited eyes, and everything in the right places. But when she turned, Stephanie didn't look at him. She looked at someone else, far behind him.

Chapter Thirteen

STEPHANIE HAD WORKED A LOT OF LATER HOURS AT THE OFFICE IN THE LAST while, and tonight she felt as though she might actually get everything on her list done if she stayed just a little longer.

"Hey!" Grant said, sticking his head into her office doorway before leaving. "You don't have to stay late again, you know."

She looked up at her boss and smiled. "I know, Grant. I just think if I stay an hour, or two at the most, I might finally get caught up. Besides, I want to take one last look at the proposal for tomorrow and make sure it's perfect, and I need the extra hours to get my condo furnished."

Grant laughed, looking at the list he saw she'd written on a small paper on her desk. Stephanie saw where his gaze fell, and she smiled. "Never mind," she laughed, covering the list.

"You and your lists." He shook his head. "You're young—why don't you use your phone for those?"

Stephanie shrugged, smiling. There was nothing like pen-stroking something off paper when it was completed. Her mom had always done that, and she'd learned from the best.

"Never mind." She laughed again. "Go home or I'll never get anything done."

"Okay," Grant agreed, but before he left, he added, "Not too late, promise? You're making me look bad, Steph. I'm the boss. I should be here later than you."

"You have a family waiting for you, Grant. I don't. Besides, this is my work, and you know I love it."

"That I do." Grant nodded appreciatively. "I think you're the best employee I've ever had."

Stephanie couldn't help but redden a little. When Grant complimented her, it always felt so honestly genuine. She'd never had a boss like that before, and she appreciated him as much as he did her. He and Trish had been so welcoming to her, and she loved them deeply.

Grant cleared his throat, feeling sorry that he'd embarrassed her. In that way, she and Trish were very similar. He smiled again and left her office, locking the main door to their offices behind him.

Stephanie sighed, looked at her computer screen, and got back to work. When she next glanced at the time on her phone, she couldn't believe how she'd let it get away on her again. She smiled, thinking how she must sincerely think her job was fun, since time did fly when she was working on new marketing strategies or the more creative parts of her occupation. She quickly decided that she'd do just one more thing on her list, jotted down a few informational points that she needed from the site she was on, and got up to grab a folder out of one of the filing cabinets that sat just outside her office door. As she pushed the cabinet drawer closed, she stopped and listened. The faint sound of music was coming from somewhere. Stephanie went into her office and placed the file on her desk before slowly walking to the other side of the large main room to find the source of the music. The office secretary, Alicia, often played the radio while she worked, but the music seemed to come from somewhere else. It grew louder as she moved closer to Grant's office, and when she opened the door, which he seldom locked, she slowly moved inside. That was strange. Music was playing. As Stephanie came around his large desk, she peered at the computer screen. Stephanie felt her throat constrict as she sat down in Grant's leather chair, watching and listening to the words as Francesca Battistelli sang "If We're Honest." It was as if the artist was speaking right to her.

Stephanie often felt like a mess too, and she felt broken. She hadn't been honest, and she needed mercy.

"Bring your brokenness ..." the song invited.

She'd made so many stupid mistakes and poor choices. Trish had told her many times that God wanted everyone to come to Him, no matter what they'd done or said. That's why He'd sent his Son to die—to cover everyone's baggage. Trish was convinced that God loved everyone. They just needed to choose Him.

The video ended and another began. Stephanie immediately recognized the song as one that Grant had listened to many times. He'd told her he liked the songs sung by this vocalist, but she'd never really paid much attention. Now as the song rang out, she read the lyrics, and her heart began to beat faster. As she listened to the words of the song "Mended," everything that God needed to say to her was made clear through Matthew West's words. The wounds she'd suffered, even as a young child, *could* be healed. She wasn't too far gone! She wasn't just damaged goods! She could be mended! Suddenly, in that dark office, with only the glow of the screen surrounding her, Stephanie understood.

As she continued to listen, she started praying—not like she'd been taught in Sunday school, in rhythmic memorized verse, but in a soul-wrenching confession of what she'd been and, better yet, what she wanted to become—a child of the King. Stephanie gave herself fully and entirely to God that night, and suddenly what her Grandpa Jack had said to her when she'd first met him came to the forefront of her mind like a wrecking ball. She belonged to him, and now she *belonged* to God.

When the song was over, the computer went dark, as if it had never been on. Stephanie wiped her tears and stood up. A chill ran through her as she walked quickly back to her own office and glanced at the list that lay, almost completed but not quite, on her desk. She felt different, somehow, and suddenly all the work she had planned to get done didn't hold the same importance. She turned off the remaining lights, locked the office, and left, leaving the file and the uncompleted list lying on her desk.

When Stephanie arrived at her condo, even though the hour was late, she felt compelled to call Joe. She didn't want to think of Abigail any longer without telling him the truth. She would come clean, and she was certain that God would take care of the rest.

Chapter Fourteen

WHEN JOE SAW STEPHANIE'S NUMBER ON HIS PHONE, HE JUMPED TO wakefulness.

"Hey," he said, clearing his throat and trying to sound casual but feeling worried. It was one o'clock in the morning. Something had to be wrong.

"Joe," Stephanie sounded excited, "I have to tell you something, and it couldn't wait."

"Sure," he answered, wondering why she sounded happy if some emergency was happening.

"I know what everyone's been talking about, Joe! I was in the office tonight, and the coolest videos came on Grant's computer, which was weird because he doesn't usually leave it on. Anyway, they were there, and I heard them, and I just ... I was listening to them ... and they talked about being broken and that God's okay with that and that He can fix anyone and ... well ... I get it now! I believe it!"

"Did you drink and drive?" demanded Joe, confused by what she was trying to say.

Stephanie laughed. She was rambling. Of course he'd think that. "No!" she answered, laughing. "I'm trying to tell you that I think ... I understand the whole God and Jesus thing, Joe. I believe in them. All of it! Like Trish and Grant and everyone's been telling us."

"Hmm ... right," Joe smirked with a grunt.

Stephanie could hear the cynicism in his voice, and somehow it hurt more than she'd expected. Suddenly, she didn't know why she'd felt so driven to call him. They had spoken a few times since Jack and Sandy's wedding, and they'd texted a few times too, but mostly it had been surface talk. Why would she feel that calling him was so important tonight? Right! She needed to come clean about Abby. But he sounded so ...

Stephanie shook her head, coming to her senses. "I'm sorry, Joe. It's really late. I shouldn't have called. I'm not sure—"

Joe stopped her. "No!" It was his turn to feel sorry now. He was glad she had called him. He hadn't been able to stop thinking of her. In his eyes, she was wonderful, and he wanted to get to know her even better. "You know you can call any time, Stephanie. Really. Even if you have weird news."

It wasn't weird news to her, and Stephanie couldn't help the hurt she felt. An inner battle began as she debated telling him about Abby again. When she'd dialled, she'd been so excited about it all, and now, listening to him, she felt deflated and full of self-doubt. Of course it would seem strange to him. It would have sounded weird to her too, even an hour ago. What had she been thinking? She should've shared her news with Trish and Grant, or her Grandpa Jack and her parents first. They would've understood. As her mind reeled, she decided to back off.

"How's your job going, Joe?" she asked as nonchalantly as possible.

Joe was glad for the question, deciding to ignore what she'd just told him. At least she was staying on the phone and talking. After all, what she wanted to believe about God was fine with him. Whatever.

"I like it," he replied. "My boss is great. He's thinking of sending me to school to get my journeyman papers."

"Cool," she said, feeling glad for him but wishing for something so much more.

Silence followed, but soon Stephanie said, "Well, it's late and I should go. I'm really happy for you, Joe."

"Me too," he agreed, "and ... I'm happy for you too, Stephanie, about whatever makes you happy."

"Thanks," said Stephanie quietly, knowing he just didn't understand.

"Is there anything else?"

His question hung in the air, and Stephanie took in a quick breath. He was giving her an opening, and she knew she should, but ... she just couldn't. It wouldn't be fair over the phone, anyway, she justified in her mind. "No. Nothing else."

Joe was quiet before he tentatively said, "Well ... goodnight then, Steph."

As she hung up, all she could feel was a profound sadness for Joe. She'd been thinking about him so often lately, and when she had seen him on different occasions, she'd been drawn to him more and more. Although they'd had a one-night-stand years ago, and that had produced a baby girl, they had become more like friends in the last few months. Did she want it to be more? Probably. Maybe. Yes. After talking to him tonight, however, Stephanie knew in her heart that it couldn't be more—not yet anyway, and maybe never.

Stephanie suddenly knew what she was going to do. She was going to pray for Joe—that he would know what he believed in. But from this night forward, she was moving ahead with God and would seek what He had planned and wanted for *her.* The advice her grandmother Helen had given her now resonated in her mind. *Decide what you believe, Stephanie.* She would do just that. She would read her Bible and pray and decide what she believed.

Then, feeling guilty for not telling Joe about Abigail again, Stephanie prayed that she would have the courage to do that also when the time was right.

Chapter Fifteen

"I HAVE GREAT NEWS, GRANT." STEPHANIE COULDN'T HELP GRINNING. SHE'D just gotten to work and had headed straight for his office instead of her own.

Grant had just sat down at his desk with the hot cup of coffee he'd made when he got to the office. From the excitement in her voice and her glowing countenance, he thought he could guess at what was coming. He waited, but he didn't have to wait long.

"I get it, Grant! I finally understand what you and Trish and Grandpa were talking about! Last night in the office here, your computer was on, and these music videos were playing, and I started praying and—"

Before Stephanie could finish, Grant sprang out of his chair and hugged her. He laughed and she grinned, tearing up, and both of them just knew that "something" that's impossible to explain. Stephanie had given herself to God and knew, without a doubt, that she belonged to Him.

As Stephanie told Grant all about it, they both couldn't stop smiling. She didn't tell Grant about speaking with Joe. She'd been disappointed in his reaction and thought Grant might be too.

As they walked out of Grant's office to where Alicia sat, the secretary looked up from the work she was doing. "What's up?" she asked, smiling at them.

Stephanie suddenly felt nervous. She'd been so caught up in how differently wonderful she felt, but she knew Alicia had made fun of what

Grant believed in before. That hadn't bothered Stephanie then, but now, as she looked at the secretary, she felt scared to tell her. She would probably think she was crazy—kind of how Stephanie viewed Christians just a day ago. Instead of saying anything, Stephanie looked up at Grant, who easily answered. "Stephanie gave her life to Christ last night. She became a Christian."

Alicia sat back in her chair and nodded slowly. "Good for you," she said, her smile fading.

"Yeah ... good for her!" exclaimed Grant, giving Stephanie a high-five. Stephanie couldn't help but laugh before going to her office to start work.

Grant had almost reached his office when he heard Alicia softly say, "Jesus freaks."

He didn't turn around but resolved, again, to keep praying for her as he went to call Trish and then get back to work. It would be a busy day.

• • •

"Come for dinner," Grant said close to the end of the workday while leaning on the doorway to Stephanie's office. "I told Trish your news. I hope that's okay. I couldn't keep it to myself when I checked in with her."

"Thanks, Grant, but maybe not tonight. I'm really tired. I think all my late nights are catching up with me. Would it be okay to make it another time soon, though?" asked Stephanie, almost sorry she was turning him down.

"Trish isn't cooking, if that makes a difference," he winked. "I'm picking up something instead."

It wasn't a secret to Trish, or many others who knew her, that cooking wasn't her gift, and it had become a family joke of sorts.

Stephanie smiled. "No, it has nothing to do with what's being served, Grant. I'm just wiped."

"Okay," he returned. "Soon, though. Kylie's missing you too."

The thought of her little sister made her smile.

"Soon," she promised.

"I'm holding you to it," said Grant, pulling his coat on. "Quitting time," he added, holding Stephanie's coat toward her.

Stephanie got up and sighed. She looked at the list of things she'd wanted to accomplish and wished she'd gotten more done, but Grant was right. Tomorrow was another day. Grant ushered Stephanie out of the building and hugged her again.

"I'm so glad you're part of our family, Steph," he said. "Now you really belong—in every way."

Chapter Sixteen

ANNIE WAS A PROFESSOR IN A UNIVERSITY FOR ONLY THE BEST AND BRIGHTEST. Although Helen had initially felt intimidated by that, the more the two chatted via phone or text, it seemed to Helen that Annie seemed more interested in the events she was planning with Melissa than the important things she did for a living. Helen guessed her explanations were simple distractions for her friend, who had a much more important life.

Over the months that had passed, Helen had confided a little in Annie, and she had been a good listener. When Helen told Annie how much she missed Ted, she would say things that made Helen think she knew exactly where she was coming from. Sometimes after only a few short minutes of conversation, Helen felt as if Annie had helped her more than the counsellor had after her husband's death. Although Annie didn't share much about her past relationships, she seemed to know just what to say to make Helen feel better. Annie also talked more about Jack and how she was convinced that as a child and into her early teen years, he had so often been her saviour. She held her brother in the highest regard, although she didn't talk about their lack of relationship after his incarceration. Annie only spoke about him as the big brother that had saved her from a lot of bad things, and Helen would again be left wondering just how bad it had been for them.

Helen knew that Annie did well for herself financially. She seemed very proud of that. When they'd gotten close to talking more deeply about relationships with other people, however, Annie would back off, changing the subject to something that Helen thought probably felt safer. A few times Helen had mentioned church, or something about God, but Annie always needed to get off the phone then. Now as Helen stared at her phone, she realized the same thing had just happened. She had only mentioned Stephanie's upcoming baptism, and Annie had been unwilling to continue.

"That's great, Helen," she'd said, interrupting her friend, "but I have to go."

"Please try to come, Annie. She's Jack's granddaughter—your relative too. She'd love to see you there, and I'm sure it would make Jack really happy."

"Yes, I suppose it would, Helen, but you know how busy I am. Jack invited me too, but I just can't ... get away."

Helen had heard something that she wondered about again in Annie's voice. She couldn't help but think of just how sad Annie sounded. Helen thought back to when she had hidden all her sadness behind her smiles and busyness. She suspected her friend was feeling something similar to that, but how could she judge? She didn't know Annie really well yet. Helen sighed, deciding that she would pray more for Annie. She needed someone in her life, but didn't realize it yet, so Helen would keep being the friend who would try to help her find Him.

Chapter Seventeen

STEPHANIE LOOKED UP, FEELING THE COOL AIR ON HER CHEEKS BEFORE stepping into the water. As the pastor took her hand and led her deeper, she couldn't help but smile even more. The pastor asked her questions about her belief in Jesus Christ. She thought she'd be nervous, but she wasn't at all. She listened carefully and answered with complete honesty.

Although it was a sunny day, the few white clouds that dotted the sky moved in waves in front of her as Stephanie opened her eyes underneath the cool water. As she was lifted out, she felt different but couldn't name how—much like that night at the office. It was as if she'd been wiped completely clean by God's love. With surprise, Stephanie thought of her mother, Stacy, who may have neglected her as a small child but who had experienced the same thing she now was. As she was raised from the water, Stephanie felt something move within her. In many ways she'd been like her mother, so if God could forgive her, Stephanie felt an overpowering strength to now fully forgive as well. The freedom she felt was exhilarating. She wiped the water from her face, pushed her hair back, and grinned. When she looked up at the sky again, the clouds had changed back to fluffy puffs.

She looked at her parents, Doug and Vi, who beamed as they watched her being baptized. Grant, Trish, Jack, Sandy, and Helen all looked on as well. Trent and Melissa had brought little Abigail with them. She didn't know why, but Stephanie was glad that the child she'd given birth to would watch her be baptized also. This was her family—hoping for her, her best life, full of the joy that comes only from God.

Although she was often self-conscious when soaking wet, Stephanie laughed as she wiped the water that dripped down from her long wavy hair from her eyes. She didn't care about how she looked today, or if her mascara still kept to her lashes. In that moment, with the people she belonged to, Stephanie only thought of her many blessings, and she thanked God for the freedom He had given her.

• • •

After all four people were baptized and were drying off, Helen went to speak to Stephanie, who was under a tree by herself. Helen would've preferred Stephanie get baptized in the church, but Stephanie had requested the lake.

"You need to get those wet clothes off, dear," observed Helen. "It probably won't be enough to just towel off."

Stephanie looked at her grandma and smiled. She lifted up the long white T-shirt she wore to reveal the bikini beneath it. "It's okay, Grandma," she laughed. "I was ready for this. A bathing suit dries quickly enough. Then I'll just put my jeans over it until we get back to Grant and Trish's place."

Helen looked at her granddaughter and thought she was probably right, since the skimpy suit she wore wouldn't take long at all to dry. Helen shook her head and chastised herself inwardly for being judgemental. Then she thought of what she'd come over to say.

"Your Grandpa Ted would be really proud of you today," Helen said sincerely.

Stephanie had thrown a dry shirt on immediately when she'd seen her grandma's expression and now came close to hug her tightly. "Thanks, Grandma," she whispered.

When she pulled away, she saw the tears in Helen's eyes, and her own teared as well. Although months had passed, the pain of losing Ted was still very raw—especially during special celebrations. Helen's husband, Ted, hadn't been her blood relative, but he had meant a lot to Stephanie, and she to him. He had always been encouraging and loving, and Stephanie had felt his love, unconditionally, toward her. Suddenly she missed him all the more. It had been a shock and an incredibly difficult reality for Helen, and Trish especially, but knowing that Ted was in heaven made it easier to accept. Today, Stephanie could smile, knowing that someday she would, without a doubt, see her grandpa again.

Stephanie's baptism meant that more extended family would meet for the first time. Although Doug and Vi had visited with Grant and Trish before, they hadn't met other members of the family, including Abigail. They were excited to meet her and had enjoyed spending time with her at the lake that afternoon.

"Grandma," said Stephanie, "Trish can pretend all she wants that she's making supper tonight, but I know you've done all the work. I want you to know that I really appreciate it. I'm hungry, and you're the best cook I know, but don't ever tell my mom I said that, okay?"

"I won't, sweetheart," Helen promised, squeezing her hand. "As long as you don't let on to anyone tonight that you know I'm the one who cooked. I think Trish thinks it's a secret."

"No one will believe that anyway, Grandma," laughed Stephanie.

As she watched Helen glance in the direction of her grandpa and Sandy, Stephanie hooked her arm in her grandmother's and asked, "Can I grab a ride with you? I came with my mom and dad, but since they're not coming to dinner, I think I'd like to go with you."

Helen appreciated her granddaughter's sensitivity and was more than happy to agree. On the way to the car, Stephanie told her grandmother just how she had felt as she'd been baptized, and Helen remembered back to that same time in her life. As she drove, Helen glanced at her beautiful granddaughter. Although Helen had experienced much emotional pain in her past, she suddenly felt overwhelmingly thankful. She was surprised to feel grateful that she had gotten pregnant at fifteen. For so many years, she'd only seen that as a horrible thing, but all these years later, she realized that because of it, she had received the most wonderful gift—Stephanie. For the first time, Helen's guilt over all of that genuinely left her. She was together with a young woman whom she treasured and who loved her as well. What more could she possibly ask for?

"Are you okay, Grandma?" asked Stephanie, breaking the silence.

Helen broke from her thoughts, glancing again at her granddaughter. "I'm so fine, Stephanie," she said, her throat catching. "Really … just fine."

Stephanie smiled her radiant grin just for her grandmother, and Helen returned it.

As they entered Grant and Trish's home, Helen, for the first time since seeing him again, felt a peace about being in the same room as Jack. She felt genuinely happy for him and Sandy. As she greeted them, she didn't care anymore about what people thought or said, or if people would find their history strange. As Stephanie had explained about being raised up out of the water on that beautiful afternoon, Helen Holmes too felt a newfound freedom—freedom to move on. Freedom to be who she was meant to be. Freedom in God and through His Son. Freedom.

Chapter Eighteen

OUR FAMILY AND A FEW FRIENDS GATHERED AT OUR HOME TO CELEBRATE Stephanie's baptism. I thought I'd give them a treat and cook instead of ordering in something, and although Grant had almost insisted it would be fine to bring in Chinese or something else, I was adamant that, since I had all day, I'd be more than happy to cook. Little did he know that my mother had offered to help out, and she would probably "help" by making most of it. It would be a win-win nonetheless, and no one really needed to know who had prepared the meal. That was my plan, anyway.

Everyone who was important to Stephanie was invited, including her parents, Doug and Vi. Trent, Melissa, and Abigail came as well. Kylie was ecstatic that her friend was there. They were both over two-and-a-half and very giggly. They always had much fun when they were together. In the end, it was Doug and Vi who decided they wouldn't join us after attending her baptism. Grant and I had spoken with them several times, but they politely declined. I couldn't help feeling a bit of relief, and I think Stephanie did too. It took more pressure off of her to tell Joe about Abby. On one hand, it might have been a good thing to force her hand, but I also suspected from what Stephanie had told us that her parents had a problem with meeting Joe. I couldn't really blame them about that, but Grant and I prayed that after Stephanie did tell him, there might be some sort of reconciliation. After all, Stephanie had become such an integral part of our family, and we wanted Doug and Vi to feel part of us also. Sometimes I found myself just wishing Stephanie would tell him already, but it wasn't up to me. I reminded myself of this as I greeted Stephanie.

"Come in!" I hugged her as she and my mother came into the house. It was still a few minutes before dinner would be ready, so I assured her that she wasn't late. She was so much like Grant and I in a few ways. Being early for everything was one of them. The more I'd gotten to know her the more I loved my niece. She was radiant tonight and hugged me back hard.

"Oh! Sorry!" she said, stepping back and looking at my growing abdomen. "Did I squish them?"

"Of course not," I laughed. "They're tucked right in there, safe and sound," I assured her.

"You're sure growing," she commented, looking a bit surprised.

"Tell me about it," I said, rolling my eyes. "It's crazy. I look like I'm ready to pop, and they're only just over half-way baked. I won't be able to move by the time they're finished."

Stephanie laughed, her arm through my own mother's.

"Come, sweetheart," said my mom, taking Stephanie with her. "Dinner won't be long."

Stephanie looked at me and I rolled my eyes.

"Home-cooked meal tonight," I admitted secretively, "but your grandma made it."

"Whew!" Stephanie smiled, mocking me by wiping her brow in relief.

"Funny," I said drolly, "and don't pretend you didn't know."

She laughed. I was secretly elated that my niece was comfortable enough with me now that she could joke about my consistently pathetic attempts at cooking.

It didn't take long before we were all enjoying the delicious meal my mother had, mostly, prepared earlier.

"I'll have you know, I did help," I said in defence of myself.

"Yes … she did," said my mother. "She tossed the salad and cut a few vegetables."

Everyone laughed as I tried to take the joking in stride. I'd been constantly hormonal lately and was trying my best not to take things so seriously. Sometimes it worked and sometimes not as much.

Not everyone could fit around the table, so people spread out, eating wherever they could find a spot. Small groups of not only family but a few of Stephanie's friends congregated, and lively conversations filled our home.

After a delicious dessert of individual honey-cakes with a berry sauce and whipped cream, I saw Melissa and my mother conversing in the kitchen, and I walked over.

"Trish!" Melissa turned to me excitedly. "Just the person we need. Tell your mother she has to do this!"

"Do what?" I asked, completely in the dark.

Melissa looked toward my mother and asked, "You didn't tell her?"

My mother looked at me and shrugged. "It didn't come up," she said.

"Wh ... what?" I stammered, suddenly anxious that I had missed something important. "Mom," I continued, "we talk all the time. What wouldn't come up?" I had been talking to my mom almost daily since my dad had passed away. I would have felt more concerned if Melissa hadn't been smiling so broadly.

Melissa couldn't stand it as she blurted, "I asked Helen to partner with me in the business. She's been such a great help to me, and I think we could add a huge dimension if we were partners and could even cater most events ourselves."

Both Melissa and I turned to stare at my mother.

"That's a fabulous idea!" I almost yelled in my instant excitement. "Oh Mom, you have to do this!"

My mother looked back and forth between me and Melissa, and rolled her eyes.

"Now this isn't fair. Two against one," she commented, with a smile playing on her lips.

"Seriously, Mom," I said, "what could possibly be holding you back?"

"Nothing is holding me back, Trish," she started. "I just think it will be a lot of work, and I had to think about it first." She looked at Melissa and nodded. "I was going to agree to it tonight, but you girls haven't given me a chance."

"Oh yes!" exclaimed Melissa, grabbing my mother in a hug. "This is going to be absolutely fantastic!"

Melissa had become more heavily booked in her event planning business than she had expected. Although she loved all of it, she had told me that she was considering getting a partner. I don't know why I hadn't thought of my mother. She had planned more events than I could ever count, mostly in our church, but also for some of my dad's medical meetings. She'd be perfect for this. I suddenly felt a relief that I hadn't felt since my father died.

"Mom, Dad would love this idea. I bet he's smiling down from heaven right now!"

My mother moved around the counter to hug me and whispered, "I doubt he's looking, but I think he'd agree with my decision. I'd like to help Melissa out as well."

As I looked at my mother, I had to admit that she seemed to glow. In fact, I hadn't seen her look this radiant since before my father died. As I watched her smile and talk to Melissa, I thought about how alike we were in some ways. We were much more rooted and happy when we had goals to accomplish.

My mother was already offering to take responsibility for the booked events when Trent and Melissa had to be away for Abigail's medical appointments. No doubt Melissa had thought of that too. I almost left them there to talk about further plans for all their upcoming events when Melissa stopped me.

"How was your last ultrasound?" she asked, suddenly changing the subject and placing her hand gently on my abdomen. I tried not to complain about my aches when she was around because I knew she would take those bothersome pregnancy pains in a heartbeat if she could. I looked at my friend and smiled, appreciating even more that she was still excited for me.

"It was all right," I replied. "Twin B is still a bit smaller, but the difference in their weights is still acceptable, so we just keep watching."

"Twin B," my mother sighed. "By now you must know what gender these babies are, Trish. You have an ultrasound every two weeks. I wish you'd share it with the rest of us. I'm tired of hearing Twin A and Twin B."

I smiled at my mom. "That's what we call them in obstetrics, Mom. A is the one coming out first, usually. B is second."

"You know what I mean, daughter of mine," she replied, giving me a pointed look.

Grant and I had discussed learning the babies' gender, but when asked at every ultrasound, we had declined. One of us would say, "Maybe next time," and leave it at that. Seeing all the other details about our babies, and knowing that they were both all right, was all that mattered. Most everyone in the family assumed that we must know, and we couldn't convince them otherwise, so we would simply smile and decline commenting.

"How is Abigail? How was her appointment this week?" I turned my attention over to Melissa.

"It was as good as it can be, I guess," she said, her smile fading a bit. "She still is getting weaker on her right side. We're doing all the physio exercises, but the latest MRI showed a little more calcification on the left side of her brain. We were really hoping it would stop, or at least slow down, but it doesn't seem to be ... not yet anyway."

"We'll keep praying," I promised, aching for my friend.

"Thankfully, she hasn't had as many seizures lately, and she's a happier kid most of the time now," Melissa said as Abigail and Kylie came tearing into the kitchen. "And really busy," smiled Melissa.

"I hear ya," I agreed, looking at a red-faced Kylie. I knelt in front of her then and said, "Hey, slow down before you hurt yourself, young lady. You're all sweaty from running around. Can you and Abigail go and find a book to read? Maybe Uncle Joe can read to you."

Kylie shook her head. "Uncle Joe is chasing us, Momma."

That made sense. Joe could never sit still either.

I stood up, albeit a little clumsily. "Joe!" I said loudly, suspecting he was close by. "Quit getting the girls all worked up. They won't settle down for hours, and if that happens, you're the one staying up with them."

I meant it. Since Joe had been staying with us, we'd had more than our share of late nights with Kylie due to her Uncle Joe instigating her hyperactivity before bedtime. Tonight Trent and Melissa had accepted our offer when we'd invited them to stay with us. Joe would have two girls to settle down before bedtime if he didn't watch it.

"Okay! Okay!" Joe laughed, coming around the corner and looking a little red faced himself. He grabbed Kylie and threw her up in the air, saying, "Sorry, kid, your mom is raining on our parade."

Abigail reached up then and squealed, "My turn, Uncle Joe! My turn!"

He put Kylie down and picked up Abby to swing her around.

"I agree with Trish, cousin," agreed Melissa. "You'll be stuck with these two if you keep this up, man."

Joe put Abigail down beside Kylie, and as the girls both begged for more antics, he shook his head at them and shrugged. "Two against one, girls. Our number's up. Blame your moms."

I grabbed a tea towel and smacked him with it but couldn't help smiling at his smirking face.

"You are such a brat," I grinned.

"And you are such a drag sometimes, sister-in-law," Joe half-heartedly laughed.

Melissa and my mother moved into another part of the house to visit as I looked at Joe.

Suddenly, Kylie broke the momentary silence with, "I get a book, Uncle Joe!" like it had been her idea. We both laughed as she quickly hugged Joe's legs before grabbing Abigail's hand to pull her to her room.

"Okay, kid," he agreed as they ran out of the room. "One book and I've gotta go downstairs," he added loudly behind her.

Kylie knew that, for now, our basement was her Uncle Joe's space. They had gotten into a bit of a routine with him reading to her before he'd go down to bed. It had been nice for her, and Grant and I knew she'd miss him when he was gone.

A rather unexpected decision had been made very recently. Joe had announced his plan to move to the family's cabin, situated at a beautiful lake, just thirty minutes away from the city. Much discussion between Grant, Sandy, and Joe had led to the final decision. The biggest surprise, however, came from Joe the night before Sandy and he were to sign the final documents declaring him as the new owner.

"What do you mean, you're buying it outright?" Grant had asked, not hiding his shock. "You don't have money for that, Joe."

"I'm not the idiot you still think I am, Grant," his brother had returned quietly.

Grant had waited, and after Joe spilled the news that he had never used the stipend his brother had sent him over the years from the profits of the business, Grant's jaw had dropped.

Joe had smiled then. "You thought I was spending it all irresponsibly everywhere I went," he stated with a quiet accusation in his tone.

Grant wasn't able to deny that. "But how did you live?"

Joe had laughed then and said, "I may not be like you, Grant, but I know how to work, just not work like you do, and"—he'd looked away from his brother's stare then—"maybe not always the best choices of work either."

Grant didn't know exactly what Joe meant by that, but his respect for his brother had grown a little that evening, and I had to admit that after Grant told me details of their conversation, mine had too.

Although Sandy owned the cabin by the lake, she was more than willing to sell it to Joe. It hadn't been used much in recent years, and it needed some work. Joe was more than willing to do the work and, once it was in a better state of repair, he said he'd be agreeable to letting family use it too, when it worked out. He told us that his plans included travelling again someday, so he would be willing to have us all enjoy it when he was away.

Sandy and Grant had told me about the cabin when I first joined their family, but I'd only gone there once. Although it seemed to me to be in more than "just a little" disrepair, Grant and Joe hadn't seemed bothered by it. Instead, they had ignored all that and reminisced about the fun times they remembered when they had spent their summer holidays there.

"Not all packed up for your move yet?" I now asked Joe, smiling at him.

"Oh, I'm packed. I don't have much. When you backpack all over the world, you don't accumulate a lot of stuff. I just wanna get up early, and I think I need some downtime tonight," he replied.

"I get it," I agreed, totally understanding. "I love me-time too."

Joe looked at me, thinking. "When I get some stuff done out there, Trish, I'll come back and take Kylie off your hands so you can have some alone time too. I'm gonna miss that kid a lot." He looked in the direction Kylie and Abigail had gone.

That touched my heart, and when the girls returned with more than one book, I looked from Abigail to Joe, and my heart skipped a beat. Stephanie had come into the kitchen at some point, and when I turned, I saw her staring from Joe to Abigail as well. As soon as our eyes met, hers teared up before she quickly turned away.

I wanted to follow her as she exited the kitchen, but Sandy had come into the room and caught my eye.

"Trish," Sandy said, looking at me with tenderness, "thank you for having all of us here. What a lot of work for you. Are you feeling all right?"

"Never mind me," I said, ignoring her question. "How are *you* feeling?" Grant had once again mentioned his mom's headaches, and I'd finally said more about it. Although Sandy insisted there was nothing much else going on except the headaches, I felt she was leaving something out.

"Oh, I'm fine," she waved off the question. "I do have an appointment in a few weeks for a CAT scan, though. I took your advice and saw the new doctor who's taking over for mine. He isn't really worried. He examined me and said everything looks okay, but I did tell him what you told me to say, so he ordered the scan."

"Well, good," I smiled. "It'll make me feel better after that's done. I still don't think you should have that many headaches. Hopefully we'll find out some reason for them ... although, you do babysit for us, and that daughter of ours could be the reason for at least some of them."

Sandy looked at me and laughed, shaking her head. "That girl just brings me smiles and more smiles, Trish." Then she came toward me, glancing at my stretched abdomen.

"Trish Evans," she said quietly, touching my cheek, "you just concentrate on growing my grandchildren and taking care of Grant and Kylie. Don't overdo it, and promise me you aren't going to worry about me. I'll be fine. Nothing can happen that God hasn't already seen. You just take care of you."

I couldn't help tearing up then. She was the most unselfish person I'd ever met, and I wished I could be so much more like her. As I sunk into her hug, I suddenly and strongly felt that I didn't want to let her go.

Chapter Nineteen

STEPHANIE LISTENED OUTSIDE OF KYLIE'S ROOM AS JOE READ TO HER AND Abigail. When the girls dragged Joe to Kylie's bedroom upstairs, she had felt compelled to follow, but now she felt that maybe she shouldn't have. As she sat outside the room listening to Joe read the different characters' voices with funny expressions and intonations, she had smiled at first, but then she'd started to cry. She tried to stifle it, but as she thought about Joe not being aware that he was reading the book to his own daughter, she couldn't help it. She breathed into her sleeve, trying to keep her crying silent, and she thought she'd been quiet enough until she heard silence. Joe had stopped reading.

"That's enough for tonight, girls," Stephanie heard him say. "Time to brush your teeth and go give your parents hugs."

Stephanie's heart skipped as she jumped up, turning quickly to run down the stairs. She'd just started down when she heard Joe behind her.

"Hey, I can read to you too, if you want. You could've just joined us," he said with a smile in his voice.

She swiped at a tear and tried for a smile before turning to look up at him.

"I was just … uh …" she stammered, not knowing what to tell him.

Joe's smile grew, confused by her nervousness but liking it for a reason he was unsure of. Then he saw a tear fall and he moved closer to her.

"What's wrong, Stephanie?" he asked, seeing her chin quiver.

Since telling him that he could call her by the shortened version most of her friends used, Joe hadn't called her by her full name very often. For some reason when he said it now, it felt more intimate, and she found herself wanting him to use the shorter version. He'd become her friend—at least on some level—and she wanted to keep it just that way.

She shook her head and denied her tears. "Something in my eye maybe," she answered feebly, looking down as she turned to descend the flight of stairs.

Joe had no idea what was going on with her but said nothing more as he followed her down to the main level. When she grabbed her purse from the front entrance, he made a decision. It might be dangerous, but he was too curious to let this go. Too many questions were in his mind. How long had she been listening to him read? Did she think he sounded stupid when he animated the characters in Kylie's book? The kids loved it and always begged for more, but maybe it seemed silly to Stephanie, and Joe didn't want to be seen that way.

"Can we talk?" Joe asked, thinking it might have sounded more like a command than a question.

Stephanie started to shake her head but then she looked up at him and changed her mind. She hadn't been fair to Joe, and she knew it. Even Trent and Melissa had told her to come clean with him. They were willing to accept his reaction, whatever it would be. With time, Stephanie had felt more and more guilty about not telling him, and today she'd declared publicly that she wanted to follow God in all things. Of course—it was time to come clean.

Joe stared at her as Stephanie bravely looked him in the eye. Just as quickly, though, her eyes deviated. Every time she looked at him, she felt things she knew she shouldn't, and now she was a ball of nerves about more than telling him about Abigail. As she looked away from him, she prayed for strength. Finally, when she turned to him again, she nodded and whispered, "Okay. Let's talk."

Joe grabbed her hand and led her across the house. When he opened the door to the stairs leading to the basement, her breath caught. Maybe this wouldn't be the best place to go, but where else would be an option?

Maybe it was wise not to go anywhere else. At least there would be people still mingling upstairs.

She nodded again and walked down the stairs, holding on to the rail. Joe followed, snapping on a brighter light. When they reached the bottom, he turned on another light, and Stephanie couldn't help but smile, relaxing a little. At least there wasn't just a bed to sit on, like she'd imagined.

He or Grant or Trish or someone—Stephanie wasn't sure who—had set up a sort of living room area and a separate bed area. Although it was one big room, it seemed cozy, and at least it wasn't just a bed.

Stephanie shook her head, embarrassed by where her mind had gone. *God*, she prayed silently then, *please give me the right words to say so he won't be angry*.

Joe had been watching her with a puzzled expression. "Are you okay? You look … like you're not."

Stephanie looked directly up at him and immediately stepped back. Too close. Eyes too blue. Too tempting. She moved to the small love seat on one side of the room and stared at the chair across from it. She wished she could push the furniture even further apart. Before she could entertain the thought, however, Joe sat down beside her. Right beside her. Way too close. He smelled so good.

Almost instantly, Stephanie stood up and started to pace away from him. Why did she feel so drawn to this man? She almost couldn't control herself. She had to get her bearings immediately. If she could just spit out what must be said and be done with it, it would be over.

She faced away from him and took a deep breath. She'd almost started speaking when, instead, she felt him. He'd gotten up quietly and now stood directly behind her. She felt his hands move up her arms and rest just below her shoulders. Her eyes closed as she sunk back into his body.

"Stephanie," he whispered beside her ear.

Suddenly, with the distant memory of him, her eyes flew open, and she came to her senses. She tried to move so quickly that she lost her footing a little.

"What the …" he started, confused. When he saw that she might fall, Joe didn't even think about it. To keep her upright, he grabbed her waist and turned her to face him. They stood, each staring at the other and breathing harder than they both expected. Then—without thinking—he kissed her.

Stephanie was thrown off kilter by the kiss, but she didn't want it to stop. It was so deep and full of longing that when she finally did break away, her face had flushed brightly, and she was completely out of breath. Why had she let that happen? Suddenly, she felt so embarrassed that she wanted to apologize but wasn't sure if she was sorry only for the kiss or how much she'd wanted it.

"Joe," she said with a gasp, "I didn't come down here for anything else but to tell you …" She choked.

Joe stood still as he watched the woman he had spent way too much time thinking about grasp for words. He'd only had one thing on his mind, but looking at her expression and hearing the sudden strangeness in her tone, he'd become wary of what was coming. His heart ached a little when he saw the tears begin to fall down her cheeks again, but he felt rejected by her reaction to his kiss as well. This girl seemed only to confuse him.

"What?" he said with more frustration than he meant.

"I don't even know how to tell you this, but …" She paused, with a pain so deep in her eyes that he almost moved to hug her but knew he couldn't. She obviously regretted the kiss. She wouldn't want a hug.

"Abigail is our child," she said quietly.

Joe stared at Stephanie, not sure of what he had just heard.

"What?" he asked, thinking he needed her to repeat it but not wanting her to.

"Abigail," she started, pointing toward the upper level of the house.

"Don't say it again. I heard you," he stammered, looking from confused to sad to almost angry at her then. Joe didn't know what to do with the emotions he felt racing through his body. "I've got to sit down or something," he said, turning toward the love seat he'd been on just a few moments before. Suddenly he felt tired. Tired and confused, frustrated and angry. His physical attraction to Stephanie faded as the questions in his mind started. He sat for long minutes as Stephanie stood, unable to move. "How long have you known this?" he finally asked, darkly.

Stephanie felt a shudder run through her as she looked at him. She wondered if she should stay standing where she was, sit down again, or just run upstairs. She glanced toward the stairs but knew that wouldn't be fair.

"Since Grandpa Jack and Sandy's wedding when I saw her birthmark," she finally admitted.

"That long and you didn't tell me?" Joe asked with more hurt than anger in his voice. "Six months?" he whispered.

"Joe," Stephanie started. She had to explain herself and try to get him to understand. She hadn't meant to keep it a secret, but now she could see how unfair she'd been to him. He'd had a right to know. "When I gave her up for adoption, all I knew was that she had a heart-shaped birthmark on her cheek, much like mine on my—"

"On your lower back," Joe interrupted. "I remember, Steph," he finished in a soft but still dark tone.

He turned his face upwards, and his eyes pierced hers. She couldn't break from his gaze, but she wouldn't let her mind return to the one night they'd shared together, nine months before Abigail was born. Stephanie knew she had to finish this quickly. "When I saw her at your mom's wedding, I knew she was my baby, but I couldn't tell you then, Joe. I was so shocked, and I wasn't ready, I guess," she finished, knowing that sounded lame even to herself. Why hadn't she just told him then?

Joe slowly nodded, the shock building and something else infusing into his soul. "You call yourself a Christian," he accused, still so darkly before his voice turned to mocking. "And we're all here to celebrate Stephanie's baptism! She's got a relationship with God, folks! Look how wonderful she is." He looked at her with a cynical smile. "You're one of the most selfish people I've ever met."

Stephanie couldn't have been more surprised than if Joe had slapped her across her face. His accusations had hit her to her very core. True, she'd turned her life over to God, but that didn't make her a perfect human being. And selfish? She thought about that as her ire grew. How dare he say that! If anything, she'd been trying to spare him from the same feelings she felt every time she gazed at Abigail. Or was it something else? The power of holding the secret from him? To hurt him somehow?

Stephanie couldn't think straight, but she knew she wasn't going to let herself feel sorry for Joe. She walked closer to him but didn't sit down.

"How dare you!" she breathed. "How dare you say that, Joe! You have no right. You talk about selfish, but look at you! You sit here, judging me, when you've done absolutely nothing that isn't selfish your entire life! At least that's all I see."

They stared at each other, their pride keeping each of them from admitting anything, including fault.

"Just go," he finally said, turning his face from hers.

Stephanie suddenly felt panic. What would he do? What would he say to Trent and Melissa? Before she could say another word, however, Joe asked one more question.

"Does everyone else know?"

He'd asked it so softly and with such pain in his voice that Stephanie's heart couldn't help but threaten to crack. Suddenly, she didn't want to be angry at him. She wanted to wrap her arms around him and try to make it all better. She wondered if she had been selfish.

As silence fell around them, Joe looked up to where Stephanie still stood. The pain on her face and her falling tears almost had him feeling sorry for her again. Almost. Instead, when she wouldn't answer him, he stood up and came toward her like a tiger stalking his prey. She stepped back, but he caught her arms with both his hands. From her silence he knew the answer, but he needed to hear her say it. "Does everyone else know?" he said, louder this time.

Stephanie only whispered, "Not everyone," but before she knew what was happening, Joe ran toward the stairs, taking them two at a time. Stephanie felt the rush of air as he passed her in his haste. She stood for just a second or two before she tore after him.

"Joe," she called out, but Joe was already up the stairs before he would've heard her.

Chapter Twenty

I HAD JUST CLOSED THE DOOR AND SAID GOODBYE TO THE LAST OF OUR guests, except the ones staying in our home overnight and Sandy and Jack, when Joe came bursting up from the basement. The look on his face said it all. Although I had suspected it would be a difficult scene when Joe found out about Abigail, it was still shocking to see my brother-in-law's wildly hurt and angry face staring at me. Thankfully, the little girls had fallen asleep and wouldn't hear our conversation.

"Joe," I said quietly.

"You knew and you didn't tell me, Trish," he accused in a soft tone that was no less threatening than if he'd yelled it at me. I could say nothing to that, so I looked over to Grant for back-up.

We all gathered quickly in the living room as Joe began his rant. Stephanie had come upstairs behind him, looking distraught, and now sat next to me on the couch. I couldn't help but put my arm around her with an ever-increasing feeling of protection for my niece as Joe continued. Her tears wouldn't stop, and my heart broke for her. This is what she had hoped wouldn't happen.

Joe made it very clear how disappointed he was in all of us "Christians," and he chastised each one of us for a long while, not leaving anyone out.

Sandy and Jack had been the only ones who didn't know up until this point, and it was Jack who looked hurt when he glanced at both Stephanie and I. Abigail was his great granddaughter, and she'd been close to him so many times without him knowing, but Jack said nothing as Joe kept on.

As much as I could understand why Joe was angry, after hearing his continued tirade, I suddenly felt my patience at an end, and Grant must have noticed. I took a deep breath in preparation to defend myself and all others who had known, but before I could lash back at Joe, Grant stepped in.

"Are you done?" he asked his brother calmly when Joe finally stopped to take a breath.

You could have heard a pin drop as Joe bore an incredulous look at his brother.

"What the—" began Joe again.

"I'm serious, Joe," Grant said louder, not backing down. "I think you should take a breather. You've made us all feel horrible about not telling you, and you're probably right."

"Ya think?" Joe yelled back.

Grant continued, unmoved. "As I was saying, maybe you're right that someone should have told you sooner, but—"

"It was me!" Stephanie exclaimed. "I should've told you as soon as I knew, Joe. I know that now."

"Ya think?" Joe repeated, rolling his eyes but speaking more softly. "Geez," he breathed in frustration. He ran his hand through his hair before finally moving to sit, slumped on the floor. No one moved or spoke for some time, and most of us averted our eyes away from Joe.

Finally, Jack cleared his throat and looked at Stephanie. He had agreed with Joe at first, as he experienced the shock of the news as well, but then he'd been watching Trent and Melissa, who had stayed very quiet and just appeared ... sad. What was this doing to them—Abigail's parents? Sure, it was by adoption, but from what Jack had seen when he'd been around them, they loved his great-grandchild at least as much, or more, than any parents could their own biological child.

Stephanie stared at her grandfather and sighed. "I'm so sorry, Grandpa. I should've told you too. She is your relative."

Jack knew how much Stephanie had grown to love this family, and he had too. It was important to her to have connection with blood relatives—with him. Although she loved her adoptive parents very much, Jack had a special connection with Stephanie—a deep belonging that he couldn't explain.

"I think you don't owe anyone an apology, Stephanie. No one ... including me," Jack said to his granddaughter.

Joe took a deep breath, and everyone braced themselves for another onslaught of his anger, but Jack stopped him with a pointed look.

"You had your say, Joe," Jack started slowly in that deep voice that commanded respect. "I know I don't say much around here about what I think, because I'm pretty new to this family, but you, young man, can listen to me now."

Everyone sat with eyes wide open, including Joe, waiting for what might be coming.

"The way I see it, you had one drunk, fun night with Stephanie and thought there would be no repercussions from it. You went on your way with no regard for the fallout of your poor choice. You had no responsibility for any of Stephanie's pregnancy and everything she suffered, making hard decisions about her life and the life of that little girl." Jack took another deep breath and looked at his granddaughter before he continued. "If anyone should be upset, it should be you," he told Stephanie. "You were left feeling all alone, with big decisions to make. In my opinion, because you loved Abigail enough to give her parents who would love her and protect her, that makes you the most unselfish person in this room." He looked at Joe before adding, "Thankfully, although you didn't know where Abigail would go, God did."

Again, the silence stretched as Joe's face reddened. As upset as he still appeared, he said nothing more and looked down.

Sandy looked between Joe and Jack and back again and sighed. "I can see why you're angry, son, but I think, maybe, it's more because no one told you right away. Maybe that wasn't the best decision, but you've found out now, as we have too." She directed her next question to Melissa and Trent. "I'd like to know how you two are holding up, actually. Abigail's your daughter."

Melissa had tears in her eyes and spoke only to Joe, who at first kept his head down. "Joe, I love you. It was a real shock for us too. Maybe I should have told you, but honestly, I guess I'd always hoped you'd be okay with me raising your daughter. We used to be close, Joe. You should know that Trent and I would never do anything to hurt Abby. We love her." Melissa's voice cracked as Joe looked up at her. "But you are her biological father. If you want to raise her yourself, Trent and I have discussed it and—"

Suddenly, a shrill cry filled the room. We all looked up to see Abigail at the top of the stairs. She had her eyes closed but she was shrieking.

Melissa's tears stopped instantly. "Trent!" she started, with an urgency in her voice. She forgot what she was saying and stood up as Trent ran, bounding up the stairs two or even three at a time as fast as he could. The room went silent before everyone let out a breath of relief when he reached the top of the staircase. As he reached for her, Abigail threw her head back and stiffened before her whole body began to shake. Trent grabbed his teetering daughter right before she would have fallen down the long flight of stairs.

None of us had ever seen her seizure before tonight, and they are never easy to watch, but as I saw Trent cradle Abigail and whisper calmly to her as Melissa joined him, I was in awe. Oh, the love they had for this special little girl. We all stared as Abigail's seizure continued for over a full minute. As they sat with her, calmly waiting for the seizure to pass, I couldn't help but tear up. When I turned to look back at the others around me, Joe caught my eye. He looked stunned, worried, and maybe terrified, but all the anger in his expression had left.

I didn't feel so angry at him then. I felt sorry for him. He just didn't get what seemed so clear to Grant and I. Abigail needed Trent and Melissa. God knew that when He'd given her to them. She was exactly where she needed to be. As I looked at Joe, I prayed that he would realize that too.

Trent and Melissa came down the stairs after Abby's seizure subsided and sat where they'd been before. Abby appeared tired and lay limply on Trent's lap as Melissa grabbed for her purse, retrieved a Kleenex, and dabbed at some blood at the side of their daughter's mouth. Trent tried to assess where it was coming from, and when satisfied, said to Melissa, "I think it's coming from her lip here. Her tongue looks okay. From what I can see, there's no oozing coming from inside."

Melissa nodded and then, as if just noticing the rest of us, simply said, "Sometimes she bites her tongue."

"How did you know she was going to do that?" exclaimed Joe.

Trent looked at Joe intently and very matter-of-factly said, "We think that's her aura. People with seizure conditions often get an aura before one starts. Abby can't really tell us, but she either screams or she just stares, kind of blankly, and won't react to anything or anyone around her."

Joe said nothing but looked down at his crossed legs. He had heard that Abigail had some kind of syndrome, and although he noticed that she walked and ran a little funny, he'd seen her as a healthy, happy girl. He had no idea that all this had been going on. He suddenly felt that he needed to leave to try and clear his head. He got up and grabbed his jacket without another word. No one said anything as the door slammed behind him.

Sandy shook her head and sighed as she got up and went over to where Abigail was lying on Trent's lap. Abby's eyes were open now as she stared up at her father with an almost vacant look. Sandy's eyes couldn't hold their tears as we all saw them fall down her cheeks. As she ran her hand gently through Abigail's auburn hair, she whispered, "My little granddaughter." If no one had thought of it before, we all did now, and we watched in rapt attention. "You have so much life ahead of you," Sandy softly whispered. "I will keep praying that God will take those seizures away from you. I would take them from you if I could." And all of us knew that Sandy meant that from the bottom of her heart.

When I looked at Stephanie, she was crying too, and I put my arm around her shoulders again, but not for long. Jack was up and raised Stephanie to her feet so that he could envelope her in his own huge hug. I looked at Grant when I heard him sigh. When he followed Joe out the door, I wasn't surprised.

Chapter Twenty-One

JOE HADN'T DRIVEN FAR. ALTHOUGH HE SUSPECTED A POOR CHOICE MIGHT be made by his brother, Grant was still disappointed and a bit surprised when he pulled up in front of the bar. Joe's truck was parked at an odd angle, no doubt because of the haste he'd been in. Grant debated for a minute or two before following Joe inside. In a way he understood why his younger brother needed time to sort things out, but then again, he still felt somewhat responsible for him, even though they were both grown men. He couldn't leave his little brother alone tonight. Grant let out the breath he hadn't known he was holding and opened his truck door.

The bar was loud with not only blaring music but a large crowd of noisy people. Grant searched from the door, hoping to see Joe, but gave up and moved inside when he didn't see his brother immediately. Thankfully it didn't take long before he spotted him in a booth near the back. A young woman was standing over him and smiling. Grant rolled his eyes and groaned inwardly. His brother never seemed to lack for female interest, but as he came closer, he could see Joe was mostly ignoring her advances.

"Hey!" Grant said loudly over the music. He hoped that if he got his brother's attention, the girl would leave.

"Hi." She turned to Grant instead. "Wow! Just my luck—two good lookin' guys to fight over me."

Grant quickly slid into the seat across from his brother, leaving the woman still standing and gawking at them. He was about to say something when Joe surprised him. "My brother and I need to talk. Could you excuse us?"

"Whaaaat?" she pouted in a sultry voice, looking down at Joe. "C'mon, honey. We can all talk and maybe end up having a little fun too."

Grant looked at the dark-haired beauty and then at Joe. He was relieved to see that Joe looked more disgusted than interested.

"We can't talk right now. We have other business. Go bug somebody else," Joe said, none too nicely.

The young woman's expression changed from pouting hurt to an ugly anger as she turned and stormed off, using expletives Grant wasn't used to hearing anymore but which didn't faze Joe.

Joe looked at his brother and huffed. "What?"

Grant said nothing at first. He wasn't even quite sure why he'd followed his brother, but he'd been praying for wisdom and now prayed again. His heart ached for Joe. In actuality, Grant's heart hurt a little for everyone in his family right now. He had tried to see everyone's perspective about the secrets that had been kept over the years, and he knew continued healing was needed in all of their lives, but especially Joe's. Joe didn't recognize God in his life, and Grant just couldn't understand how he could function without Him. Now, looking across the booth at him, as much as he felt sympathy for his brother, Grant also saw immaturity and didn't know how to help him with that. Maybe he needed a change of scenery and time away to reflect on his life and his choices.

"Ready for your move to the cabin tomorrow?"

Joe looked surprised by the question. He'd expected a lecture. Maybe that was coming.

Joe slowly nodded. "Yeah." He paused. "I've got a few days off. Shouldn't take me that long, though. I don't have much to move, but I've got a lot to do out there."

Grant watched as Joe brought the drink that had been sitting in front of him to his mouth for a deep gulp. Although he didn't comment, Grant found himself feeling incredibly disappointed. Joe had come so far and had quit drinking, as far as Grant knew, months ago. He knew Joe would be sorry tomorrow, but that was his decision.

Joe watched Grant, waiting for a lecture again, but none was forthcoming.

The silence stretched before Grant spoke. "I get why you're upset, Joe. I know I'd be too if she were my child," Grant said with empathy.

Joe looked surprised again and couldn't reply.

"But," Grant said then, "I get why Steph didn't want to tell you either. I think she's scared that you'll want to take Abby away from Trent and Melissa, and it's always been very important to Stephanie that Abigail have stable parents. If you want to raise Abigail, you probably could, but is that best for her, Joe?" Grant leaned forward, closely looking at his brother. "Joe, ya gotta ask yourself, man … why are you so mad? Do you want to raise this baby by yourself, Joe? Is your pride hurt because you didn't see it for yourself? Or is it just because you didn't know until now?"

Grant waited, but Joe couldn't answer. He stared at his drink instead, swirling the ice around as he moved the half-empty glass in his hand.

Grant leaned back again in his chair and sighed. "Well … you know now. I'm not here to tell you what you should do, Joe. Honestly, I don't know what I'd do if I was in your shoes." Grant paused, feeling sorry for the pain he saw in his brother's eyes. "I guess you have to ask yourself—are you ready for that kind of responsibility? When I look at Kylie, I can't imagine living without her, but that's me and my daughter, Joe. Are *you* ready for that kind of responsibility? Or are you just mad because you were left outta the loop?"

Joe still couldn't reply but looked deep in thought as he stared at the ice cubes now left at the bottom of the glass in his hand.

"One more thing and I'll be done," promised Grant. Joe glanced up at his brother's face as Grant continued. "I haven't known Stephanie for all that long, but one thing I know for certain is that she did give up your child because of her love for her."

Grant wanted to say more but then decided against it. When he got up to leave, however, he was relieved that Joe followed him outside.

"You okay to drive?" Grant couldn't help asking.

"Yeah … perfect. Only had one drink, man," Joe stated with a bit of irritation in his tone. Before Grant could say anything more, Joe got into his truck and sped away.

Grant sighed, praying more than ever that his brother would soon get his act together.

• • •

When Joe returned to Grant and Trish's home, it was late. He'd driven around for a while and had even stopped in front of another bar—the one where he'd met Stephanie again. She'd been so mad at him when he hadn't recognized her that night. He almost smiled thinking of her rage and how her face had almost matched the bright red colour of her hair. But then the memory faded as he thought of their conversation that evening. How could he have left her alone to make those important decisions regarding her pregnancy and their baby? Suddenly, alcohol and the possibility of a warm woman for temporary pleasure held no appeal for him, and he spun the tires of his truck, leaving the bar behind him.

He was relieved that everyone had either left or gone to bed, as he made his way downstairs and flopped onto his bed. He glanced at the time on his phone. It was close to 2:00 a.m. Of course everyone would be in bed. Joe couldn't stop thinking about Abigail. He relived her sweet begging for getting chased, and he smiled as he remembered swinging her in the air. Then his memory darkened when he closed his eyes, seeing again every detail of the seizure she'd had. Trent had been so capable, gentle, and familiar with her. Melissa had remained pretty calm too, but Joe hadn't been able to move.

Suddenly, he couldn't stand it. He got up and walked as quietly as possible upstairs to where she and Kylie were supposed to be sleeping in Kylie's room. He held his breath when he saw Trent leave the room. He must've been checking on Abby. Joe waited in the dark, not wanting Trent to see him. Joe's heart ached. He almost changed his mind and turned to go back downstairs, but something stopped him. He had to just take a peek at her. If Trent could check on his daughter, so could Joe. She was, after all, his too.

Trish or Grant or someone had set up a small tent structure in the bright pink girl's room and there, on a small mattress on the floor, were the two little girls, lying fast asleep together. As he pulled the covers back just a little to see Abigail better, Joe saw that they seemed to be holding each other's hands, which made him smile.

Joe thought that it might seem weird, but he sat down beside them anyway and watched them breathe. They were so cute and innocent and sweet in the soft light of the Winnie-the-Pooh nightlight. He looked at Abigail and tried to see if she looked like him at all. Her nose maybe was a little like his. He wondered if her hair would lighten up if she spent time in the sun like his did. It was a darker red than Stephanie's but still quite like hers. And that heart-shaped birthmark on her cheek ... Abigail had just turned over in her sleep, and Joe couldn't help it. As soon as he saw it again, his mind went to the one night he'd spent with Stephanie, and he remembered the same heart on her body.

Joe shook his head. What a mess he'd made of everything! Why had he lost it so badly on Stephanie tonight? Jack was right. He hadn't been around when Abigail was born. What would he have done if he had known about the pregnancy? Would they have gotten married and kept Abigail? He was embarrassed to admit that he probably would've run.

Joe was lost in thought when he heard something behind him and glanced toward the open door of Kylie's room. It was Trish's mom. He'd almost forgotten she was staying over too. He couldn't remember if she had been there when he lost it on everyone. He didn't remember seeing her. He didn't know Helen well and felt immediately self-conscious.

She cleared her throat softly and looked at him from the doorway. Joe got up quickly and moved quietly toward her, thinking she'd move and he would excuse himself.

She almost surprised him when she said, "I couldn't sleep either."

Joe nodded at her, expecting her to move aside as he came closer, but she still didn't.

"Beautiful little girls, aren't they?" she whispered.

Joe paused and couldn't help but glance again at the two toddlers on the floor, whom he had just covered up before he heard Helen. When he turned back to look at Trish's mother, he guessed that she had tears in her eyes by the reflection he saw, even in the darkened room.

"I think I know how you feel," she said tentatively.

Joe's heart skipped a beat as he stared at her. He didn't know her, so how could she understand anything about him?

Helen motioned him into the hallway with a slight nod of her head and stood close to Joe to not awaken the girls.

"This is probably not my place to say, but I have to admit that I heard some of the conversation you had with your family when I was cleaning up in the kitchen. I'm sorry, but I couldn't help it," she whispered, shrugging.

"Well," Joe acknowledged, "it wasn't a quiet conversation."

Joe followed Helen down the stairs to the main level. He thought he'd keep going to the basement, but when Helen motioned to him to follow her to the kitchen, he felt compelled to go.

Helen turned the light to a softer glow over the kitchen island and grabbed two glasses from the cupboard. "Water? Juice? Milk?" she asked Joe, walking to the fridge.

"Nothing for me," he answered, wondering why he had followed her into the kitchen at all.

Helen couldn't help herself from being the hostess and filled two glasses with water anyway, placing one in front of Joe. She put her elbows on the opposite side of the island from where Joe sat and leaned her chin on her hands.

"I don't know if you know this, but I had a baby and was forced to give her up for adoption when I was really young," stated Helen, looking down at the counter.

Joe had heard about that and asked, "Grant's first wife, Stacy?"

Helen nodded and looked back at Joe. "Stephanie's mom, yes," Helen agreed. "I didn't have a choice and, in all honesty, if it would've been up to me, I might have kept her, which would have probably been … a mistake. I'll never know, but I think Stephanie did the right thing by loving Abigail enough to give her a better chance in life, and I do think Abigail is with good parents. But I can see how you'd feel angry that you didn't get the opportunity to be part of that decision," Helen acknowledged as she looked at Joe but thought of Jack. She'd often wondered if he'd ever felt angry because he hadn't known about Stacy. Whenever she'd seen him since, he'd only ever been polite and kind toward her.

"Yeah, well, I guess it was my fault for not hanging around," admitted Joe.

Helen watched him and pondered before saying, "I love my granddaughter very much, and I'm so happy that we found each other after all these years, but it was just as much her fault as yours that you didn't find out about the pregnancy. At least, that's what she told me. She wanted you to find her, but she regrets that she didn't seek you out. She knew she probably could have."

Joe looked surprised by this news. Ever since he'd found out about the baby; he'd blamed himself—at least until tonight—and Stephanie had never indicated that she wished they'd found each other again.

"I may be way off here too, but I'm guessing ...," Helen swallowed.

Joe stared at her, waiting for her to continue.

"I'm guessing that one reason you're upset is that Abigail was right in front of you, and you couldn't see her, or you're mad because that's how you've felt for so long—like no one is seeing you for who you are. I know a little bit about that too. Maybe you feel alone and angry about everything, and anger is the safest emotion to run with. Or is it the only one that's comfortable anymore?" Helen sighed. "Take it from someone who spent a lot of years stuck in that same state but wasn't smart enough to admit it, Joe."

Although Joe's expression held confusion, Helen continued. "Can I leave you with some advice?" she asked with empathy in her eyes.

Joe's heart was pounding, and all he could manage was a nod. It was like this woman—a stranger to him, really—knew him. He could hardly breathe as she smiled gently at him.

"Don't let all the bitterness and anger take your joy away. I don't want to sound preachy, but if you give God all—the sadness, the guilt, and the real gut-wrenching anger that's running all over inside of you—believe me, He'll take it."

When Helen saw that Joe was still listening, she continued. "And you'll realize that either the situation you're in is where you belong, or God will show you how to change it. That's what happened with me." Helen looked away from Joe's stare then. After taking a deep breath, she looked directly at him again and bravely said, "But don't try to kill yourself before you get to the joy part."

Joe gaped at her abruptness. He had heard something about Helen's suicide attempt, but not from her. As she'd been talking, Joe had thought she was starting to preach ... until that. Hearing someone freely admit to that gave him pause.

Seeing his shock, Helen smiled. "Not my best decision," she added, shaking her head.

Joe didn't know what to say, so he took a drink of his water. When he was done, he looked at her. "You remind me of Trish."

Helen couldn't hold in her laughter. "Now that's not something I've heard often."

"Really?"

When Helen didn't answer him, he smiled. "She tells me exactly what she thinks too."

Helen's smile waned as she thought about that. "Well," she started, tentatively, "maybe we're more alike than we know. I hope I'm a little like her, actually. I kept my real feelings to myself for too long. I've often thought she's too open about things, but maybe that's not such a bad thing."

Joe sighed and then smiled a little at Helen as he got off the stool. "I guess I better—"

"Yes," interrupted Helen, nodding quickly, grabbing their glasses, and putting them quietly into the sink. "Those children will be up before we know it, and we adults will be the ones who are exhausted. Have a good sleep, Joe."

He nodded once and turned.

Helen watched as Joe left the kitchen. He was in so much pain. If Helen had to guess, it probably wasn't just because of the paternity issue either, but maybe because of a whole lot more. She would pray that he'd turn his life around before things could become dire. She knew about that. She'd been there.

As he made his way downstairs to try to catch at least a few hours of sleep before his move to the cabin, a few things that Helen said repeated themselves in his mind. Had he been so angry about so many things that he'd lost all joy in his life? Drinking made him feel better sometimes, but it didn't take away his anger. If he was honest, he did feel angry about a lot of things. He was angry that he'd never known his dad. He was angry that he never seemed to measure up to Grant's standards. He was angry about a lot of other poor choices he'd made too. But if he was really honest with himself, he was angry most of all for not being there for Stephanie. With that, Joe felt even more guilt and anger for the drink he'd succumbed to tonight. He'd gone months without it but had let the temptation get the better of him. What an idiot! Maybe he did need some help.

Joe was suddenly and overwhelmingly tired. He couldn't think about anything any longer. He flopped on the bed, hoping to forget by sleeping all of it away.

• • •

Across the city in her condo, Stephanie couldn't sleep. Although Joe had been so mad at her and hurt her incredibly, she still couldn't deny the strange kind of bond she felt with him. She convinced herself on her drive home that it had only to do with their one-night stand and that they did, indeed, share a child in only a biological sense. But why had she kissed him back tonight? In all the drama that followed, she almost forgot the kiss, but now, as she lay alone in her dark bedroom, it seared itself into her mind. She pleaded with God that she would be able to forget Joe and everything that was behind them, choosing instead to really move on with her life. Her Grandma Helen was right. She had to figure out where *she* stood and what *she* believed. After tonight, Stephanie knew with practical certainty that Joe Evans was not for her. Kiss or no kiss.

As she drifted off to sleep, she did what Trish had told her to do after Joe left the house that evening. She prayed and tried to give all of the mess she felt she'd made to God.

Chapter Twenty-Two

JOE GLANCED AROUND FROM UNDER THE BRIM OF HIS COWBOY HAT AT THE people seated in the circle of chairs. He didn't usually wear his hat off the ranch, but somehow it felt like a form of protection tonight. He squirmed in his seat, clearly uncomfortable with the entire scene. Why had he even come? Although he knew the answer to that, he still berated himself for everything stupid he'd done to get there. He thought he had a handle on the drinking, and for a while he had seemed to. But then … Stephanie and the news about Abigail had sent him reeling in a way that he'd never experienced before. He hadn't handled it well at all. He'd been angry at first, but now, more than anything else, self-loathing filled him to his very core. As Joe sat waiting for the meeting to start, his mind recalled what little he could remember from the night that had brought him here.

A few days after Stephanie had given him the news about Abigail, he'd agreed to go with the guys when they invited him, again, to join them for drinks after work. He'd stayed strong and ordered a non-alcoholic drink at first, telling them he'd be their designated driver. When they'd declined his offer and all laughed at him, he'd started with a rum and Coke and just didn't stop. He'd been in rough shape when it was time to leave the bar, and he knew he wasn't in any shape to drive out to the cabin. No cabbie was going to want to drive him that far out of the city either. None of the guys he'd been with offered him a ride, so Joe had pondered his options. Feeling a great aversion to going to either Grant or his mother's place, he'd made a worse decision.

Stephanie had recently moved to a place of her own, and Joe had phoned her, asking if he could come over and apologize to her. Although she had sounded hesitant, she eventually agreed. He remembered how surprised she'd looked when she saw him.

"What the …?" Stephanie had said with a shocked expression when she opened the door. "Joe?"

He remembered how she'd looked at him when she realized how drunk he was—as if he was completely pathetic.

"Stephanie," he began, suddenly sorry, even in his drunkenness, that he'd decided to go there.

"What?" she said, turning angry.

"I just wanted to say I'm sooorrry for the other night. I shouldn't ha … ave been so stupid."

Stephanie had looked at him then—really looked at him—like he was a bug under her foot.

Suddenly shame had engulfed him, and he couldn't help but start with the excuses. She'd slammed the door in his face then. That had fuelled a fire within him that wouldn't be abated, and he'd banged so hard on her door that she eventually opened it again.

"Are you kidding me, Joe?" she'd hissed at him. "You're going to bust the door and wake up the neighbours!"

"If I … have to," he'd drawled loudly. "I just wanna say … I am sorry. I neeeed you to forgive me, Steph."

He'd taken a cab from the bar to Stephanie's place, but the driver had left as soon as she dropped him off. Joe had asked the cab driver to stay and wait for him, but now as he remembered vignettes of the whole embarrassing evening, he didn't blame her for leaving. He wondered if he'd even paid her for the ride to Stephanie's place. He couldn't remember that, but there was one vague memory that held on …

Now as he looked around the circle at the people who were supposed to help him get a handle on his drinking, he sighed.

"Hello, everyone," the leader began. "Welcome to all, including the new faces here. We might be expecting a few more people, so we'll wait a couple more minutes and start shortly."

In a few minutes, Joe heard the door opening behind him again, but he didn't turn around. If he would have, he might have decided against the meeting. The man who entered let out a low grunt before sitting next to Joe in the last empty chair available. As Joe peeked up at the familiar profile beside him, he let out a small gasp and turned away quickly, grimacing, as he slumped lower in his chair and tried to hide under his hat.

"Really, Joe?" stated Jack in a low whisper.

Joe sighed, wishing the floor would swallow him up right there and then. Why had he listened to his boss and come to this place and this particular group?

After he didn't answer immediately, Joe heard Jack sniff and then he thought he heard what might have been a snicker. When he looked up again, however, Jack's face held only a stony gaze that caught Joe's eye.

"About time you do something about it," Jack stated, looking past him.

The leader began to speak, and both Jack and Joe fell silent. It wasn't the most comfortable meeting for either man, and by the end, Joe was more than itching to leave. Jack hadn't said much, which didn't surprise Joe and seemingly didn't bother the leader either. From what Joe knew about Jack, that was pretty typical of him—at least, up until the last time they'd seen each other. Joe still felt a little of the sting from Jack's words on that night.

Joe had planned to run from the building as soon as the leader dismissed them, but Jack's deep voice stopped him.

"Hang out a minute," Jack said in a soft command that left Joe no choice.

Joe said nothing to anyone as he stood by the door, waiting. Jack went to talk to a man standing by the coffee urn. The two men spoke for a few minutes, and just as Joe decided that perhaps he could leave, Jack nodded his goodbye at the man and walked over to where Joe stood.

"What'd you think of the meeting?" asked Jack.

Joe shrugged, not knowing how to answer. On one hand, it was good to know that other people struggled with alcoholism, but on the other hand, it was depressing to be there in the first place.

"Yeah," started Jack. "I wasn't sure about the whole thing when I first came here too, but I knew I needed to change something."

Joe nodded, adjusting his hat while looking down at his feet. The anxiety of coming to his first meeting and then seeing Jack was catching up with him. He suddenly felt tired.

"I didn't know you needed this too," Joe sighed, looking up at Jack.

It was Jack's turn to take a deep breath as he adjusted his bandanna with his strong hand. "Yeah," he nodded. "Been coming here for almost two years. I don't make it as often now, but I still need the support sometimes. That never goes away, Joe."

Joe nodded, looking at the scar on Jack's face and wondering about it again. It seemed strange that this tough guy who'd led a wild life and even had been incarcerated for assault was married to his mom. He didn't know how his religious mother ever hooked up with this sort of guy. Jack intimidated Joe on a good day, and he didn't feel much differently tonight, but he had to ask, "Don't the people at yours and Mom's church help you out? I woulda thought you'd go there for help."

Jack looked at Joe with a half-grin and shrugged before answering. "Just more comfortable here, I guess," he began, before surprising Joe with another admission. "Nothing against Christians, Joe, but some are pretty judgemental, and here I don't feel any of that."

"Right?" Joe couldn't help but spit out. "That's totally what I've always thought too! But if you feel that way"—Joe looked confused before continuing—"why would you even want any part of the whole religion thing?"

It was a loaded question, but Jack didn't pause for even a second before he answered. "Because it isn't about religion, Joe. It's about a relationship with God—and a personal friendship with Jesus Christ. It has nothing to do with any other person on earth. It's just between me and God."

Joe had heard that since he was a kid, and at some point he had believed at least a small part of it, but he'd left that kind of thinking behind long ago. Something in Jack's voice now, however, made Joe think. It was that conviction—the same one his mother had always had in really believing in something so much deeper—that alluded Joe.

When Joe thought of his mom, he smiled. "You sure it's not more about my mom?"

Jack looked at Joe with fleeting irritation before answering patiently. "Your mom introduced me to Him. I love Sandy more than my own life, but my relationship with God excludes her. That's between me and Him."

Suddenly, Joe didn't want to hear any more, and he felt relief when Jack moved to leave. As Joe drove back out to the cabin, he couldn't help replaying a lot of the evening in his head, including Jack's declaration.

Chapter Twenty-Three

SANDY WATCHED AS JACK ATE THE SNACK SHE'D MADE FOR THEM. HE'D come home right after his meeting and had seemed quieter than normal. Now that she thought about it, Jack had acted similarly after last week's meeting too. Although he had always kept everything from the meetings he attended confidential, he'd usually be in a good mood after attending one. Sandy knew something was bothering Jack but couldn't imagine what. He attended the meetings when he felt he needed them, and he had been honest about things being a little more difficult since finding out about Abigail. She had understood and did now as well. She was glad that the group he was committed to helped him so much.

"How was it?" Sandy asked Jack tentatively.

"It was all right," he answered. They'd finished eating and were in the kitchen. As Sandy handed Jack their dishes, he absent-mindedly placed them in the dishwasher.

"Just all right?" she asked.

Jack closed the door to the washer and turned to look at his wife. He looked deep in thought as he pushed his long hair behind him. He knew he couldn't divulge anything about his meetings, and it made him ache, which it never had before. He wanted to give Sandy hope for her son, but he just couldn't tell her about seeing Joe at the meetings. He decided to say nothing and moved toward her to envelope her smallness in a hug. He rubbed her back and heard her sigh.

"You're avoiding my question," she sighed again, hugging him back.

His low chuckle was all he returned when they both heard the front door open.

"Hey!" Joe's voice rang out.

Sandy smiled up at Jack and whispered, "This'll have to wait." She let go and walked to the living room to welcome her son.

"Hey, Mom," he said, wrapping her in a hug. "How are you?"

"I'm good, honey," she smiled. "Even better now that you're here."

Joe laughed. "Big guy not enough for you?" he teased, looking to where Jack stood tall in the kitchen doorway with his arms crossed.

"Very funny," Sandy laughed.

They all sat, and Sandy asked Joe if he wanted some dessert.

"Nah, I'm good, Mom," he said with a mischievous expression. "Did Jack tell you we've been seeing each other?"

Sandy shook her head, confused, as she glanced at Jack, whose expression was unreadable.

"Yeah," Joe said, waiting for some reaction from Jack and guessing that he'd shocked him. He smiled as he laid the cowboy hat beside him on the couch. He ran his hand through his hair. "They're okay—the meetings, I mean."

Sandy's eyebrows lifted and she couldn't help but smile. A sudden feeling of hope filled her heart. Had Joe finally seen and admitted what she and others had been praying so earnestly about?

"Thought that might make you happy," said Joe smugly.

Sandy immediately replied, "It's not about my happiness, Joe. This is about you and what you need to do to—"

"To what, Mom?" Joe cut her off. "To get right with God? To be a decent person? Or to not embarrass you?"

"Hey!" interrupted Jack, instantly fired up. "That's not fair, Joe, and you know it. Your mother has only ever done right by you, man. In fact, she's had nothing but patience with you. From what I've seen, you should be thanking her—not disrespecting her."

Jack looked like he could strangle Joe, so before that could happen, Sandy stepped in. Turning her attention to Jack, she asked, "Honey, could you excuse me and Joe for a minute?"

Jack looked from Sandy to her son and back to his wife. He nodded once, saying nothing more, but walked into the kitchen. He'd leave the room but wasn't about to be out of earshot.

"Look, Mom," Joe started, "Jack's right. I don't know what's wrong with me. I think I'm just a little overwhelmed with starting on this road to recovery, or whatever they call it. I didn't mean—"

"Yes, you did, Joe," interrupted Sandy. "You did mean—all of that. You think I preach too much at you, and clearly you think I'm embarrassed by you." Sandy took a deep breath to stop the tears that threatened. "I'm not preaching at you, Joe. I'm just telling you the facts—you aren't right with God, but I think you know that, so any time I do mention it, it makes you even more angry. That, my son, is your conscience bothering you. And just for the record, there has never—ever—been a day that I've been embarrassed of you. Some of your actions have bothered me, yes, but I've always been proud of you, Joe, and I love you ... more than you will ever know. If you're feeling that way, maybe it's you being embarrassed by your own actions. It's time for you to take a good, long look in the mirror, Joseph Evans."

Joe stared at his mother and wasn't able to move or speak. To say he was surprised would have been an understatement. His mother had been firm with him at times, but she had been more of a patient and loving picture of parenthood. She had apologized a while back for not being a better parent to him, but was this what she meant?

Joe's surprise and his aching expression gave Sandy pause. She didn't want to hurt her son, but she also wouldn't be responsible for trying to make him feel better about himself when he clearly needed to grow up. Sandy looked down at her lap and sighed. When she raised her head, tears did fill her eyes, and she shrugged as she said, "I only love you, Joe, and I believe there is a decent, authentic man inside of you somewhere." She took another breath before finishing. "You listen to me now. Even if I want to shake the sense into you sometimes, I *will* love you ... always and forever!"

It was a simple declaration that his mom had told him so many times, but this time, in its simplicity, something larger ached in Joe's heart and caught in his throat. He knew he hadn't made loving him easy on her, or for many others in the family.

Nothing more was said as Sandy stood and excused herself, saying that she was tired and needed to rest. Before Joe could reply, his mom left the room, and he was alone for only a short moment before Jack crossed from the kitchen to the living room to follow Sandy to their bedroom.

"You'll let yourself out," he stated quickly, glancing at Joe.

Joe nodded and was about to say something, but Jack disappeared before he could.

Chapter Twenty-Four

JACK LOOKED AT SANDY, BUT ALL SHE COULD DO WAS LOOK STRAIGHT AHEAD. The CT had just been done yesterday, and already her doctor's assistant had called and told her the doctor wanted to see her. She'd also said that she could bring someone close to her along. Sandy didn't have a medical background, but she knew the wheels of medicine often only moved quickly when the news was less than wonderful. As they sat in the waiting room, Jack held Sandy's small hand in his large one.

"How long have your headaches really gone on?" he asked quietly.

Sandy sighed before answering. "A few months," she admitted. "I'm sorry, Jack. I really thought it was nothing. I thought they'd go away—and the doctor I saw a while ago said they were from stress."

Jack nodded, reached over, and placed his arm around his wife. "It's okay. We don't even know what he's going to tell us yet." Jack wanted to be strong for Sandy, but even he knew the news that was coming was probably not the positive kind.

They'd come into the full waiting room, and they'd had to wait a long time already. It was getting to Jack, but there was nothing they could do but wait. When the office nurse called Sandy's name, Jack was on his feet first, taking her hand. The nurse looked surprised, as often was the case when Jack was in the room. He towered over everyone and could look rather foreboding, but he was oblivious to that right now. The nurse led them into an examination room and told them each to sit. The doctor would be right in. Neither Jack nor Sandy had much to say as they waited, again.

The young doctor came in not long after and greeted them both. He'd met Sandy once and had ordered the CT scan for her then. He was new to the office, but he smiled at Sandy and shook Jack's hand before he started asking questions. "How long have these headaches persisted?" he asked Sandy, getting right to it.

"Well ..." She paused. "Like I told you a few weeks ago, I think they've been getting worse for the last few months, but I thought it was because of the wedding plans at first. Then there's been a few other things—you know, normal life stresses everyone has. But they haven't really stopped, and I seem to need more Tylenol and Advil too."

The doctor nodded as he looked at the computer screen in front of him. He keyed in something and stared at the screen again. "Is there anything else you can tell me about how you're feeling, Sandy? Any other strange symptoms that you haven't had before?"

She took a deep breath and softly said, "I've noticed, just in the last few weeks, that I feel nauseous sometimes, and maybe a little dizzy occasionally. But it usually passes quickly, and I think the dizziness is just related to not eating as well as I should," she guessed.

Jack looked at his wife with concern etched over his features. She had told him none of that, and he highly doubted that her symptoms could be caused by ill eating habits. Sandy only ever ate well, as far as Jack knew, but maybe not as much as he thought she should lately.

"You fainted on our honeymoon, Sandy," Jack said quietly.

The doctor looked at Jack. "Fainted?"

Sandy turned a little red and had to nod her head. "Just that once, though," she admitted.

Sandy looked down and then up again. "But I hadn't eaten for a while. I was fine after. There really isn't much else except for these more constant headaches. It's probably hormones or something, right?"

The doctor didn't answer immediately, and Jack looked with sad eyes toward his wife. He knew she was downplaying everything, and he wanted to take the worry and fright away from her, but he also wished she hadn't ignored what could be a big problem.

"Unfortunately, Sandy, I have some rather grim news for you." Her doctor looked at the computer screen again as Sandy and Jack glanced at one another and then back to the doctor.

"I think we should move to doing an MRI as soon as possible but ..." The doctor paused, but not before Jack couldn't stop himself from jumping in.

"Doc," he started, "can you just tell us what's on the report?"

Sandy looked up at Jack and gently placed her hand on his forearm. He looked down at his sweet wife and sighed.

"Yes," agreed the doctor, nodding.

Sandy couldn't help but feel sorry for her new doctor, who likely hadn't given bad news to patients many times in his short career. As she looked from Jack to the physician, she tried to smile her encouragement to both of them.

"I'm so sorry to tell you this." He looked away from his screen and stared directly at Sandy. "This report states that you have a tumour in your brain, but we'll have to do a few more tests to see exactly what's involved and what type it is."

Sandy nodded, unable to say anything to that. Jack too was dumbfounded.

The doctor asked a few more questions and then needed to do a few neurological tests on Sandy, but Jack didn't hear him. Sandy only went through the motions, for the doctor's sake. He seemed thorough and had said "hmmm" a few times as he examined her, but he wasn't forthcoming with any further answers.

When the doctor left the room to arrange the MRI, Sandy tried to smile at Jack. "This is the most serious I've ever seen you, Jack," she said, her voice catching. "You know ... it will all work out for good."

"Oh Sandy," Jack managed, trying with every cell in his body not to fall apart as he pulled his chair even closer to her.

When the doctor re-entered the room a few minutes later, all he saw were two people wrapped in each other's arms, praying to the God of the universe for healing and strength.

Chapter Twenty-Five

PRIOR TO BECOMING PREGNANT, I'D OFTEN SAID THAT IF EVER I WAS, I WOULD only work until I couldn't fulfill all of my nursing duties as well as I had in a non-gravid state. Since I'd been assured that our twins were growing appropriately and everything looked as normal as it could be, I decided, against my doctor's suggestion, to work beyond her suggested twenty-eight weeks. With pride, nearing my thirty-second week in the heat of summer, I waddled into work one day and flopped into the most comfortable chair I could find in our report room.

"Still goin' hard, huh?" asked Shauna with a dubious expression. She'd agreed with my obstetrician that I should be off work and had voiced her concern before, as did a few of my other friends, but I had assured them that I would go off soon enough and that they shouldn't worry.

"Yep," I smiled, feeling suddenly larger and more uncomfortable than ever before.

"Well, I'm glad your running shoes are on, Trish. Our lull is over," she stated. "You might decide to do the smart thing and listen to all of us after this shift."

When I didn't return a rebuttal to that, she started in on the rather long report about the many labour patients presently on our unit. Kindly, I'd been assigned one early labour patient and one patient who was nearing delivery.

I smiled when Anne, another colleague with whom I'd worked for years, offered to watch my early labour patient when I'd be busy with the delivering one.

"Thanks," I said, hoisting myself from the report room chair. "I'll try to cover for your breaks too. I'm thinking we'll all be regrouping a few times today."

"You've got that right, Trish," she nodded. "Gonna be a busy one."

As I went to introduce myself to my patients, I knew without a doubt that the one baby, at least, would be born within a very short time. As I was readying the supplies for that little one's entrance into the world, a sharp pain I hadn't felt before suddenly grabbed into my left side.

"Are you okay?" said my experienced labour patient, who had noticed my sudden expression of surprise.

The pain was there and gone so quickly that I resolved just as fast and smiled at her. "I'm fine. Let's concentrate on you now."

"You might have to," she winced, starting to breathe heavier with her next contraction. As soon as I heard the grunt of her first involuntary push, I pulled the call bell. Soon after the doctor had gloved, a beautiful baby boy let his presence be known to all of us.

Later, when I was doing her fourth stage care—checking her vital signs, uterus, and flow—she smiled up at me. "Your first baby?"

I looked at her. "Yes." She was easily nursing her third child, and I couldn't keep myself from smiling. So many times I'd been there, helping to bring little people into the world. As my patient seemed to glow, comfortably holding her third boy, I couldn't help but appreciate the miracle of it all again.

"You must be soon done work, no?" she asked tentatively in her broken English.

"Maybe," I admitted, feeling a strange tightness spread across my belly.

"When will baby come?" she inquired, clearly seeming more interested in me than the baby at her breast.

"Babies," I said, turning to look directly at her and placing one hand on top of my swollen abdomen.

"Oh!" she exclaimed then. "Two? Two blessings!"

I couldn't help but grin at her enthusiasm, and no matter how I tried to bring the focus back to her and her newborn, she would only tell me how blessed and fortunate I was. She told me that she wasn't planning to quit having babies until she had at least one girl. I had to laugh when she told me that next time she would wish for twin girls and hoped that was what would happen for me.

As my shift progressed, I could no longer ignore the more regular tightenings that had chosen to persist no matter what I tried to do or how I moved. Near the end of my shift, as I ran down the hall holding on to the bottom of my belly for the fourth c-section of the day, Lisa saw me and in no uncertain terms said, "That's it, Trish. You're done—today."

Any other time I probably would've argued, but the tightness I felt just then made me wince as it took my breath away.

• • •

Grant didn't often get angry with me. His patience, in fact, had always astonished me. I mean full disclosure. I'm self aware enough to know I'm not the easiest person to live with. When Shauna called him from the hospital, however, to tell him that I was in threatened premature labour, the frightened and worried demeanour he presented with changed. His expression turned to a scowl when he learned from my turncoat of an obstetrician that I'd been ignoring contractions in my determination to finish my shift.

"In my defence," I started, feeling it fruitless but willing to try to explain my position, "the place was full to the rafters, Grant. Patients needed my help. What else could I do?"

I knew that hadn't helped in my plight when he quietly but with frustration clearly lacing his words returned, "Trish, God doesn't expect us to pray for safety and then do the dumbest thing we can to test Him."

Not only did I think it unnecessary to bring God into the conversation, but I instantly felt put out that he'd called me dumb.

I huffed, looking away from his handsome face. I focussed instead on the fetal monitor's print-out of our babies' heartbeats. I felt relieved to see that the contractions, which had previously been occurring every two to three minutes, were now much further apart. The medications I'd received and the rest, which I'd already heard would be ordered by my doctor, were clearly working.

As I looked back at Grant, I softened. He was right. Twins often came early, and why wouldn't I, an experienced obstetrical nurse, have been more aware of what was happening to my body? As my eyes teared a little, I felt Grant come to sit beside me on the bed.

"Careful," I warned him. "You might fall off. I take up a lot more room now."

When I heard him sigh, I glanced up and whispered, "I'm sorry, Grant. I really thought it was nothing. I wasn't thinking straight."

His gentle kiss stopped me, and we both turned when we heard Lisa re-enter the room. "Hey, you two," smiled my doctor and friend.

She looked at the fetal monitor and her smile grew, relieved as we were that the tightenings seemed to be abating. Grant and I listened as she told us about the ultrasound I'd had about an hour before. Although the babies were fine, my cervix had started to thin.

"So," she finished, "the good news is that it's not so thin that you need hospitalization at this point, but it's definitely shorter than a week ago at your last scan, so as far as the plan goes—off work and off your feet as much as possible, at home for now. You got that?"

As she and Grant looked at me, I nodded, finally willing to listen to the sound advice from the others around me.

"And," she smiled at me, "I probably shouldn't have to tell you this, but as you'd tell all our patients with threatened prem-labour, Trish ... no sex."

Grant reddened a little but kept nodding his head with the same serious expression that had been on his face the whole time Lisa had been speaking. Poor Grant. He wasn't as comfortable with the sometimes-blatant instructions needed when explaining things to patients. I, on the other hand, while not embarrassed by it, didn't feel it necessary that she tell us every instruction that I very well knew.

Lisa must have read my mind because she winked at me before leaving. "You be good, Trish Evans. This place will survive without you, you know. Just try to enjoy the few weeks you have left before those boys come. You'll be glad you did."

Grant and I both stared at the empty doorway long after Lisa left. Apparently she hadn't been aware that we didn't know the gender before that moment. As I absorbed that new revelation, suddenly it all fell into a totally new perspective. I don't know why it took that long, but in that moment it all became real to me. This wasn't just another "twin pregnancy." This was our pregnancy. Our miracles. These were our babies. Real babies. Boy babies.

As I turned to Grant, feeling intense and overwhelming guilt that in my denial I could've caused the early arrival of our ... sons ... my breath caught. I was beyond speaking as my eyes welled with tears. I suspected Grant could see the coming torrent when he looked down and, placing his strong hands on either side of my face, whispered, "I didn't call you dumb."

"Wh ... what?" I asked in my befuddlement, seeing the smile in his eyes.

"I just meant ... you did a dumb thing. *You* are not dumb."

Suddenly remembering what he'd said when he first arrived, I could only smile back. With all the news I'd just had to digest, the one little thing he'd said out of frustrated concern paled in comparison.

"Can I still kiss you?" he asked, looking a little concerned.

"You better," I smiled, kissing him and, like a kid being told they can't have something, wishing there could be more.

"How long?" Grant whispered.

"Thirty-six weeks," I laughed, hitting his arm.

"There she is," he laughed back, the small wrinkles around his eyes deepening.

• • •

Later that evening after Grant had put Kylie to bed and had arranged some additional care for her while I'd be trying to rest more at home, we were watching a sitcom that neither of us were paying much attention to.

"I guess we can seriously focus on just boy names now," I ventured.

I was living large on the recliner, trying to adjust my right hip into a more comfortable position as he glanced at me from his place on the couch.

"I guess so," he nodded.

We kept nodding at each other before blurting out what had been on both our minds.

"Let's not tell anyone!" we both chorused and then laughed.

We agreed that the special secret we'd accidentally learned that evening would stay just between us, for a little longer anyway.

Chapter Twenty-Six

GRANT AND JOE SAT ACROSS FROM SANDY AND JACK IN THEIR LIVING ROOM and stared. Grant was the first to speak after the long, shocked silence. "How long?" he asked with a raw voice.

Jack looked at Sandy before she answered. It had been a few weeks since the second specialist had told them the same answer that the first one had—about the tumour in her brain. They'd done a few more tests and even another biopsy, just in case, but the tumour in her brain was a glioblastoma, one of the most aggressive brain tumours anyone could have. For a few weeks, since the diagnosis, Sandy had been rather evasive with the family. Everyone was busy with their own lives, so no one really took notice until Grant asked her about babysitting a little more to help with Trish's needed bedrest. When she'd turned him down, Grant had wondered about it, but other plans were made quite easily, and he hadn't thought about it much since.

Sandy and Jack were thankful to have the time together alone to deal with their own thoughts and to pray for guidance for the days to come. Decisions needed to be made, and with Jack beside her, they'd made them together. Although she hadn't wanted to tell the family yet and was nervous that it might further affect Trish's pregnancy, Jack had talked her into it. Joe had been asking more questions at the last AA meeting too, so Jack had pushed Sandy a little more after that.

As Grant's question hung in the air, Sandy sighed. She thought she'd cried all the tears she could, but as she felt them threaten again, she took a few deep breaths.

Jack, seeing his wife struggle, spoke for her. "The doctors don't exactly know, but they think months, or maybe a year."

"A year?" echoed Joe, dumbfounded. He'd been punched in the gut a few times, but even those times had never felt as awful as this.

Sandy nodded, agreeing with what Jack said.

"Well, what about chemo or radiation or surgery or everything they do for people with cancer these days?" asked Joe, feeling the same panic that Sandy had felt at first.

"Joe, we've discussed all of those things at length with the specialists. They all agree that we could try some of them, but at most it would prolong my life for only a very short time, and the quality of my life would likely be worse. Right now I'm not feeling all that bad, except for the headaches and some nausea and dizziness, so I've decided ..." Sandy paused, knowing that she would break their hearts no matter what she'd say now. She squeezed Jack's hand tighter and glanced at him quickly for strength. "I've decided to ... to live my best life, every day, until ... I don't. I just want to enjoy the time I have left to the fullest."

As Joe continued to argue with their mother, Grant sat back and watched. Although he'd thought something was off, never in his wildest dreams did he imagine this sort of news. As he looked around, he saw sadness and worry in his mom's eyes, but he knew the sadness wasn't for herself. She had prayed for Joe and seen her son struggle for so many years. Grant suspected that now, more than ever, the concern etched on her face was most likely for Joe.

Of course his mom would choose no treatments. She'd always been practical and wise. Grant knew his mother believed that her time on earth was fleeting. She'd always said her real home was in heaven and that everyone's time on earth was, like the Bible said, a vapour. But she had always told her sons that what they did while on earth counted for eternity. Although Grant knew no one could earn their way to heaven, but rather it was what had been done for them on the cross, as he watched his mother smile at Joe just then, he knew that her reward there would be great.

"Joe," his mom said again, "it's fine, honey. It really is. I know what you're saying, but I don't want to have surgery and treatments just to prolong my life for a few weeks down here. I know where I'm going, and although it might be hard until I go, and hard for you after, I want to spend the last while I have just being with my family … until I go home."

"Home?" asked Joe in a conflicted voice. "This is your home, Mom, and we need you to stay here!"

Sandy sighed again. She didn't have words to help him through the shock of her news. Her poor Joe just couldn't understand.

"Yes," nodded Jack. "This is your home, Sandy." As she turned to him and smiled, he added, "And we're going to make it the best, however long you'll be here, starting right now."

Joe and Grant looked from their mom to Jack and back again.

"So … what do you want, Mom?" asked Grant, still in shock but knowing his mother probably had worked out a plan for the rest of her time with them.

"Well," she swallowed, "we've decided on something called palliative care. It's basically just keeping as comfortable as possible and enjoying life as much as possible, until the end."

Joe huffed as Grant continued to mull that over.

Sandy and Jack looked at each other again, and when she looked back to her sons, Sandy's expression was nothing short of glowing.

"And," she started, looking at Joe pointedly, "I want to ask you for a favour, Joe."

Grant looked at his brother but was relieved when Joe replied, "Anything, Mom."

"I know you've just started living out at the cabin and haven't finished with all the beautiful things you're doing out there, but if it's okay with you, I'd like to move out there. It doesn't have to be right away, but nearer to the end. I have such good memories there, and it's so peaceful …" she trailed off, looking down at her lap.

Joe's expression was unreadable as she looked back up at him.

"I know you're in the process of fixing it up, Joe, but I don't care if it's not finished, and I don't want you to rush to get everything done. I just … I guess what I'm saying is … I want to go home there."

Joe felt numb as he got off the chair he'd been sitting in to cross the room to where his mother sat. "Yeah." He cleared his throat as he kneeled in front of her. "Yeah ... of course, Mom. You can move in any time."

Sandy smiled as Joe wrapped his arms gently around her. "If you want to," she said, "you can stay here, or stay with us out there. It's up to you."

Joe shook his head, getting back up to return to his chair. "Nah," he said softly. "You and the big guy can have the cabin. I'll hang out sometimes, but I can stay here."

Grant watched his mother's nod and serene smile. Whatever she would ask, he knew he'd try to move heaven and earth to make it all work for her, and obviously Joe felt the same.

"And ..."—she paused, looking up at Jack before returning her eyes to Grant—"now we wait for those babies and enjoy them and Kylie to the fullest!"

"I still can't believe this!"

Sandy stared up at Joe, who had stood up and was now pacing in front of them. As he rammed his hand into his hair, he stopped in front of Sandy again. "Geez, Mom! I can't believe this! I really have to say that I doubt all of this because you've always been so healthy. I mean ... are you *sure* they know what they're talking about?"

"They do, Joe," said Sandy gently. "Numerous doctors have reviewed the tests. They all say the same thing, honey." Her heart broke for her angry son as she prayed silently for him again.

Joe's anger continued. "But ... if what you're saying is true—that you only have a little bit of time left— you're acting like this is no big deal, Mom! You sound like you've got this list, and we're just going to discuss a few things like it's nothing! I don't know why you won't fight! I mean, this is nuts!"

Joe stepped back when Jack stood up to move in front of him. They stared at each other as if they were in a showdown before Jack spoke. "Joe," he said softly, unexpectedly placing his hand on Joe's shoulder, "we know you're in shock. We are too, but"—he looked at Sandy, who looked up at him encouragingly—"your mom is just asking that you support her decision."

Joe stared up at Jack, and his shoulders sagged. If this wasn't some sort of horrible joke, Jack was right. His mom had made a decision, and now she'd need his support more than anything else. Suddenly, a feeling of deja vu infused Joe's mind. This reminded him of when she had told him about Grant's decision not to sue the hospital after his first wife, Stacy, died. Although he wanted his mom to fight with anything medically available, she'd made up her mind to let the cancer take her. Grant hadn't fought either. Joe sighed. Maybe he'd never understand the medical decisions his family made.

As Jack removed his hand from Joe's shoulder, they both moved back to their seats. Joe looked at his brother and blinked.

"I know this is a lot for you to take in, boys. I still feel overwhelmed about it all too," said Sandy.

Grant sat further back in his chair, swirling thoughts running through his mind, but utmost was his concern for his mother. He leaned forward with his elbows on his knees, as if trying to capture his mother's complete attention. Ignoring his brother, Grant spoke softly.

"I know what you've said, but have you thought this through completely, Mom? Jack?" Grant glanced at the man beside his mother. "I mean, if there's any chance at all to beat this thing, shouldn't you try? We can send you anywhere, Mom, for any treatment. We'll make it work."

"Yeah!" Joe chimed in, gesturing with a hand toward his brother. "Someone with some sense!" he added.

Sandy looked at Jack and smiled again at the man she loved.

"I can only tell you this one more time, Grant, Joe ... this isn't the kind of tumour that can be fixed by any kind of medical treatments. It just can't, but it's going to be okay. This has happened for some reason we don't know, but"—Sandy swallowed—"I need to know that you're going to be here for me and Jack and everyone in the family, and that you'll try to prepare ..." Sandy's eyes teared as both of her sons came around her then.

There were hugs and promises—of support and encouragement—as would be normal for any family where there is love for one another, and in most moments such as these. Impossible, sad, and heartbreaking moments.

• • •

Sandy hugged both her sons for a long time before they left, and now, staring out the window as she watched them pull away from her small home, her eyes teared a little again.

Jack came beside her and placed his arm gently around her shoulders. "They'll be okay."

Sandy nodded. She knew Grant would be, but she couldn't help but feel great concern for her youngest.

Jack leaned over and kissed Sandy gently on her cheek before he turned around, picked up two of the still full cups of now cold coffee, and walked to the kitchen with them.

Chapter Twenty-Seven

JOE SIGHED AS HE STARTED HIS TRUCK AND PULLED AWAY FROM THE HOME Sandy had moved to after her sons had grown. Now she wanted to go back to the cabin. He could understand that. She'd always said some of her best memories lay at the cabin and on the lake. He almost smiled as he remembered some of the fun they'd had there. Grant could remember a few things about their dad during those years, but Joe had been only two when he died. Although he couldn't remember him, their mother had made many great summer memories for them during their childhood and teen years. She obviously had loved it as much as they had.

Joe's eyes teared. His mom was dying. Dying. And not in years from now, but any time. Would she even be around for any more celebrations? Even for Grant and Trish's twins' birth? Joe thought about the long hug his mom had given him before leaving tonight. How many more of those would he get to have? As much as he didn't always agree with everything his mom preached, he certainly didn't feel ready to lose her. She was the best woman he'd ever known. But what was God good for now? Joe huffed. Good for nothing God. Joe didn't know what to do with himself, but he knew what called to him.

As he started his truck, he debated. He wanted a drink so badly right now, but he hadn't had one for a while. He knew he'd not only let himself down if he gave in, but he'd be letting his mom down too. How could he do that to the woman who had only shown love and care for him her whole life? And now she was dying. Joe closed his eyes and took a deeper breath, trying to calm the anxiety that infused his every cell.

The sudden buzz of the phone in his back pants pocket made him jump a little as he scrambled to see who would dare bother him right now.

It was a familiar number and he readily answered it.

"Hey, Joe," said Glenn. "How ya doin?"

Joe paused, wondering. This seemed to be suspiciously coincidental. "I've had better days," admitted Joe to his boss.

"So I hear, Joe," Glenn returned with empathy in his voice. "Wanna meet somewhere for coffee?"

"Maybe," Joe countered.

"I'm not forcing you, Joe, but I'm here for ya, man."

Joe thought for a short moment before asking the question he felt he needed an answer to. "So ... how did my sponsor know I'd need a coffee tonight?"

"A mutual friend of ours told me," answered Glenn.

They decided on a place to meet, and as Joe pulled away from his mom's place, he glanced back. He saw her at the window, looking out into the night, and then Jack coming alongside her. Joe couldn't help himself. Maybe Jack wasn't such a bad guy after all.

• • •

Grant's mind reeled as he tried to assimilate everything his mom had just told them. He felt shocked, overwhelmed and even angry.

"Why, God?" he yelled inside his truck. He knew from what he believed that God had a purpose in everything, but tonight he couldn't possibly imagine any good purpose for his mother's diagnosis. She didn't deserve this—a brain tumour of all things! She had lived such a good life, been faithful to God, and was so wise and unselfish. The saying "only the good die young" came to his mind, and he suddenly wondered if that had originated in the Bible or if someone had made it up. In any case, apparently it was true.

She had acted so calm and accepting of all of it. It was almost like many other conversations they'd had, except this one ended with news of another death. Her death. Death had been all too real to Grant: first his dad when Grant was six; then Trevor, his son; and then Stacy. Grant shook his head. Ted. Trish's dad was gone too. That brought his mind to his lovely wife. How would he tell Trish? Or did his mom want to tell her? He hadn't even asked. Kylie was too young to understand, but he knew she would miss her grandmother terribly.

Grant pulled into an almost empty parking lot to think. He couldn't help it. He hadn't fallen apart often, but tonight, in the darkness and aloneness of his truck cab, Grant Evans wept. He cried for all of them and what was to come, and then, a long while later, as was his go-to, he started to pray.

• • •

When Jack was done cleaning up the rest of the cups, he came back to where Sandy still stood, looking out at the now darker night. He hugged her and tried, again, not to cry. He'd asked God so many times in the last days why He was allowing Sandy to go through this and why she would be taken away from him now. They hadn't known each other that long, but the time they'd had together had been wonderful—something he often thought he didn't deserve. Jack had learned so much through knowing her. She'd answered so many questions for him, not only about God but about how he could live an honourable life, even after all the many mistakes he'd made.

Sandy looked up at her husband and stared deeply into his eyes. What a man he'd become! His faith had grown so much, and as they'd travelled the difficult path of the last few weeks, it seemed to surpass her own. She hoped and prayed that he'd always go to the Rock for the strength she suspected they'd need more than ever with what lay ahead for them.

"Tough for the boys tonight," Sandy broke the silence. "I hope they're okay." She put her head on Jack's chest and treasured his hug. "There's just no easy way to break this sort of news."

Jack's heart ached for his wife. She'd been so strong and only seemed to worry about everyone else around her and how it would affect each of them. Her love for everyone around her and her seemingly endless generosity toward others had been a huge attraction for Jack when he'd first met Sandy. She truly was the kind of person he wasn't sure he could ever be. He had been instantly angry when the doctor had given them the news. He wanted a second and, if necessary, a third and fourth opinion—until they would find someone who would give them some sort of hope. But the two specialists they had seen had both agreed that there was nothing that could be done. Sandy seemed to accept it with the grace Jack would have expected. Jack had struggled more, but she, again, thought of him and was very matter-of-fact that he should accept it as part of God's will, even though they both didn't understand why.

Now they both sighed at the same time before Jack took Sandy's small face in his big hands and kissed her. He had vowed that he would love her and stand alongside her "until death do us part," and although it was much too soon, he would treasure this woman until that vow was completed.

Chapter Twenty-Eight

"I'M REALLY SORRY, GLENN. THIS ISN'T A GREAT TIME TO ASK FOR TIME OFF, BUT I really need to right now," Joe said, sitting across from his boss in Glenn's small office.

Glenn stared at Joe, thinking. He really needed him right now, but he also knew that Joe needed time with his family. He normally would have turned him down flat, but since learning about some of the tough stuff he was going through, Glenn knew he couldn't. Clearly Joe's mom meant a lot to him, and for gosh sakes, the woman was dying. How could he turn the guy down?

Glenn had quickly felt responsible for Joe after meeting up with him at AA. He couldn't help liking the guy, no matter his addiction to alcohol. He'd been there himself, and someone had seen potential and hadn't given up on him either, and neither would Glenn. Joe seemed to really like his work, and he did good job. Employees with a good work ethic were getting harder and harder to find, and because of the potential he saw in Joe, Glenn had to allow it.

Glenn had paused long enough that Joe surprised himself when he said, "I'm really sorry about this, but if you can't spare me, I … I guess I'll just have to quit, because I have to get this done. It's not that my mom is asking me to, but I need to do this for her before she moves into … well, I have to finish the cabin for her," he ended in a rush.

Silence continued between the two men, with Joe soon becoming uncomfortable. Why was he being so insistent about finishing the cabin? His mom had said she didn't care about the state of the place, and she'd be okay with Jack there. Nonetheless, as questions fired through his mind, something he couldn't figure out drove him to insist that he had to do it.

"You must be very close to your mother, Joe," Glenn started and then paused before something else occurred to him. "Is she, perhaps, the one who keeps you even more accountable than your sister-in-law?"

Joe didn't need another conversation about accountability. The last time Glenn had talked about that, Joe hadn't slept well for a night or two when he'd thought, again, about Stephanie. Joe hadn't always listened to his mother. Sadly, he had rebelled against a lot of the things she had taught him since he'd been a small boy, but now he looked at his boss, considering.

Joe shrugged after a few seconds and looked away from Glenn's stare. "I don't know," he shrugged.

"Hmm," Glenn pondered. "Well, Joe, I know your family is going through some tough stuff right now, and since you feel this strongly about getting that done, you better get going. I don't want to lose you, however. You do good work, and I really think you're a good fit for the company. You'll be welcomed back when you're ready," he said.

Joe almost couldn't believe it. He'd actually thought he might be leaving without a job today. "Yes, sir!" Joe exclaimed.

Just before he was out the door, Glenn stopped him. "I'm really sorry about what's going on with your mom, Joe," he said, watching him. "Call me anytime if you're getting overwhelmed, okay?"

Joe turned in the doorway with sudden wetness in his eyes. He inwardly chastised himself for the tears that threatened, swiping a hand over his face. "I will," he nodded, genuinely appreciating it.

Chapter Twenty-Nine

IT WAS SHOCKING, TO SAY THE LEAST, TO HEAR OF SANDY'S DIAGNOSIS, AND after Grant shared it with me, I began berating myself for not seeing things more clearly much sooner. I know I'm not alone when I say many professionals in the medical field blame themselves—unnecessarily and unrealistically—when something they perceive they've missed is brought to life. I am no different. Compound this with pregnancy hormones and being forced into way too much time to think, and my guilt began to grow exponentially.

"Stop beating yourself up, Trish," repeated Grant one evening.

After taking Abigail for a visit to Sandy and Jack's place, Trent and Melissa had brought Chinese food over to ours. They'd been in the city for one of Abigail's appointments, and we'd enjoyed sharing dinner with them.

"Like Trent said, the headaches my mom had could have been caused by so many other things. You can't blame yourself or the doctors she saw earlier. Mom ignored some of her symptoms too, Trish. I mean—she didn't tell us about the fainting spells she'd had. But she believes that everything happens in God's timing, and she's right."

"Well," I huffed as I climbed into bed beside him that night, "I just wish I'd insisted she see someone sooner. And I should've questioned your mother much more thoroughly about her symptoms. I mean ... what kind of nurse *am* I?"

As my frustrated tears threatened again, Grant leaned over me and placed one hand on my ever-enlarging abdomen. He looked deeply into my eyes and sighed. “Say it,” he said, with the quiet patience of a man who was determined for me to believe it this time.

“I know,” I replied, my eyes rolling while filling with tears.

“Then please say it and mean it this time,” he stated.

“I’m a nurse. I’m not ... God.” I blinked and a few tears fell.

“You know my mom’s tumour was never your responsibility, Trish, and I want you to believe that. No one blames you, and you have to stop beating yourself up. It’s not healthy—for you or these two,” he said, looking down at where our babies were not-so-secretly held.

I nodded as I reached up to touch his cheek and look into the fabulous blue of the eyes I’d fallen in love with. He wanted me to believe it, and I did too. He kissed me then before smiling at a kick we both felt. We had to laugh when the opposite baby kicked back.

“They’re playing already,” Grant grinned, getting to a kneeling position to kiss both sides of my stretched belly.

“I think maybe more like fighting,” I returned, putting my hands over the babies Grant told me on a daily basis I was blessed to carry.

I could feel him smile as he looked up at me, over the mountain between us. “Glass half full, Trish,” he whispered.

I couldn’t help but smile as he moved beside me to continue reading his devotions. So often when I saw the worst-case scenario, he’d see something wonderful in the middle of the chaos. Before falling into another uncomfortable sleep, I thanked God again for giving me a man with strong convictions, the kindest of hearts, and endless patience.

Chapter Thirty

AS THE NEXT FEW WEEKS PASSED, SANDY'S SYMPTOMS REMAINED MUCH THE same, and after the initial shock ebbed, life seemed to almost fall into the routine it had followed before the news. We all knew a more serious time was ahead of us, but for the short time being, more moments in our days seemed almost normal again.

Kylie kept Grant busy when he'd return from work in the evenings, and her caregivers, helping in the daytime, were much appreciated by both of us. Sandy insisted on caring for her as often as possible, but we could tell by Jack's attentiveness that both of them didn't leave his watchful eye for long.

Between her responsibilities with all the events that needed prepping in the business that Melissa and my mother now co-owned, my mom had also been coming into the city more often. She often came to our house and cooked for us, making delicious meals that we would freeze and save for use after the babies were born. When I told my mother about Sandy's diagnosis, she had cried with me and told both Grant and I how deeply sorry she felt for all of us. My mother would often think of Sandy and Jack and would send soup or a casserole with Grant to take to his mom's so she didn't have to cook as much either. Our church friends, my hospital colleagues, and a few people we hardly knew stepped in significantly for both Grant and me, and his mom and Jack. I felt constantly overwhelmed with how people rallied around us, but I was relieved as my thirty-sixth week of pregnancy neared. I hoped that when I was finally allowed to get off the couch I might even repay some of the kind things that had been done for us.

The day before the calendar marked the magical thirty-six-week point, I couldn't wait any longer. As soon as Grant left with Kylie that morning, I rose out of bed, feeling ridiculously excited about the plan I'd made for the day. Enough lying around!

As I opened the door to the room we had deemed the "nursery," I smiled and looked around at what Grant had accomplished with a little help from Joe. Of course I'd seen it, as he'd worked on it in the evenings and on weekends, but today I looked at all of it with more of a critical eye. I know my gifts don't lie with decorating by any means, but something had been niggling at me ever since we'd found out the genders of our babies. Although we had agreed not to give away this one secret, I was becoming more driven to make the room a little more gender specific.

Although I had told Grant that they could sleep in the same crib, he had insisted on setting up two anyway. The room was large enough to accommodate both comfortably, as well as a change table I'd found on an online garage sale. I sighed as I sat down in the beautiful rocking chair Joe had made. It didn't match the white of the cribs either, but I didn't care about that. It was so comfortable, and as I'd told Joe, it would be a family heirloom from that day forward. As I rocked, feeling the smoothness of the wood under my hands, I looked around the room and the lack of colour surrounding me. I hoisted myself up, walked to our room, and went into the walk-in closet Grant didn't use. Melissa had made some suggestions on a few things I might consider to add "splashes" of colour in the otherwise neutral room, and I had listened. As I wedged myself between the too many boxes and bags I'd squirrelled away in the closet, looking for the one I needed, I thought back to the night before.

As well as some personal reflection, praying, Bible reading, and all the things I knew I should do while lying down and growing our babies, I found another wonderful outlet that helped pass my boredom on bedrest. And that would be—specifically—online shopping. Before I was afforded the opportunity for rest, I hadn't ordered much from over the internet, but that quickly changed in the weeks I considered myself forced to.

Grant had never commented much before on things I'd buy for us or our home. I'm a huge fan of consignment stores and consider myself quite frugal, but I learned, as the days passed, that even I could go broke on a good deal.

As we were relaxing in the living room the evening before, we both didn't miss the now familiar quick knock and plop of a package being dropped off on our front steps. Grant jumped up, went to the door to retrieve the box, and then waved at the courier as he drove away. After Grant closed the door, he turned to look at me, and I couldn't help but redden a little. I knew I'd been pretty busy ordering things, but at the same time, I was prepared to defend our need of them.

"I guess I should feel relief," he started, placing the box on the coffee table across from me. "As often as that guy comes here, I might think you're having an affair."

I couldn't help my burst of laughter as he added, "Nice to know you're just breaking our bank account instead."

"Funny," I smiled, hoping to curb my impulse a little more in the future. "Like anyone would care to have an affair with all of this." I gestured at the hidden humans that certainly weren't hiding anymore.

He grinned mischievously and whispered, "I'm just waiting until the magic thirty-six, lady. Only two days away."

"If you think that's happening, Grant Evans, think again. I mean ... look at me! There's no way!"

He'd settled back to sit on his end of the couch and threw me a smouldering look. "We'll see," he shrugged, before becoming more serious about a commercial playing on the TV.

I slowly got to a sitting position and began tearing open the box in front of me. Which treasure would it be this time?

• • •

Although Stephanie was busy with her office work, she would occasionally drop in on her lunch break and bring me an iced cappuccino or some such luxury that I'd taken completely for granted when I'd been more active. It was on the day I'd finally decided to get up and stand on my own two feet again that Stephanie found me sitting on the floor in the nursery, rereading the instructions for the wall-writing letters I had, so far, unsuccessfully placed.

"I thought you weren't home, Trish, and then I got worried when you didn't answer the door," she started.

"Huh?" I looked at her blankly. "How did you get in?"

"You gave me a key, remember Auntie Trish?" she laughed. She had called me aunt earlier in our relationship, and although theoretically I was, we'd both decided just Trish would suffice.

I'd been so engrossed in the instructions in front of me that I hadn't heard her knocking or the ring of the doorbell.

"Okay, niece Stephanie." I shook my head and smiled. "I'm gonna blame that on pregnancy brain."

"Hmm," Stephanie sounded doubtful before shrugging. "Maybe. Hey!" she added, as if struck by a thought. "Aren't you supposed to be resting?"

"I'm done with that, Steph," I said, almost proudly. "Tomorrow is thirty-six weeks. One day won't make a difference, and I've had enough resting anyway. I have to get ready for the bo…" I stopped, having almost tripped up.

"The babies?" she laughed. "I'm guessing they're boys by the blue lettering all over the floor."

"Uh …" I managed, knowing that I couldn't deny it now. "I guess my number's up, huh?"

She smiled as she retied the messy ponytail behind her head. "Here … let me help. I may not be very good at this, but I put some of these up in my condo, and they're pretty nice. Mine are removable. Are these?"

As I let her take the instructions, I lifted my body to a standing position and explained where I thought they should go. As we worked, we talked about the family, and I held her in a hug when she spoke about Sandy and her grandfather, Jack. I noticed that Joe's name didn't surface, but I couldn't help my curiosity. When she began admiring the rocking chair, I saw my opening.

"Joe made that," I began. "Isn't it perfect? He even put this removable brass plaque on the back so that we can get it engraved with the babies' names. He said we can put all the children's names who we rock in this chair on it."

I hadn't noticed Stephanie turn away until I looked up. Although she didn't face me then, from her slumped shoulders and audible sniffles I knew she may be staying longer than just for her lunch hour.

"Oh Trish," she said, turning as she dabbed at her eyes and blew her nose, "he was so weird that night, and somehow I just can't get it out of my mind. We've talked since, and he's told me over and over that he's sorry and that it'll never happen again, but I just don't trust him."

To my knowledge, Stephanie hadn't told anyone about the night Joe had ended up on her doorstep, completely drunk and out of control. As curious as I'd been about that, I wasn't even sure I wanted to know about any of it. I'd actually found myself thankful not to have more possible reason to disrespect my brother-in-law. He had never been a stellar person, in my mind, but I still couldn't help but like him at the same time. It was confusing for me. I couldn't imagine what it was like for my niece.

"I mean"—she was now determined to continue—"some of the things he said that night were right, but other stuff didn't make sense. At the same time, what if he does it again?"

Instead of replying, I shrugged. How could I give words of wisdom, much less any advice, if I didn't know the whole story? And I didn't really want to know … but maybe I did.

"Can I tell you what happened?" she asked, giving me my own answer. "I don't want you to think less of Joe, though. That's why I haven't said anything to anyone, but since I've had the time to think and pray about this, I need some advice. I won't tell you all the things he said because I couldn't tell you everything anyway. He couldn't seem to shut up. He talked and talked, but I don't think he remembers much of it, actually. But I need to bounce this off someone, and you're always so great, and you get me, so do you think—"

"Of course," I interrupted her. "But first … I have to pee."

Stephanie laughed as she sat on our nursery floor to await my return.

On the way to our bedroom ensuite, I texted Grant that Stephanie might be late returning to work. When he didn't text back, I hoped that he'd get it and that it would work out.

When I returned to the nursery, I sat down in the rocking chair, and Stephanie revealed a few things about Joe from that night. Surprisingly, what seemed like huge problems to her somehow didn't appear so to me. Maybe I was growing up. Turning thirty, although it had bothered me a little at the time, had actually brought with it more wisdom.

When I'd given her assurance and could see that my advice was seeming to help her consider a few things from a different perspective, she suddenly blurted, "He told me he loved me!"

Sure! Just when I thought I had wise answers!

Stephanie glanced at her watch as soon as she'd said it. "I better get back," she rushed, starting to get up. "Now I'm going to be late, and I hate that."

"Wait!" I said, stopping her. As I held up one hand and pointed my finger at her to stop her from moving, I fleetingly thought of my mother. I looked at my hand and saw hers, but I didn't have time now to evaluate that psychology. Besides, I wasn't this girl's mother. "Wait a minute, Steph. You can't drop that on me and just leave." I'd stopped my rocking and glanced at the phone I still held in my other hand. I hadn't heard the text back from Grant, but it was there, and I quickly read it.

"I texted Grant before," I continued, glancing at Stephanie. "He says stay as long as you want, unless you have a meeting lined up that he doesn't know about. Do you have one?" I added, hoping she didn't.

Stephanie shook her head and seated herself on the floor again. She smiled. "Thanks, Trish."

"Don't thank me," I started. "I may not have any good advice to give you."

The scene that Stephanie explained now changed everything in the surety I had about my own wisdom, so I started to pray silently in desperation for the wisdom I'd read is ours in James 1:5.

As she gave more details of that night, I could just imagine the scene ...

When Joe had entered her condo, he'd immediately flopped on the couch and asked for a drink. She'd gotten him water but suggested making coffee for him instead. He had turned that down but took the glass of water and eventually spilled it when trying to grab at it with his uncoordinated hands.

"I just ... I'm just so sorry, Steph," he'd said to her.

"For what?" asked Stephanie.

"For ev-er-y-thing," he'd drawled.

"Not good enough," she'd returned, "but ...

She told him then that she was truly sorry for not telling him sooner about Abigail, but it was no excuse for his now irresponsible behaviour and that he needed to grow up. He'd argued with her, with some rude words thrown her way, but she'd told him exactly what she thought as well, in no uncertain terms. After she'd called him an immature child, he hadn't denied that but rather had looked, according to her, into her eyes so deeply that the intensity had made her feel a little weak. Then he'd told her that he loved her and would never feel differently and that he was sure she should love him back.

When she told me that, I couldn't help but remember back to not long after I'd started seeing Grant. Although he hadn't been drunk, which in Joe's case did make the validity of his declaration questionable at best, I had been equally astounded by his very early admission of love for me. I found myself feeling a little sorry for Joe in that moment, and I wasn't at all sure of why.

"He didn't seem so drunk when he said it, Trish," Stephanie was saying when I refocussed. "But then he fell off the couch, and I left him on the floor till morning."

I couldn't help but laugh at the picture of that in my head. Unfortunately, I didn't wait for wisdom then but blurted out, "Do you think you love him?"

Stephanie looked at me with surprise on every feature, and I was immediately sorry I hadn't prayed harder. "How ... how could I possibly love him?" she gasped.

"Right," I agreed, nodding my head. "Sorry. Not sure what I was thinking there."

Stephanie stared at me, and to my surprise, her chin started to quiver. "He's such a jerk," she managed, "but ... I'm crazy about him. I don't know if it's love or if I'm insane, but I'm *so* attracted to him, Trish. No matter how stupid he is, I just keep thinking about him and can't seem to get him out of my mind."

When I saw her tears begin to fall, I stopped the rocking I'd started again, got up, and wrestled my body to the floor to give her a hug. I had no past experience with any of this. Grant had been the only love of my life, and although I suspected he'd always be the stronger one, we'd both been believers when we met. Joe didn't seem to have any kind of faith, but Stephanie did, and as she'd told us, she wanted to make God her life's priority.

I couldn't imagine what to tell her now, but suddenly I knew what God needed me to do.

Stephanie nodded her thanks as I began to pray.

• • •

Before Stephanie left, I promised that I wouldn't tell Grant the details of what she'd shared with me if she would be kind enough not to tell him that she now knew the gender of our babies. We even pinky-swore, which we both knew was completely ridiculous but seemed fun anyway.

I decided to temporarily forego the decorating I'd planned and instead try for a nap. I didn't want to walk back upstairs anyway, so I grunted and moaned a little as I settled myself on the couch.

I almost wished my water would break right then. I'd call Grant, he'd take me to the hospital, and we could get this over with. I knew now that the countless women I'd cared for were absolutely correct when they'd told me they could no longer find a comfortable position to sit, stand, or sleep in. I had smiled at them then—smiled!—thinking that I was sure it was an exaggeration. As good a labour nurse as I thought I'd been, I was quickly learning that perhaps I had been more judgemental, at least in my inner thoughts, than I cared to admit. As I wedged the pillow, who many who'd gone before me insisted I would need, between my legs, I scowled at it too. No pillow was going to help me now!

I had just started dozing off when my phone buzzed loudly. I had left it on the coffee table, which I should have thought to move closer, but hadn't. As I reached for it, I almost fell off the couch. Teetering on the edge, I slammed my hand on the floor instead, caught myself, and hoisted my body back, successfully grabbing the phone in the process. I assessed my hand and wrist. Everything was moving normally, and the wild movements I felt in the rest of my body gave me relief that we were all fine. I berated myself for not keeping the table closer as I glanced at the length of the text. Why did my mother seem to have to text every little detail of her life in long, drawn out explanations almost every time she texted? As I looked at its daunting length, I felt immediately guilty that I thought her simple text too much effort to read. After all, I was the one who had shown my mother the "talk and text" option when I'd watched her typing slowly and painfully into her phone one day. I gave my head a shake. What was wrong with me? I should be glad that she even wanted anything to do with her ungrateful daughter. Before I could finish reading the text, however, our front doorbell rang.

I sighed in frustration, taking a deep breath before yelling, "Come in!"

My impatience soared now. Would I ever get my nap?

Suddenly, I didn't care who entered our home. If it was a thief, I was willing to give them anything, as long as they'd be kind enough to grab the water bottle I'd forgotten in the fridge and throw it at me on their way out. Fortunately, my dream of this didn't come true, as my mother opened the door slowly and brought her smiling self inside.

"Mom, I didn't know you were coming to the city," I smiled, thinking of my reaction to her text and now being as friendly as I possibly could manage.

"Hi, honey," she answered, coming to sit across from me. "I texted you."

"Oh, yeah," I hesitated. I hadn't read to the bottom. There it was, as I glanced down at the phone still in my hand. Her last sentence read, "I'll be right there."

"Can I get you anything?" she asked before sitting.

I smiled and thanked her when she returned with my water bottle, and I couldn't help but admit, "Mom, you're always so kind and hospitable. I wish I was more like that. Were you ever grumpy when you were pregnant?"

During our short visit, she told me about being pregnant with me and, inevitably, of her pregnancy with the half-sister we'd never known. We laughed at some of the things we both felt and rolled our eyes at a few others. Again, my respect for her grew as we realized more things we had in common and some we did not.

"Well, I suppose I should go, Trish. I just thought I'd drop in and ... get you your water bottle, apparently."

I couldn't help but laugh. "Good one, Mom," I smiled. "I am needy, aren't I?" I asked, knowing the truth.

She rose from her chair. "Well, in your defence, honey, you have had us all a bit worried, but hopefully now that you're this far along, we can all breathe easier."

I appreciated how much she cared. My mother didn't always express that, but I knew it.

As she neared our front door, she turned toward me. "How is Sandy?" she asked hesitantly.

"Much the same, Mom," I replied, seeing sadness and concern in her eyes.

She hesitated again. "And ... Jack?" she asked quietly.

I looked at my mother and saw a raw pain I had never seen in her eyes before.

"He's doing all right too, Mom. I guess ... they're both as good as they can be."

She nodded, the pain wiped away by the small smile she so often held.

"I love you, Trish," she said, before turning away from me again.

"I love you too, Mom," I said, but she was gone before I could be sure she'd heard me.

Chapter Thirty-One

THE CHURCH WAS FULL, BUT WE ALL TRIED TO CROWD INTO OUR FAVOURITE bench anyway. Like I always say, people who attend church are creatures of habit and comfort, and Grant was, and is, most comfortable sitting second bench from the front. Since we have a busy two-year-old and babies on the way, I tried to convince him that closer to the back might be wiser, but he was unlikely to change. He said he hears better from the front. To my knowledge, he shouldn't need hearing aids yet, but who knows? It's an argument I continued pursuing for a while, but once I gave up, I learned to relax, sitting way too close to the front.

When eight months pregnant, however, feeling this visible and trudging down the aisle of a church is not my favourite thing. As everyone knows, I'm pretty klutzy on a good day, and pregnancy hasn't made that better. This time my tripping was over the book that Kylie dropped on our way up the aisle, causing me to crash my thigh into the end of a bench and nearly fall into one of our elder parishioner's laps.

"I'm so sorry, Mr. Hudson!" I gasped, trying to right myself as quickly as I could. Unfortunately, my misaligned centre of gravity and quicker motions only served to make me slip again. As my huge belly loomed closer to him, I could only imagine the poor man thinking that he may be headed toward suffocation, but pounding my hand down on his shoulder kept me upright.

"Almost landed on you there!" I tried to laugh it off while pretending to lightly dust off his shoulder from where my hand had been.

Mr. Hudson didn't see the humour I was trying for, however, but loudly answered back, "You could've squished me like a bug!"

I didn't think that was called for, but I managed to apologize again and carry on up the aisle. I was sure all eyes were on my reddened face, but then again, it was a fairly large congregation, so I hoped maybe not more than a hundred people saw it.

As I struggled into "our" bench and sidled my way to Grant, I whispered, "I think I'll be done coming to church soon."

Grant smiled at me as I plopped my heavy body on the bench next to him. He pulled Kylie onto his lap and started bouncing her gently up and down.

"If you're going to start to take out the people in the congregation, I guess that would be wise," he smirked.

Okay ... maybe more than a hundred people saw.

"Very funny, Evans," I said, unimpressed and wishing that even one man could experience what pregnancy was like. I was pretty sure no babies would ever be born again if even one man gave birth.

As the pastor opened the service and asked us to stand for the first few worship songs, I sighed.

"You can stay seated, Trish," Grant said as he stood. He had the good grace to at least look down at me with sympathy.

"Nope," I said, smiling. "I used to think pregnant women were wimps if they used pregnancy as an excuse not to do stuff, so I'm standing or else I'm a hypocrite."

As he helped me up, I felt more pressure in my pelvis than I had ever felt before, and I silently prayed for forgiveness for judging pregnant women when I'd known nothing of their plight.

Shauna had come to church today as well. Her "like-affair" with a certain pastor at the church we'd attended together before had ended, and she felt she needed a change of scenery. She'd also met a guy at our church with whom she was getting serious, so it was easy for her to change things up and start attending here. I, of course, was thrilled to see her. She'd come over a few times since I'd been off work, but we hadn't seen each other a lot, and I missed her.

Shauna always loved laughing at me, and today was no different.

"I saw you laughing at me from across the church," I told her after the service.

"Well, I couldn't help it, Trish. You're just so … funny," she smiled.

"Did the whole church see me almost kill Mr. Hudson?" I asked.

"No," she answered. "We all heard him, though. A bug? Really? The guy has to weigh 350 pounds, Trish. You're nowhere near that," she said, obviously in my corner.

"You're a good friend," I replied, smiling, "but I feel like I am."

"Only a feeling. Believe me, you look beautiful," she said with sincerity … or maybe she was a good liar. Strangely, I felt so much better after that, if only for vanity reasons.

"I really miss you at work," Shauna said, changing the subject.

"I wish I could've held out longer." I missed the delivery room a lot. Caring for labouring women was definitely my calling, and I missed the excitement of helping women bring their babies into the world.

"Well, soon enough you'll be panting and pushing out your own babies, and I hope I'm there when you do," smiled Shauna.

I laughed. "Are you sure you'll want to be around for that scene? You know what they say—be careful what you wish for. I'm thinking I'll not be one of the calmest or quietest patients, Shauna."

"No worries, Trish," she said. Then she whispered, "You know, we have drugs that help for that."

We both laughed our agreement as Grant approached.

"Shauna," he acknowledged her. "Ready?" he asked, coming alongside me with Kylie pulling on his arm.

"Ready," I answered. "Can we pick up something for lunch today and take it home instead of going out, Grant? I'm really feeling wiped."

"Absolutely," he agreed. "Kylie's on the grumpy side anyway. The sooner we can get her down for her nap, the better. A restaurant would be asking for trouble again."

We had learned a valuable lesson the last time we'd taken Kylie out for lunch after church when she wasn't in the "mood." Without going into every embarrassing detail of that adventure, let's just say we learned a lesson. As the unimpressed waitress stood in a pool of macaroni and burger bites, she scowled and slammed the bill on the table. It listed the suggested tip, written with a bold marker and circled. Grant was more than happy to even exceed the ridiculous amount written, and we promised we wouldn't be back anytime soon. As the tantrum we both were not expecting continued, we ran our embarrassed selves outside, and I suspect the patrons and restaurant employees may have cheered when we exited the establishment. At least, if they did, I wouldn't have blamed them for it.

We left the church quickly after Grant acknowledged Kylie's bad mood, and on the way home we talked about what the pastor had spoken about. It had been an excellent sermon on the Holy Spirit and the work He constantly does in the believer's heart. I'd paid more attention to my aching hips than to the sermon, but with the little guilt I felt about that, I was glad Grant was excited to reiterate what he'd heard.

"When you think of the power that's in us, it's ... overwhelming," he said, amazement in his voice.

I smiled at him as I adjusted myself again in the passenger seat. Grant's faith never wavered and only ever seemed to strengthen, no matter what was happening in our lives. I was suddenly again thankful that he'd married me. God knew I needed someone like him—stronger than me in so many, often different, ways.

When Kylie was fed and tucked in for her nap, I came downstairs with the goal of napping as well. I'd sit in my favourite recliner and hope to doze off. Grant stared at me as I put my feet up, sighed, and closed my eyes.

"Stop staring," I said quietly, knowing without seeing that he was still looking at me after a minute or two. "This is not my best look."

He remained so quiet I was compelled to open my eyes and look at him again.

"What's wrong?" I finally asked, feeling a little self-conscious.

He got up from where he'd been sitting on the couch and came close to me. He kissed me gently and for a long time, and I knew that if he didn't stop, I might not get my nap.

"You're gorgeous, Trish Evans," he whispered before he went back to lie down on the couch.

"You're crazy," I laughed, "but I'll take it."

"Well, I mean it," he smiled as he closed his eyes. "God knew I needed you, for a lot of reasons."

I couldn't help but smile, thinking of how I'd just so recently thought that of him. I closed my eyes as well and sighed, bending my legs to try for a more comfortable position.

"We're like two old people having an afternoon nap," I said with a twinge of irritation in my tone.

"Enjoy it now, honey," Grant mumbled. "Once these babies come, we won't be napping. It'll be like we're instantly young again."

I smiled and relaxed into the recliner. Both Grant and I slept, but he was right—it wasn't long before we were going to feel young again.

Chapter Thirty-Two

"PUSH," SAID SHAUNA NEXT TO MY EAR.

Push. That word can mean so many things. Push a shopping cart, push someone on a swing, push your feelings away, push a baby out … wow … definitely a different kind of push. Painful. Finite. Difficult-to-explain kind of "push."

I wanted to tell Shauna where to put her "push," but another contraction overtook me, and when I grunted, everyone in the room knew my number was up.

"C'mon, Trish," Lisa, my physician, said from the end of the bed. "You can do this. Don't give up now. You're so close."

I nodded and took the deepest breath I could. The words we use—"contraction," "bearing down," "pushing," "labour"—none of them explain the overwhelming amount of pain that lightnings through a woman's body as it works to give up the treasure inside it. It is powerful and impossible to control, and now, while labouring and soon to deliver the babies Grant and I had waited for, all I could do was yell, "I can't do this!" as loud as I could.

As their nurse, I'd stupidly told women that I would try to give them the most beautiful birth experience ever. What a fool I'd been! What a liar I was! This was supposed to be a beautiful experience? When pushing so hard that blood vessels were bursting in my face, I somehow failed to see the beauty in any of it.

"You can do it, Trish," chorused Lisa and Shauna as they coached me.

"You can," echoed the masculine voice from the other side of my head. "You've got this, babe. Let's go!"

I turned my head to the side and peered at Grant before my next contraction hit. Grant—my faithful and loving husband. The man who had put up with my many mood swings, cravings, and worries about the pregnancy. I tried to return his smile. I did … but somehow, hearing those encouraging words from him at that moment, when my body felt as though it would split apart… well, it all just irked me. Even though I thought of so much more, all I could squeak out was, "Grant, just … shhhh."

I could feel Shauna smile and probably mouth something to Grant in the lines of, "Don't take her seriously. She doesn't mean it," over my head. How nice for them—to have a little "moment" while I push my brains out and my bottom to smithereens.

In that moment I realized it was true—on the last leg of the journey pushing your child out, you're not yourself. Or maybe you become your true self. Nonetheless, when my next contraction hit, I threw out an expletive that I knew Grant wouldn't approve of, but I didn't care.

"Okay," Lisa smiled. "You're doing it! The first baby's head is almost here. One more push and you'll be crowning, Trish."

I was just catching my breath after the last valiant push, and all I could do was nod in acknowledgement of her comment. Grant said nothing now, so I managed to glance his way again. I threw a painful smile up at him. I did. Weirdo. So many emotions and, as usual, a little guilt since I'd told him to shush and then swore a little. I was somehow relieved when he smiled back, but he didn't speak again either. I know it's impossible for a man to ever imagine what it's like for us women having babies, but in that one quick smile was the encouragement I needed.

"Okay," I breathed. "Ready."

Shauna placed a freshly cooled washcloth on my forehead and whispered, "You're gonna hold baby number one right away."

I nodded as I felt the contraction spread across my abdomen. Two pushes later and some controlled panting and there he was—the first boy we'd waited for. His cry filled the room with, as I've said before, the most beautiful music that can ever be heard on earth.

As he was placed on my chest I cried too, and Grant couldn't have grinned more widely. He hugged us both as we "ohhed and ahhed" over what God had allowed us to make together. The moment faded quickly, however, as the second baby threatened to make his presence known.

Donna, another friend and colleague, smiled her encouragement as she took our first boy off my chest and over to a bed warmed up just for him. I'd laughed and cried with her many times as well—in the intense moments, as nurses, that bond our hearts. Even though we didn't see each other outside of work as often as we would have liked, as with many "work" friends, we always knew we would be there for one another when we needed to be. Before another contraction began, I saw her gently begin to assess our son. What wonderful women I was surrounded by!

"Wow!" said Lisa. "Number two is in a hurry. His head's right here, Trish. I didn't even need to break your water for him."

I groaned as I felt the gush of water and the pressure intensify. Not again! I'd often thought when I'd helped a woman give birth to twins that one passenger stretching out everything was pain enough, but another right after? How horrible would that feel? Now I knew, and I'd been right. This was not fun, but at least it wouldn't take long!

Again, encouraging voices filled the room as I managed to hold it together to, once again, give birth. As his slippery form slid from my body, the relief was so great I couldn't help but verbalize it. "I'm done," I breathed, my eyes closing as I relaxed my head back on the pillow. I smiled, expecting the beauty of two babies' cries to reach my ears.

We waited for our son's cry to join his brother's, but it didn't come. I forgot all about my relief and propped myself up on my elbows, only focussed on the waiting. I stared as the NICU team worked through the steps it took to get a baby to cry. They were present for all twin deliveries, but they hadn't needed to do anything special for our first baby. He'd screamed and acted normally when he was born. Now on the warmer, he was still crying and was pink and totally fine. I stared at him and wished his crying would wake up his brother. What was I thinking? I knew that wasn't how it worked. It seemed like forever, and I hadn't noticed Grant had put his arm around my shoulders until I glanced at him. His eyes had teared as he stared toward the people surrounding our quiet son.

"He'll be okay, Trish. His oxygen saturations are looking all right. He's probably just a little shocked because he came so fast and the cord was quite tight around his neck," said Lisa as she tried to examine me. She was attempting to get my mind off the pale baby I'd glimpsed between the cracks of where now even more medical people stood. He hadn't attempted to breathe on his own, and any attempt to assuage my worry was futile. Our second son hadn't taken his first breath. As I laid my head back on the bed again, I could hear the NICU team talk about his too-slow heart rate and his lack of respirations, and although I knew they were doing everything to help him, I heard no cry.

In the minutes we waited, the placenta came, whether I was ready or not. Like a huge clot it came, soft and lifeless from my body, and suddenly I thought of the stillborns I'd helped deliver.

Oh God, I breathed in silent prayer as tears sprang to my eyes, *don't let our son die*.

As if Grant read my mind, he leaned closer to my ear and started to pray. He had only whispered a few words when our first son's crying stopped, and a strange kind of calm seemed to infuse the room. I don't know how long it took, but just as if he was saying, "I was waiting for my turn," our second baby boy let out a very sudden and angry scream. Immediately, the chorus of the two of them reached all of our ears, and everyone in the room laughed.

How many times had I waited for other mothers' babies to cry and felt relief when they did? This familiar, albeit today much more intense, feeling of relief overwhelmed my soul. Grant and I smiled, kissed, and hugged one another, as if congratulating our own selves for what had happened. "Thank you, God," breathed Grant into my hair as he hugged me hard.

I smiled up at him with all the love my heart could hold—both of us knowing just exactly who really deserved the praise.

"He just needed a turn," stated the neonatologist after finishing with his examination of our son.

"Thank you so much," said Grant as he shook the doctor's hand. "He may need to fight to be heard in our house."

I looked at Grant and smiled again. Then I grabbed him in a huge hug before telling him to take some pictures of the boys.

"You'll need a few stitches," said Lisa, examining all the sore things down there that I now more acutely felt.

"Only a few?" I asked. "That's a miracle. I thought I was splitting apart."

Lisa and Shauna smiled. "That's what a lot of women say," said Shauna.

I agreed. "I know ... and they're right. No lie. That's exactly how it feels."

"I'll get this done and you'll heal well," assured Lisa as she instilled some local anesthetic into the area of my concern. After finishing with that, she turned toward the table that held all the needed instruments and placed a suture on the needle driver, but when she turned toward me again, she turned more serious and told Shauna to massage my uterus. I could feel Grant's breath catch.

"Is everything okay?" he asked, with worry unhidden in his tone.

Shauna nodded after they assessed my bleeding. Lisa remained serious, and as I lay on the bed, I winced. It really didn't feel good to have anything touched now, much less rubbed down. I'd done this like it was nothing on other women so many times. I'd always apologized but kept to it to be sure they wouldn't bleed too much. I'd even done the same things to Stacy ...

I glanced up at Grant, who seemed pale and looked like he should probably sit down.

"It's okay, Grant," I winced again. "They have to do this."

It may have seemed like it, but it didn't take long before Lisa and Shauna were satisfied with my condition, and more medication had been given to assure my bleeding slowed. Donna had offered Grant a seat in the recliner in the room, and as Lisa finished with the suturing, I turned my attention to him again. He looked relieved when he glanced up at me, both babies in his arms.

When my shaky legs had calmed and the labour bed was put back into its previous state, both babies were laid on my chest, and warmed blankets covered all three of us. Every time Shauna or one of the other nurses would check on me, I could feel Grant tense a little, and I knew he was praying.

"It's normal to bleed a bit more after having two babies, Grant," I assured him again. "Everything's great ... right, Shauna?"

"It's perfect," agreed Shauna. "And I'm so glad I got to be here."

"Me too," chorused Grant and I. We smiled at each other, and I was thankful to see Grant relax more as the first hours passed.

Of course he would be nervous. Although we'd prayed and given all of it to God, it didn't stop the memory of the few short years before. We had talked a little about it, and I'd tried to allay his fears with statistics. After all, maternal deaths in labour are, indeed, rare. No matter how remote the chances are, however, when that "rarity" happens to you or someone you love, it no longer matters that it "hardly ever happens." And it had happened ... to him ... to Stacy ... and to me. As I looked at Grant now, I remembered our prayer time in the truck after finding out about the twins. I knew I had prayed a lot since, and I suspected he had prayed more often than I could ever know in the last few months.

I looked up at Shauna as she helped me latch the first of our sons. My colleagues were great, and although I'd had some of them care for me in my labour, having my closest friend beside me as I'd given birth held a special place in my heart. I hadn't been sure if I'd even wanted to deliver where I knew everyone and where they all knew me, but when labour started, I only wanted to be here—where I belonged and where I knew everyone would take, as with everyone else, the best care of me and my family.

After the babies were fed and I learned that breastfeeding wasn't as easy as I'd expected, Grant and I were alone—or at least as alone as we would be from now on. The boys had been weighed and measured and lay in one bassinet, together, sleeping. As we gazed at them, I suddenly remembered.

My labour hadn't been full of shining moments, and although I couldn't recall every word I said, I did remember shushing Grant, as well as at least a few expletives I wished I could deny. Looking at Grant now, I felt compelled to right my wrongs, and after debating how to broach the subject, I finally decided to just say it. "I hope you can forgive me for what I said," I blurted.

Grant looked at me with a serious expression before putting his face down, pretending to look at the babies. When he glanced up again, the smallest of smiles played at the edge of his lips but was quickly gone as he shrugged his shoulders and said, "I don't know what you're talking about."

My mind raced back to our first "date" and how he'd told me later that he didn't remember how I'd ugly-cried all night. Once again, I marvelled that such a good man could belong to me, and I to him.

It's hard to focus on anything else but the newest members of your family when you're holding those precious people in your arms. What an exhilarating sense of accomplishment! And then it hit me. Here it was ... the "beautiful" in "a beautiful birth experience." Sitting there then, holding our babies after all the grunting, groaning, and sweating was over, I knew I hadn't lied to all those women after all.

Later, Kylie came up for a short visit. She didn't see her new brothers as precious people or any kind of accomplishment at all. Dolls that could be poked and prodded and made to cry, yes, but not any sort of miracle. Oh well, it would take time. Grant soon took her back to Sandy and Jack's. We both could see that her adjustment would be a work in progress, as we were sure it would be for all of us.

Later, Grant came up to the hospital again. I'd just had dinner and so had the boys. I had them on the bed between my legs, and I'd unwrapped them a little from their swaddles to look more closely and count every finger and toe.

"I wish I could capture this moment and hold it forever," said Grant, entering the room quietly.

I hadn't noticed him come in and lifted my eyes slowly to have him capture them.

"You're beautiful," he whispered, coming over and sitting beside me on the bed, looking at all of us.

I couldn't speak for some reason, and I looked back down at the babies before me. They looked so perfect, so complete, so wonderfully made.

"God is so good to us," I whispered.

As Grant placed his arm around me, he looked down at our sleeping sons. I could feel his pride when he agreed. "Yes, He is."

There have rarely been moments that I would like captured, to go back and review when I'm not feeling "it," but that minute, just sitting with Grant and adoring the new lives God had given us to care for, was one I will hopefully remember forever. There would be many moments ahead—when woken by the screaming miracles at two, three, and four in the morning, for example—when I wouldn't feel this way. But in this one fragment of time, all I felt was the total goodness and faithfulness of God. It's in clinging to even a very few of these types of memories that spurs us on, to go the distance and finish the race that God has given us to run.

Chapter Thirty-Three

JOE SIGHED AS HE SAT ON THE TOP STAIR OF THE CABIN'S VERANDA. HE DRANK his warm coffee and gazed out at the lake. He was nearly done fixing up the place and he had to admit that even though it had been a lot of work, he was happy with the result. The weather had been mostly good too, which had helped. Summer was over, but it was uncharacteristically warm for fall.

The cabin had been in rougher shape than he'd initially thought, but it had come together nicely, and Joe was proud of the work he'd done. His mom had asked him a while ago if he would consider fixing it up and redoing some of the things that quite badly needed fixing. She'd had a vision for it, and although he'd only just started some of the improvements, he had dragged his feet. Since he'd bought the property, and since knowing of his mom's diagnosis, he knew he needed to finish it now—and he was determined to.

Joe brushed his now even longer sun-bleached hair away from his face and smiled as he thought about Grant and Trish. They had told him that he was still welcome to stay in their basement, especially when their mom would come to the cabin, but Joe had doubted he'd get any sleep there. All it looked like to him was a loud, complicated mess. But Grant seemed to be in his element and so did Trish, when she wasn't acting stressed out. He'd heard the word "hormones" one too many times, and he was even more thankful he'd made the decision to move out here.

As he took another gulp of his coffee, Joe's mind returned to where it often did. He wondered if Stephanie had ever blamed anything on hormones when she'd been pregnant, or after. Joe shook his head. He had to stop this. If he wasn't dreaming about her, he was thinking about her.

He stood up, threw the remnants of some coffee grounds at the bottom of his cup into the shrubs, and walked into the cabin. Time to get to work. The weekend wouldn't last forever.

Chapter Thirty-Four

SANDY SMILED AND JACK LAUGHED AS KYLIE AND ABIGAIL PLAYED IN THEIR living room. Sandy had asked if she could spend some time with both granddaughters, and both young couples had been happy to agree.

Trent and Melissa had come into the city again for Abigail's appointment with her paediatrician, and they hadn't received good news. Although they both worked with her diligently, doing the exercises the physiotherapist had taught them, Abby had regressed even more. Her seizures had increased also, so the specialist suggested that they try a medication that was fairly new. Trent had done limited research on it, but both he and Melissa had agreed—something different needed to be done.

"Sandy, just call us if anything at all happens with her," Melissa said before leaving. "We won't be long, though."

"Go and have fun," smiled Sandy. "We'll be fine." Jack stood beside his wife, and Trent nodded at him, as if with unspoken understanding.

Grant had dropped Kylie off earlier, and now the girls were laughing over a stuffed animal they were trying to fit into the toy playhouse clearly meant for smaller dolls. Jack sat close to them on the floor, but out of the corner of his eye he watched Sandy, who had reclined back on the chair. When she opened her eyes again, she smiled down at the busy girls.

Sandy had begun to feel more tired as of late, and although she didn't talk about it much, he had noticed that she seemed quieter. He suspected her headaches were more constant now, and he'd found her, the week before last, on the bathroom floor after fainting again. When he carried her back to bed that night, she'd agreed to call the palliative nurse the next day. The nurse had come in the morning and arranged a few more medications for her—something different to help with the nausea and headaches. She had seemed to feel better after starting those, and Jack had breathed a sigh of relief.

She smiled at him and mouthed "I love you" across the room. He'd nodded to her and may have returned that, but both Abigail and Kylie had run to him just then with books to read. He welcomed them into his lap and reached for his reading glasses that lay on the side table.

"I'll go and get us something to eat," smiled Sandy, slowly getting out of her chair.

"I can do that, Sandy," returned Jack, moving to get up.

"No, Jack," Sandy stopped him. "I'm fine. It's not a big deal to get us a little something. I'll be right back."

He watched as she headed for the kitchen but then looked down at the girls when they begged again for his attention. He'd read one book and was well into the second when Abigail looked up.

"I go see Nana," she said in her sweet voice.

"Okay," smiled Jack as he helped her to stand. He watched her make her way to the kitchen, where he could hear Sandy humming. Abby seemed to limp a little but that wasn't unusual for her. Jack smiled as she turned and waved at him with her left hand. She didn't seem to use the right as much anymore.

He waved back and then returned his attention to Kylie, who was grabbing his face to get that very attention back to her.

Jack finished reading the book and, after Kylie begged for it, tickled his granddaughter as she gasped with loud laughter.

"Grandpa," she said when he told her that was enough, "you're so funny."

"I'm funny?" growled Jack, smiling at her sweet face. "I think you're the one who's funny." He tickled her tummy and didn't stop when Abby joined them again.

"Heard us having fun, huh?" he joked as they both jumped on him. "Wanna piece of this action, Abby?"

The little girls both giggled loudly as Jack continued to play with them on the floor.

"Hey," he said a few minutes later as he stood up. "I better go help Nana."

Jack looked toward the kitchen where he no longer heard humming.

"Nana aseep," Abigail stated sweetly.

"What?" asked Jack, looking down at the little girl.

She repeated it, but by the time she'd said it, Jack had run into the kitchen.

There on the floor, Sandy's body shook uncontrollably.

• • •

By the time the ambulance arrived, the seizure had subsided, and Sandy, feeling completely drained, agreed to go to the hospital. A doctor had examined her and ordered another CT. Although Sandy had been against having it, the medical people around her had agreed that perhaps they needed to know if there had been changes in the tumour's growth. After the results were reported, the news wasn't surprising, and Sandy and Jack left the hospital with a prescription for another medication that would hopefully keep further seizures at bay. Sandy had smiled at that, knowing that for her type of tumour, this was probably going to happen and that there really was nothing that would stop the process ahead.

When they arrived back home that evening, Trent and Melissa and both of Sandy's sons were there. Trent and Melissa had quickly returned when Jack called 911 earlier, and they'd decided to stay in town overnight. Grant had called Joe, and both of them had driven over as well.

Now as the group sat in their living room, Sandy and Jack looked at each other. Sandy nodded before he spoke.

"Joe," Jack turned his attention to his stepson. "We think it's time to come out to the cabin. You okay with that?"

Joe looked at his mom, whose eyes had teared. He slowly nodded at his mom before answering. "Anytime, Mom."

"Thank you." Sandy smiled at her son. "You can still stay out there with us, Joe."

Joe nodded again, in deep thought. His impulse was to run—anywhere else. He didn't know what was ahead for his mother, but he was sure none of it would be good. Even Grant and Trish's place might be appealing right now. He'd thought about it a lot over the last few weeks, but now that he had to make the decision, he was conflicted. It would be all right to stay somewhere else, but for some reason, he'd been feeling more and more compelled to stay with his mom and Jack, and he didn't know why. There was more than enough comfortable room. He looked at Jack, who had the expression of a man in deep pain, and sighed.

"I'll probably stay then," Joe stated finally. "If you're sure."

"Of course, honey," Sandy agreed while Jack stared at the floor.

They spoke quietly of the plans to move the next day, and after that short conversation, their guests intended to leave, but Sandy stopped them.

"I'm so sorry the girls had to see all that," she said, looking toward them as they played with Joe on the floor.

"It's no big deal, Aunt Sandy," Trent replied before anyone else could speak. "Abby thought you were asleep anyway."

"Maybe initially," Sandy stated, with tears filling her eyes again, "but when the ambulance came, I'm sure they were both scared."

Grant stepped in with, "Mom ... it's okay. Really. Look at them! They're fine."

Sandy smiled as she watched her granddaughters play. They didn't look worse for wear, but she hoped they wouldn't remember all the drama of that day.

Melissa walked over to where her aunt sat and embraced her in a hug. "We've explained a little, Aunt Sandy. We told Abby that you're like her. She just falls asleep sometimes, and so do you. I hope you're okay with that. She seemed good with it."

Sandy couldn't help the tears that fell down her cheeks then.

As their hug ended and her guests left that night, Sandy looked at Abigail with the pain she felt for her granddaughter etched inside her smile.

"They'll be all right," stated Jack as they watched their family leave.

Sandy could only nod and pray that God would make it so.

Chapter Thirty-Five

SANDY AND JACK QUICKLY SETTLED INTO THE CABIN OVER THE NEXT FEW DAYS, and with her palliative care team involved in the decision-making, Sandy seemed to feel a little better on the medications prescribed.

For a while, and during the coldest snap of winter, she seemed to almost rebound, which amazed and pleased all of us. Although she'd spend her time sleeping more often, when awake and feeling up to it, she and Jack would go for short walks by the frozen lake. It wasn't until a few months had passed and the budding of spring was in the air that things seemed to take a turn for the worst again. Jack rose to the challenge and stayed by her side, giving her the medications she needed and anything else she wanted.

"Was that Annie?" Sandy whispered one afternoon. She'd heard him talk through the haze she seemed to be in more often these last few days. It sounded like a one-sided conversation, so she thought he'd been on the phone. By the tone in his voice, she'd guessed it was his sister. They'd been speaking more frequently since the wedding, and Sandy was glad that they'd been reunited in their bond as brother and sister.

"Yes, that was Annie," Jack replied, moving back to his wife's side.

"How is she?" Sandy barely eked out before the retching began again. Her last bout of vomiting hadn't been long ago, and it didn't seem to be easily subsiding today like it had before. Sandy thought that maybe if she concentrated on something else she'd feel better. Obviously, that wasn't happening.

"Sandy … honey … don't worry about her now," Jack said, holding her forehead in his large hand. After she seemed to finish and moved her head back to rest on the pillow, he brushed back the few hairs that had come loose from the braid he'd attempted to help her with that morning. "Annie's fine. Please stop worrying about everyone else."

Sandy wiped her mouth with the Kleenex he handed her. She wasn't bringing up anything more, even with the more vigorous retching. "I'm sorry, Jack," she said, her bottom lip quivering.

"Do you want me to call Trish?" he asked then. "She'll be glad to come and stay. You know we arranged that for when things get …" His deep voice cracked.

"No," she whispered. "Not yet. She's so busy with Kylie and the boys. Maybe soon, but I'm okay for now." She looked at Jack again and sighed. "We're okay, right?"

Jack's eyes teared again, and he couldn't speak. All he could think to do was, once again, gather her small body into his chest and hold her there. He had seen a lot of suffering in his life, and had even seen men die, but nothing broke his heart like this … in this place … in these last days.

The palliative care nurses had warned them of what would happen and how things would probably get much more difficult, but with Sandy having done better for much longer than anyone expected, Jack had prayed that it wouldn't. He'd prayed for her so often and with everything in his being. He'd begged God to heal her—to make a miracle happen. They'd been so hopeful after she'd been prayed over at church too, having faith that God would, indeed, perform that unable-to-explain kind of miracle, but it hadn't happened.

When Sandy's condition had worsened, she told him one night that God still had a plan that they both couldn't see, but they had to trust that it was still the best one.

"How can this be the best plan, Sandy?" he'd argued angrily with her. "He brought us together. He brought you into my life, and He saved me from everything—because of you. It doesn't make any sense."

She had looked at him and smiled so sadly. "I know it doesn't look like it, Jack. I wish it was different too. I do. But He didn't save you because of me. Even if I had never come into your life, He would have saved you. You always belonged to Him, Jack. You just didn't know it until I showed up."

That was his Sandy ... wise and patient ... and he had the privilege of loving her. Although it was too short a time on earth, as she always reminded him, they would meet again in a much better place.

Jack took a few deep breaths before laying Sandy gently back against the propped pillows again. Her eyes were closed, and for a moment he thought she may be sleeping. As he moved to get up, her eyes opened, and her hand stayed him.

"You must never give up on Annie, Jack," she said quietly. "I think she's just been waiting for you to come back into her life. She'll belong to Jesus yet."

Jack nodded and watched as Sandy's eyes closed again. As he turned his hand to thread her delicate fingers gently between his much larger ones, he reached up with his other hand to adjust his bandanna.

Chapter Thirty-Six

AS SPRING BEGAN, FAMILY AND FRIENDS CAME AND WENT, BRINGING FOOD or just having short visits with Sandy when she wasn't sleeping. One afternoon, Grant had gone out to take some food that Helen had made for the three people staying at the cabin. He offered to stay with his mom while Jack and Joe went into town for a few other staples. Sandy was asleep when he arrived, so Grant sat beside her bed and was paging through something work-related on his phone when he heard her stir.

"Mom?" he said, lifting his head while placing his phone down on the small table beside her bed. "What can I get you?"

As he took her hand, Sandy turned her head slowly to look at him. "How long have you been here? You look tired, honey. You need to rest."

Grant smiled. "Mom, I'm not leaving. Jack and Joe just stepped out for a bit. What do you need? I can try to give you something if you tell me what you need."

Sandy started to shake her head but then winced from the nausea and pain even that small movement caused. "I don't need anything, son. Just maybe a sip of water. My mouth is so dry."

Grant grabbed at the water bottle on the bedside table and handed it to Sandy. She was getting frailer and, like the palliative care nurses had told them would happen, she'd lost her appetite. They'd all tried to push food on her, but it usually just came up anyway, so Trish had told them to lay off. They'd be sure to give Sandy whatever she wanted, but they needn't pressure her into what they thought she needed. Grant's heart ached as he watched his mom take the small sip of water. He wanted her to drink heartily—to eat until full—to be ... well. Grant put his face down so that Sandy couldn't see his wet eyes as he took a deep breath. When he'd gathered some strength, he looked up and saw her looking at him with brighter eyes.

"I'll tell Charles and Ted about their namesakes when I get there, Grant. It wouldn't have mattered what you named your boys, but I think Trish's dad will love that, and I know your dad will too."

"Oh Mom," Grant whispered, but before he could say more, she continued.

"I do need something."

"What?" Grant leaned toward his mother, willing to move heaven and earth to make anything she wished come true.

"I need you to promise me that you'll stay the course for this family, Grant. Some of them may doubt after I die, but you must tell them not to. I know we all prayed, in faith, that God would heal me, and I think Jack has really felt let down by God. But God isn't letting anyone down. We are going to see a miracle, Grant, but maybe not in the way we've all asked ... and I'd like you to remind them."

When Sandy saw Grant's look of confusion, she smiled and reached for his hand, which he readily gave her. "Grant," she said, "I know we've prayed that I would be healed, and I know I will be, but"—she sighed as a look of peace came over her countenance—"it's just not going to happen down here."

Grant nodded before swallowing. "I'll remind everyone, Mom," he promised.

Sandy smiled and closed her eyes briefly before adding, "Now I need you to hug me." As he came closer to her, Sandy's eyes opened and she smiled, "And not one of those wimpy hugs that almost everyone seems to think I need right now. I'm not going to break. Hug me like we always have."

Grant then, leaned over her bed and tightly hugged the woman who had raised him, been strong for him, and loved him unconditionally his entire life.

Chapter Thirty-Seven

SINCE HIS MOTHER HAD COME TO THE CABIN, JOE HAD SEEN HER SEIZURE, AND as he'd watched Jack quickly turn her to her side and wait for it to pass, Joe had replayed the scene from another night over and over in his mind. Abigail … having a seizure. He'd seen a lot of weird things over the years, but he'd never seen one of those before that night. How in this day and age didn't the health experts have a cure for that? It had been awful, and as often as he tried to forget it, he couldn't stop that picture in his mind. He'd just been playing with her earlier and throwing her up in the air while she giggled. She seemed normal then. But something was really wrong. Grant had been right to ask. Could he handle that sort of thing? Did he want to take responsibility for a little girl with problems like that? Probably not. Stephanie was right. Abigail was with the perfect people. As he thought back to the times he'd seen her with Melissa and Trent, he knew they were the right parents for her, and they loved her completely.

As much as he'd battled with the thought and wished he could go back and change it all, Joe admitted to himself that he'd only been the sperm donor. When he'd think of it that way, his stomach would churn, and he'd try to concentrate on something else. Today that something else was cleaning up and fixing more things around the shed at the cabin. His mom, although fragile, had told him the noise didn't bother her, and she was glad he'd taken care of the cabin and would continue to when she was gone. Gone.

Suddenly Joe was tired of sadness and stress. He needed to let off some steam. He looked toward the lake. The ice had just gone, but he didn't care. The water was cold—maybe too cold to just dive in—but Joe didn't usually think things through before acting. He just dove in, like now. He left all his clothes behind and took a run off the dock.

"Whoa!" he exclaimed aloud as his head came above the water. "That'll wake you up, Evans."

As he started to tread water, he looked around to make sure no one had heard him. Although he knew the two people anywhere nearby were inside the cabin, he still felt silly talking to himself. He started to swim, not caring how far he'd go, and almost hoping that he'd never have to come back.

• • •

Stephanie had driven to the cabin, as Jack had asked, to bring a few items he and Sandy needed. She'd dropped them off and stayed to talk to Jack a while but was now planning to go back to the city to get the other things on her list completed. It always felt so great to delete the tasks one by one.

As she exited the cabin, she took a deep breath. The earthy pine-filled scent was something she only remembered. She'd been on camping trips with her parents when she was a kid, but not in recent years. As she walked to her car, snatches in her memory of campfires and smores, singing, and swimming in a cold lake came to her mind. She looked through the trees and saw sparkles of sun on the water, and suddenly thoughts of her list faded. A few minutes walking by the lake before going back to the noisy city seemed very appealing.

Stephanie stopped to listen. She knew Joe had to be around somewhere. His vehicle was there, but she hadn't seen him. After looking in all directions and becoming satisfied that Joe was nowhere around, she smiled and set off toward the lake. It wasn't that she wanted to avoid him, she told herself. She just didn't need any drama today.

Stephanie took her shoes off and threw them on the beach, if you could call it that. It seemed to her that there were more rocks and stubble than beach. She imagined how nice it would be if it was cleaned up. The way the ground sloped, it would make for a beautiful beach, if it was cleared of the rocks and broken tree pieces.

She rolled up her jeans. It was fortunate that the legs were fairly loose and she could get them rolled up just past her knees. Then she stood and stretched, taking off the light sweater and loose top she'd thrown over her sleeveless tank. It was a beautiful spring day. After folding her clothing and placing it over her shoes, she walked to the edge of the water. For a brief moment after her toes were submerged, she thought about a swim but just as quickly laughed at herself. She didn't even have her bathing suit with her, and besides, if her feet were any indication, it was still much too cold to swim.

She'd walked for a while and thought she had gone quite a distance around the perimeter of the lake, but when she turned to go back, she realized she still hadn't walked very far. She had been at the cabin a few times recently but hadn't realized how big the lake was until she'd come closer to it. Reluctantly, she started back. She looked around as she neared the dock—close to where she'd started—and found herself not wanting to leave. It was so ... peaceful here.

As she grabbed her shirts and shoes, she took in deeper breaths, relishing the wonderful scent that surrounded her. She tucked her clothing and shoes under her arm and turned to make her way to her vehicle when she heard it. Splashing? *That's strange*, she thought as she turned. She hadn't seen anyone out there.

Sure enough, Joe Evans was swimming toward the dock and moving at a pretty quick speed. Stephanie didn't move at first. Her mind raced as she debated what to do. Maybe he hadn't seen her and she should just run to her car. No. He'd probably seen her. If she walked away now, she would look like she was running away or scared or something. She certainly wasn't scared of him, and there was no way she'd ever let him think that. Why hadn't she just left earlier? But the walk had been so nice.

She glanced at the water again. He was almost at the end of the dock. With a huff, she made up her mind, tried to smile, and started toward the beach end of the dock. As she stepped onto it, she saw them. A pile of clothes lay in the middle of the wooden dock. Men's clothes. Joe's clothes. The smile that she had to work for seconds ago grew into a genuine grin as she walked closer to the garments. What would she do with this opportune moment? As she waited for him, Stephanie placed her own attire down beside his. When he swam up, she was standing over them, her thumbs hooked in the waist of her pants and tapping her bare foot on the dock.

"Hi!" she said enthusiastically as Joe swam to the end of the dock and pulled himself up to rest on his elbows.

"Hi back," he grinned.

The sunlight glinted off his blond hair as he whipped his head to the side in an attempt to move the wet strands off his face. That hadn't done it, so he'd lifted what was left away with a strong hand before placing it back on the dock. Stephanie hoped he didn't see her take the quick breath she had. This guy was so good-looking—maybe even better wet.

"What're ya doin' here?" he asked, looking genuinely interested and nonplussed.

Stephanie tried for nonchalance, unsure how to handle what could very well turn into an embarrassing situation. What had she thought she'd do anyway?

"Ja … Jack asked me to come. He and Sandy needed some stuff, so I brought it," she stated. She was even more aware of the clothes that lay close to her feet now. What had she been thinking? She should walk away.

"What stuff?" asked Joe, still hanging loosely onto the dock. "I coulda run into town for them."

"Just some groceries and a few other things." Stephanie shrugged tightly. "I didn't mind. It's really nice out here."

They both paused, both thinking.

"Nice swim?" she asked suddenly.

"Great!" he grinned. "A little cold right now, but it was okay. Good way to let off some steam."

"Oh," she returned quietly, looking down again at the clothes next to her on the dock.

"Yeah," Joe said, staring at the top of her head.

Suddenly Stephanie couldn't help but smile to herself. He had to know what a vulnerable position he was in. She could run away with his clothes, for goodness' sake. She could dump them all in the lake too. Was he completely daft?

Instead, deciding to act with maturity, she raised her eyes to look at him again. "Well, I guess I should go so you can get dressed."

Joe burst out laughing and splashed the water with one hand.

Stephanie stared at him. He wasn't bothered by this at all. With all she knew about him, he'd probably get out of the water and ...

He *was* daft! Fortunately, as fast as he'd hoisted himself up and onto the dock, she had turned. At least three shades of red infused into her face as she looked in the direction of the cabin.

"Are you crazy?" she yelled, careful not to turn when she felt him walk up behind her. All her plans to make him squirm had turned on her.

She could hear him grabbing his things, and she hoped he was putting something on. Knowing him, he'd just stand there and not care at all if she looked at him in the nude. Stupid man.

"You could offer to get me a towel," Joe suggested, with laughter in his tone. "They're in the cabin—just there."

He'd moved so closely behind her that she could see his hand pointing toward the cabin out of the corner of her eye.

"I know where the cabin is," she said in a frustrated tone as she moved a few steps away from him. She didn't know why she simply didn't leave.

"Hey, you can turn around," he said a few seconds later. "I'm dressed."

Stephanie turned and let out a sigh as she gazed on Joe's idea of dressed. He did have his jeans on, but the rest of him was left to warm in the afternoon sun.

"Don't go," he said when he saw her step back. "It's okay. I'll be good. Promise."

She smiled, because there was nothing else she could do. After all, it was her own fault she was even on the dock. She didn't know why, but while standing there looking at his damp jeans, she couldn't help but empathize. "You can't be comfortable."

Joe looked at her and laughed again as he adjusted the waist of his jeans. "Well, they're not as easy to get on when you're soaking wet," he agreed. "Let me just get changed and I'll be right back."

Stephanie shook her head. "I should go," she said unconvincingly. "I've got a list that's burning a hole in my mind. I have to get things done."

"Screw the list!" Joe said, sounding blunter than he meant. "I'll be right back."

Before she could move, he ran past her toward the cabin, but not before he added, "You could finish getting dressed too, ya know."

Stephanie looked back at the dock and smiled as she grabbed her shoes and shirts before walking toward the cabin.

• • •

As Joe towelled off in the bathroom, he didn't know why he'd been so glad to see Stephanie. They hadn't really talked a whole lot lately, and when they had, their conversation had been stunted and didn't really amount to anything—nothing of importance anyway.

He'd been a long way off in the lake when he'd first seen her walking on the beach. She was hard to miss with that long, red hair. As he'd swum up to the dock, he'd almost swallowed lake water. She was stunning with the sun shining down on her. He'd also noticed that she stood over his clothes, and he had wondered what her plan was, but there was no way he was going to let her get the upper hand. Joe was smiling to himself as he exited the bathroom.

Jack was looking out the front window and turned toward him. "Stephanie still here?" he asked Joe.

"Yeah," Joe said, going over to the fridge.

"Hmm," grunted Jack.

Joe didn't want to talk about Stephanie with Jack. Truth be told, Jack still freaked him out a little. His size and tattoos were intimidating enough, but his whole demeanour around Joe sometimes felt less than inviting. Even though he had thought they'd come to some kind of understanding, at the meetings anyway, Joe still wasn't completely comfortable around his stepdad. Stephanie was his granddaughter, but Joe thought Jack was too overprotective, or some such thing, when it came to her.

"How's Mom?" asked Joe, trying to change the subject. He closed the fridge door after pulling two drinks from it.

"Sleeping," said Jack with a low sigh.

Joe nodded and turned to look at Jack. As nervous as he made him, Joe still felt sorry for Jack. He really did love his mom, and his hurting consumed him. It consumed all of them.

Joe stepped toward Jack and offered, "Do you need me to sit with her again? I can."

Jack stared at Joe, as if making a decision. "No," he finally said. "She's finally sleeping. We probably should leave her be."

Joe nodded, feeling the cans cold under his palms. "Want one?" he offered, lifting a drink toward him.

Jack shook his head and looked away before quietly saying, "Don't hurt her again, Joe."

Joe knew what he meant and couldn't help but feel the threat in Jack's tone. He knew that Jack's past included some bad stuff, but he had turned his life around. He couldn't mean he'd hurt him, but Joe wasn't about to take that chance.

"I won't," he said sincerely before leaving the cabin.

• • •

Jack went back to sit on the side of Sandy's bed and pray. When he looked up again, her eyes remained closed, but she had stirred, so he wanted to be there when she awoke. He'd removed his bandanna and tied his hair back. His mind went back to their wedding day and he smiled to himself. She'd liked the tail, but he still hadn't worn it that way much of the time. Maybe he should have.

The worship song that filled the cabin bedroom was by one of Jack's favourite artists. He could relate to the guy who sang it. He'd come from a rough background too but had found God's love, like Jack had. In the past few days, he had to admit he hadn't felt like listening to any of it, but it seemed to soothe Sandy, and he'd put up with anything for her.

A while later, his wife stirred and smiled up at him before closing her eyes again. Even with obvious pain etched on her face, she always tried for a smile when she looked at him. He supposed she was still trying to encourage him, as she always had. Some of the nausea and vomiting had ebbed after the palliative care nurse had come earlier and given her a different medication. Jack was thankful for that.

Oh, what he wouldn't do to stop all of this—the pain, the sickness, and what was coming. He'd cried out to God so many times in the last months, but still no healing had happened. Jack had heard of people being healed miraculously, and he wanted to believe it could happen. They had all prayed and prayed, and he had begged God, even offering his life for hers, but nothing. No answer had come. Jack didn't want to think that he was being punished, but he couldn't help it. He hadn't been a good person. He'd done some bad things. Very bad things. He'd even ended up in jail for a few years and probably deserved even more time behind bars, but he hadn't been caught for everything he'd done. But when he'd met Sandy, she told him that God would forgive all of it.

As he gazed at her now, another memory came to him.

"Jack," Sandy had laughed that day, "you're so funny." They'd met for coffee, alone, after some sort of church meeting. They'd met a few times before and had gone out with other people, but this was their first time alone.

Now as Jack thought back, he guessed that it would have been called their first "date" because after that night, they'd never stopped seeing each other. He had looked at her then and mumbled, "Wow. I've been called a lot of things, but funny has never been one of them."

She'd smiled up at him and taken a sip of whatever she'd ordered. He'd been so nervous around her then.

"I didn't mean funny as in ha-ha," she'd said. "I meant ... you're trying to dissect salvation. It's not that hard, Jack. God loves you. Plain and simple. He sent His Son to die for everything wrong you've ever done, or ever could do. All you have to do is believe that, and you'll belong to Him."

She'd shrugged then and taken another sip of her drink. It had been an everyday shrug, but Jack remembered it now as he looked at her. She'd made her complete faith in God clear to him then—great faith—quietly said within a simple shrug. A few days later he had cried out to God, and he knew he'd been changed, instantly, in those moments. It was so powerful, but like she said, simple. When he'd called Sandy shortly after, he must have sounded out of his mind because she'd laughed again, but he knew she was praising God. She told him much later how much she'd prayed for him, and he'd been so humbled by that.

Now as he gazed upon his Sandy, he prayed again that she wouldn't be taken from him.

"Jack," she whispered.

He jumped out of the memory and put his hand beside her thigh, leaning closer to hear her better. "Yeah, honey?"

"Are Joe and Stephanie here?"

"They're outside. I'll get them," he said, standing quickly. He hadn't been thrilled that Joe was spending time with his granddaughter, and he suddenly felt relief that Sandy had asked for both of them. He could hardly wait to check out where those two were at.

• • •

Stephanie had come up on the veranda and was sitting on the top step, looking toward the lake, when Joe joined her again.

"That guy is scary," he admitted, sitting next to her and handing Stephanie a drink.

"Who?" she asked, accepting it but looking around.

"Jack," he replied. Who else would he be talking about besides the hulk in the cabin?

Stephanie laughed. "He's not scary. At all."

"Well, that's because you're his granddaughter. He thinks the sun rises and sets with you."

"Hmm … maybe," Stephanie agreed as she cracked open the can Joe had handed her. She knew Jack would probably do anything for her, but she hoped he didn't think she was better than she was. She'd done her share of idiotic things too, and she knew she was far from perfect.

"Does he ever talk about his past?" Joe asked, taking a long gulp of his drink.

"Sometimes," she said, looking at Joe with a sidelong glance. "He doesn't like to dwell on it. He says it's over and forgiven so …" As she trailed off, she took a sip. "What about you?" said Stephanie after swallowing. "Everybody tells me you're a world-wide traveller. Tell me about some of the places you've been."

Joe was surprised by her question. Not many members of his family, except his mom, had ever asked much about his travels.

"Which country do you want to start with?" he smiled.

"Wow," she replied. "I guess any you want to. No! Start at the beginning. Where did you go first? How old were you?"

Joe smiled as he told Stephanie of how he'd travelled a few years after he graduated high school. He told her how he just couldn't see himself working in the business, like Grant did. So he'd taken off and hadn't ever settled anywhere since.

He wondered as he talked about his feeble attempt to work at the office again what he'd been thinking coming back to it after all those years. Had he ever really thought he'd love it even then? Or had he wanted to be like Grant so much that it had looked like the only option? He was not like his brother. His brother would never have done half the things Joe had—the bad stuff especially. As Joe told Stephanie about some of the places he'd been, she leaned in closer and seemed clearly interested in what he was saying. An hour or so passed as he talked and she listened, sometimes even laughing with him at some of the crazy antics he'd pulled.

"So when did you have time to come here?" she asked, waving her hand around her, taking in the cabin and its surroundings.

"Oh, I haven't been here for years—till lately. This place is where a lot of my kid memories are, though. Man, we had fun. See over there?" he asked, not knowing that he'd moved close enough to her so that their arms were touching. Now with his arm outstretched, he felt the warmth of her.

"Where?" she asked, looking to where he pointed.

"There, by the biggest tree," he answered. "Grant just about killed himself trying to fly off of that. Funniest thing ever."

Stephanie slapped Joe's arm while saying, "What? That's not nice ... and I don't believe you. That doesn't sound like Grant. It sounds more like you."

Joe looked at the tree, remembering. "Oh, I did it too, but he was the one who landed wrong—right in the hospital. Mom was so mad at me."

"Why? Was it your fault?" Stephanie smiled, knowing what the answer would be.

"Me?" Joe shrugged as he put up innocent hands. "I'd never do anything like that to my brother."

Stephanie laughed. "Oh, sure," she said, giving him a bump with her arm.

"Well, I guess I was a bad example, but I'm younger, so he shoulda known not to listen to me," Joe said in defence of his child-self.

Stephanie smiled and played with her now empty can. "I sure haven't lived compared to you, Joe," she said after a few moments of silence.

Joe thought before he replied. "Everyone has a different life to live, I guess."

Stephanie nodded. She stood then and walked to the bottom of the few stairs, turning to look up at Joe. "Thanks," she began, handing her empty can up to him. "This has been really ... nice."

Joe didn't want her to go. He needed to say something that had played on his mind all afternoon, and if she left now, he might never do it.

"I just want you to know something before you leave," he said, looking deeply into her eyes.

Neither one moved as they stared at each other. "I know you made the right decision, Steph ... and I was wrong to think—" Joe looked surprised at Stephanie's interruption.

"It's okay. I knew it was right—for all of us, Joe, but I am glad you know it now too. Abigail is in the perfect place for her."

Joe nodded, appreciating that she'd taken over. Not only was she beautiful and strong, but apparently she had some kind of intuition. Sometimes she seemed to read his mind. Normally that would've bothered him, but with this woman, something felt so different. Joe felt like a burden had been lifted from his shoulders. He told himself that maybe now, finally, they could move on in a better direction. They didn't have to be close, but they'd be seeing each other, so it would be nice for the tension to at least be less.

Stephanie tore away from his gaze, looking down and then up again before she added, smiling, "Enough procrastinating. My list won't finish itself."

As he watched her, he tried for a serious expression before saying, "Do you always live your life by the lists you make?"

"Only sometimes."

He thought she looked a little unnerved and wasn't sure if he liked that or not.

She took a deep breath before blurting, as if in defence, "I didn't have that whole God thing on my list. That wasn't even on my radar until I met this family." Stephanie smiled up at him then—a radiant smile that made Joe yearn for something he didn't know anything about.

Joe shook his head before he said, "Good for you." That sounded lame, but Stephanie didn't seem to notice.

"Yeah, man!" she said enthusiastically, reaching up to slap Joe on his knee. "Yeah—it's really been great!"

Joe nodded, unable to add anything more. He'd just told her of how many wonderful places he'd been and all the fun he'd had, but somehow, in all his tales, he was suddenly convinced that he'd never felt as much joy as she seemed to have in this minute.

"Well, I'm really going now," said Stephanie, looking him in the eye.

"Okay." Joe sighed, standing to stretch. Hopefully she'd see that what she'd said didn't bother him in the least.

As they walked to her car, she smiled at him again. "Thanks again, Joe. I feel like I maybe know you a bit better. That's okay, right?"

Joe saw the tentative look on her face. Of course it was okay. He didn't know why, but suddenly he wanted Stephanie to know him—really know him—and not in the shallow, physical way that they had in their history, but in a much deeper way. Something stopped him, though, as he shrugged and simply said, "Sure."

Stephanie nodded once before getting into her car but quickly opened the door again when she saw her grandpa come out of the cabin's front door. He looked worried.

"Steph!" Jack said, waving at her. "Before you go—Sandy's asking to see you."

Stephanie glanced at Joe with a question in her eyes before walking, quickly, back to the cabin.

After Stephanie had gone into the cabin Jack glanced back at Joe. Joe felt like Jack wanted to say something to him, so he waited but didn't move from where he stood by Stephanie's car. He put his hand on the hood and leaned against it as he watched Jack.

Jack waited for at least a full minute before deciding. He wanted to say a few things to this young man, but maybe this wasn't the time for it. Finally, making his decision, Jack moved his head, indicating Joe should come inside as well. "You too."

• • •

Sandy smiled and tried to move further up on the propped pillows behind her as Stephanie approached the bed. When she winced, Stephanie moved quickly to her side and said, "Here. Let me help you."

Sandy seemed even smaller than the last time she'd seen her, and it was easy to help her move up on the pillows as she turned and adjusted them behind her.

"Thanks so much, sweetheart," said Sandy. "I'm really okay. If I wasn't so tired all the time, I'd get up more. I'm just not used to lying around so much. It's not healthy."

Stephanie let out a laugh that she immediately felt embarrassed by.

"Now don't stop laughing because of this, Stephanie. I wish people would laugh more around me. It's starting to feel like a tomb in here, and I'm not even dead yet."

Stephanie couldn't help but let out another laugh as Sandy smiled. "I mean it. Everyone is way too serious. I'm glad you haven't stopped laughing. It's so nice to hear that. I wish everyone would just be themselves around me."

Stephanie looked down as she took the seat beside Sandy. When she looked up, her laughing eyes held tears. "They can't because we're all so sad that you're going away."

Sandy closed her eyes for a few seconds before opening them to look at Stephanie again. This time her eyes had teared as well. "I hope you know what a wonderful thing it is that Grant found you. God knew our family needed you."

Stephanie was lost for words but quickly swiped the tears that had fallen when she heard Jack and Joe enter the cabin.

"Hey, Mom," Joe whispered as he approached the bed.

"See?" Sandy grinned at Stephanie. "Like I said."

Stephanie couldn't help but let out another laugh as she enjoyed their private joke.

"What?" Joe asked, looking puzzled.

"Nothing," said Sandy. "Nothing at all."

"Can I get you anything?" interjected Jack, towering over the far end of the bed.

Sandy shook her head and winced again as a wave of nausea swept over her. She had to remember not to move her head.

"You need something," stated Joe, looking toward the dresser where her medications lay. "Where's Trish? Isn't she supposed to be here for that? I thought she was planning to stay more now."

"Honey," Sandy said. Her eyes had closed to get a handle on the nausea, but now she opened them and looked at her son again. "She'll be back again soon enough. She gave me something a while ago. She can't be here all the time."

Joe looked at Stephanie. "We could figure it out, Mom."

"We?" squeaked out Stephanie, trying to keep her voice soft. "I don't know about you, but I don't know anything about that stuff."

"Ah ... c'mon," Joe said, like it was nothing and she should be totally on board with his request. "You could figure it out." As he stared at Stephanie, he forgot everything else and focussed solely on her as she looked at him.

"Hey!" returned Stephanie, her ire rising. "Just because I have an aunt who's a nurse doesn't mean I know anything about ... this." She gestured to the dresser. The nerve of this guy!

"I'm sure you could figure it out," insisted Joe, clearly not backing down.

"Okay, you two," Jack started in a low growl.

Sandy stopped him with her hand. She knew he was getting impatient, but she'd been serious about people acting normally around her, and as she'd learned, this was Joe and Stephanie's "normal." "No, Jack. It's okay. Let them be."

As Jack watched the smile on Sandy's face, he turned his attention to Stephanie, who was rolling her eyes in Joe's direction. Well, if nothing else, Jack felt glad to know his granddaughter would stick up for herself.

Jack sat right on the end of the bed with Joe and Stephanie on the chairs on either side of his wife. They spoke about a few everyday things and then, suddenly, Joe thought he'd share about Stephanie finding him skinny dipping in the lake. Sandy had laughed. Stephanie hadn't expected that they'd ever share that with anyone and had tried to hide her face when he explained how embarrassed she'd looked.

After Sandy finished laughing, she winced again, which worried everyone, but she ignored her pain and said, "Joseph ... you have no shame.

You must promise me that you'll be kind to our Stephanie. At least she has more brains than you do."

Joe looked surprised at that and blurted out, "Mom! You're supposed to be on my side. What a thing to say to your favourite son." He shook his head, feigning disappointment, as a smile played on his lips.

Jack hadn't said anything as the other three chatted, and although he didn't appreciate all of Joe's story, as he watched Sandy, he knew it was perfect for her. He loved her laugh. It was good to hear it, and if anyone could make her laugh, it was Joe.

It wasn't long before Sandy's eyes began to close more frequently again. Jack knew she probably needed to sleep, and a few minutes later, after her eyes had stayed closed for a while, he wondered if she was asleep. As Joe and Stephanie continued talking in low tones, Jack was watching Sandy. Just when he'd become convinced that she'd fallen asleep, he'd see her smile a little and knew she was listening. His heart ached for her, but he was glad that she seemed content. Soon, he was sure, she'd need something more for pain, and Trish hadn't returned yet.

When the radio started to play Zach Williams's "Chain Breaker," as if on cue, Sandy's eyes opened.

Joe stopped talking and everyone in the room went silent as they listened along with Sandy. Jack had told her on their honeymoon that this had become his favourite song, and she remembered. She smiled up at Jack but then turned her head to her son. She moved her hand toward him, and Joe grabbed it.

"Ah Mom," said Joe quietly, getting up from his chair and sitting next to her on the bed.

"Joe," she whispered, looking and sounding exhausted, "I need you to remember something when I'm gone."

Joe nodded his head as he looked at his mom with a worried brow. He was surprised when his mom looked away from him and focussed on Stephanie. As Sandy's other hand came toward her, Stephanie moved closer on her chair and took it. Her eyes teared as she looked at the sweet lady who had taken her in with such love and compassion she still couldn't quite understand.

Jack knew that Sandy needed to say something important, and he leaned in closer too. Sandy held both Joe's and Stephanie's hands, and her eyes closed again. Joe suspected she'd forgotten what she needed to say and had probably fallen asleep. Stephanie waited, as Jack did, both of them suspecting that Sandy was praying. It wasn't long before Sandy opened her eyes again, and this time they seemed brighter. Everyone was surprised when Sandy, slowly and silently, placed Stephanie's hand over Joe's. Stephanie had to reach a little, but Joe moved closer to his mom to make it easier. Sandy then took her free hand and motioned toward Jack. When he offered his large hand, she took it and placed it gently over Stephanie's.

Joe wasn't sure what his mom was doing, but his heart started to beat faster, and his hand felt hot under Stephanie and Jack's touch.

"If you don't remember anything else I say, I want you three to remember this. And I'm dying, so you have to listen," Sandy said with a small smile and a stronger voice than she'd had in days. Surrounding her closely, three people who loved her so much held their collective breath.

"I want you always to remember ... Who you belong to," Sandy said with finality before closing her eyes again.

Stephanie gasped softly as her tears fell and she smiled. "I will, Sandy. I promise."

Jack nodded and couldn't help but smile either. He'd been struggling so much, but he knew what she meant, and he suspected that if he didn't heed what she said, she might come back and kick his butt.

"What?" Joe asked, looking confused.

Sandy opened her eyes with no surprise at his reaction. She had placed her hand over theirs but now lifted it from Jack's to cup Joe's cheek.

"Son," she said, more quietly, "you'll get it yet. You're just working on your testimony."

Joe guessed that what she had said had to do with God, but it was true—he didn't really get it. He knew who his family was, and that they all belonged together. He would've much rather got some sage advice about his job or finances, or something worth something.

As the music of the song faded, Joe became more aware of where his hand was situated. No one had moved since his mom had placed them there. They sat like that for a few more minutes and half expected Sandy to say more, but soon it became clear that she had, indeed, fallen asleep. Jack saw that no small smile played on her face as he slowly removed his hand. Stephanie didn't know why, but she left hers on top of Joe's for just a second or two longer. Joe looked down at their hands as she slipped it away.

"Your mom is right," she said. "We have to remember Who we belong to."

Joe smiled and found himself hoping that she meant him, but the seriousness in her expression made him doubt it.

"I better go."

Joe nodded, looking up at Stephanie as she stood but not moving from his mom's side.

Jack walked outside with Stephanie, and when they reached her car, he gathered her in a hug. Stephanie hugged him back and sighed.

"I think she meant two things, Steph," said Jack. Stephanie nodded into her grandpa's chest and sighed again. "You'll always belong to me, and we'll always belong to God."

All Stephanie could do was hug Jack harder. "Always, Grandpa."

"Not sure where Joe fits into this, but I guess Sandy's always believed he'll grow a brain and wise up someday."

"Oh Grandpa." Stephanie couldn't help but laugh then.

"I know. Not nice," Jack said with a hint of a smile. "I should be—"

Jack was cut short by the arrival of Grant and Trish, who pulled up quickly in front of the cabin.

"How is she?" Grant asked with concern as Trish ran up the stairs to the cabin. "We were gone a bit longer than we expected."

Jack held his hand up and said, "She's fine. Joe's with her. She was sleeping a few minutes ago."

Grant looked relieved as he followed his wife.

Stephanie smiled up at her grandfather again. "Grandpa," she started, guessing at what he'd wanted to say before, "please never think you should be anyone but who you are. You're perfect for me—just the way you are."

Jack quickly hugged her again before she drove away.

As Stephanie pulled away from the cabin, she remembered all the things that had happened that afternoon, and somehow, the list she'd written—the list she had been so driven to complete earlier—was forgotten.

Chapter Thirty-Eight

THE NEXT FEW DAYS PROVED TAXING, NOT ONLY FOR SANDY BUT FOR EVERYONE who loved her. Not only did her pain increase, but she was sick more often, and she'd begun to have many more seizures.

Melissa's parents, Sue and Joey, had come for a very short visit but hadn't stayed long. They, and anyone else who came out to the cabin, usually brought food, which we all appreciated.

It had been decided that Grant and I would stay at the cabin, at least a majority of the daytime hours, as Sandy's life moved closer to its earthly end. My mother had come to stay with our three children, and although I'd pumped enough breastmilk for what seemed to me at least ten babies, we had stocked some formula for her as well.

Most days at the cabin were quieter now, with fewer people coming and going. Joe would run any errands that needed to get done, and when he wasn't with Sandy, he tried to keep busy with work around the cabin. Grant would help as much as he could, only driving into town to check in with Stephanie, who was carrying the brunt of the office work while we were with Sandy. Jack didn't leave Sandy's side.

Since her diagnosis, Sandy's medical team had been surprised that she had hung on this long. We'd been told by the professionals that deal with this every day that it would be "over soon" a few times, but then she would somehow improve, and we'd all become hopeful that maybe a miracle was happening. Sandy would smile, thankful to feel better, and say things like, "I guess God's not done with me down here yet." But, as is more often the case, things would worsen again, and finally Sandy's time to rally was over. To make it easier on everyone, I didn't mind spending a majority of the last few days at the cabin with her and her closest family.

If you're a nurse in any family, you'll know why I would be the obvious option to care for her. I've watched and talked to many colleagues, and most times nurses and doctors don't mind being called upon to help when needed. That is, after all, our calling. But, that doesn't mean that we're heroes and can't get ... tired.

Maggie, an older palliative care nurse, had been out to the cabin the day before. She'd left more medication and reviewed it all with me before being satisfied that all was as "normal" as this sort of thing can be. I was walking her to her car, and we'd almost reached it, when she said what I'd apparently heard one too many times.

"It probably won't be long, Trish."

It's amazing how I can still, after all the life I've lived, say and do such asinine things, but I did just then. I stared after her and, obviously before thinking, I blurted out, "Yeah. That's what all of you have been saying."

As she turned to look at me, I begged the ground to swallow me up and not spit me out. What had I just said? What would she think of me? And was she right? What an awful thing to think, much less say! I knew it was out of our hands—life, death, and everything in between. I was losing my mind, and there was the proof.

Fortunately, the kind-hearted person who had come to see Sandy had also seen crazy before. She walked back to where I stood and enveloped me and my red face in the warmest of hugs. When she pulled away, she smiled. "Hang in there, Trish. You're doing a great job. It's so tough—sometimes on the caregivers more than the patients."

I couldn't help but cry then as Maggie hugged me again. She not only was compassionate but had a wise discernment that often eluded me.

Before I could apologize, she added. "Don't worry about anything said here. You're tired and stressed. Sometimes it's hard to put into words what your heart really feels. And it's okay to be a little impatient. You don't want to watch her suffer anymore."

With that I wanted to hang on to Maggie and never let her go, but since that wasn't an option, I nodded and let go of her.

"Thank you," I managed, wiping at my eyes.

"We're a phone call away, Trish. And if Sandy changes her mind, you can bring her into the hospital."

Maggie left with a wave as she drove away.

• • •

Most of the time the medications the palliative care team left helped, but other times it felt like I was giving Sandy nothing but water. I'd check the labels just to be sure they were correct, and they were. As is typical of me, I became even more tired and frustrated.

It was on one of those long afternoons when, again, I was humbled by the wonderful woman I will never forget. Grant had gone to the city to pick up a few things for us and check on my mom and the children. Joe had gone with him. I'd finally convinced Jack to go for a walk or swim or something to get him out of the cabin. As much as I admired him, he needed to give himself some space, and I couldn't help but think that Sandy might rest better if she didn't have someone constantly hovering over her.

After the narcotic I'd given her had finally seemed to take effect, I'd gone to the kitchen to clean a little and try for a cup of coffee. I'd just sat with my mug at the rustic, wooden table in the middle of the large main room and was admiring the work Joe had done. As my fingers played with one of the knots in the tabletop, my mind went back to the first serious conversation I'd had with Sandy. She'd surprised me then with what I'd thought were some weird questions. I smiled as I remembered her warning me that if I married her son, sometimes I might feel like running away. I had run away from a lot of things before I'd joined this family. If nothing else since I'd married Grant, I'd learned to stick more things through. When I thought of the last six months with three small children, I shook my head. If I ever wanted to run, it wouldn't be from my husband—but maybe our three wild kids. Then I thought of Kylie and the boys, and my heart ached. I hadn't seen them for a few days, and I missed them horribly. A mother's love was truly something unexplainable. They could drive you crazy, but that love ... well, there are no words for the strength of it.

"Trish."

I stood up with a renewed bolt of energy as I walked quickly to where Sandy lay in the bedroom, next to the kitchen.

"What can I get you, Sandy?" I asked, hoping that what I could offer would help in some way.

She was trying not to move so as not to bring on more nausea and probably pain. "Nothing," she smiled, her eyes only half open. "I just wanted to tell you something before I forget."

"Okay," I said, feeling some relief that she seemed fairly comfortable. As I sat in the chair beside her, she sighed.

"I was just remembering some of our conversations, and it made me smile. I would've laughed, but I don't want to move too much. You're very funny sometimes, you know."

I took her hand as I smiled at her.

"I just want you to always remember how proud I am of you." She swallowed before continuing. "Honestly, I didn't know if you'd stick it out at the beginning."

I felt just a little hurt by that until she added, "You did tell me you were a runner, after all."

I couldn't help but laugh at that. "I sure did, after I told you our family just takes more medication when things get bad."

Sandy smiled. "I remember. You did think you were funny, and I would've laughed actually, if I hadn't been so concerned about the engagement ring on your finger. I was a little nervous about you marrying Grant."

I looked down at our hands, held fast in friendship and love. When I raised my head, I could feel my tears threatening. "You didn't tell me that."

Sandy's eyes had closed, but then she looked at me again. "That's why your answer to my question was so important to me, and"—she swallowed again—"you've been so much more than I even prayed for, Trish."

Now my tears fell as she continued. "Grant couldn't have found anyone more perfect, and it makes me happy to know that you'll stick it out."

"I will," I whispered.

"I know you will," she said, more strongly and smiling at me again. "If you were going to leave, you'd have done it in these last few months. Those kids are wonderful, but they're strenuous!"

"Ha," I laughed through my tears. "I was just thinking almost the same thing, sitting in the kitchen."

Before Sandy closed her eyes again, she whispered, "You've been such a gift to Grant and our family."

Her shallow breathing told me she was probably in some kind of sleep after that—maybe aided by the narcotic I'd given to her not long before. As I stared at her, I couldn't help but smile, thanking her for the gift she'd given me in her son.

Chapter Thirty-Nine

SOMEONE HAS SAID THAT DEATH IS SIMILAR TO BIRTH, BUT I'D HAVE TO disagree. Birth, most times, is a time for rejoicing and celebration. Watching someone suffer and eventually die but not knowing how long it will take … well, that's not joyous or any kind of celebration.

I know—if eventually heaven awaits, then the suffering of the sick one is gone, and the party starts. What a relief and wonder that must be—for the person who is gone! But for the rest of us—the ones left on earth—well, the hurt and emptiness is still so great.

"Jack," I said from behind him, "I'm going to give her something more." It hadn't been long since I'd given her a dose of the antiemetic, but still Sandy's retching hadn't subsided. I walked beside the bed and slowly pushed the medication into her subcutaneous line.

She smiled her thank you at me and all I could do was nod. "Are you having more pain, Sandy?" I asked, willing to give her additional morphine if she needed it.

She didn't shake her head because it made her more nauseous. Any small movement seemed to now. Instead, she whispered, "No."

"Okay," I replied quietly, squeezing her hand. "You let me know."

I've been a nurse for many years, but I have to admit that I've not seen many people die. Unfortunately, I've cared for more babies that have passed away than adults. That is a whole other element of tragedy.

As I watched my mother-in-law, I couldn't help but think that as awful as it had been when my father died, I felt secretly thankful now that I hadn't had to watch it happen. This seemed like emotional and physical torture for not only Sandy but for everyone she loved.

However, in that beautiful cabin, where Sandy remembered wonderful summer days spent with her boys, she seemed to be at peace with her decision to die where she had chosen to. I, however, felt more and more unsure as I hovered over her. Although it had been discussed many times, and I'd felt I'd be all right with it, when push came to shove, I wasn't sure if I was the health care worker that should be here now, so my relief was great when Trent and Melissa, along with Abigail, entered the cabin that evening.

Sandy seemed to be resting more comfortably after the medication I'd given her, so I left Grant and Jack beside her and quietly exited the bedroom to meet the newcomers.

If Trent couldn't see my relief, Melissa did. "Oh Trish," she said, putting the containers of food they'd brought on the table before coming to hug me. "You look exhausted."

I'm sure I did, but somehow I didn't feel that tired—just more worried.

After the hug, I immediately turned my attention to Trent, and in a nurse-like way I reported everything I'd given Sandy. Although I knew we weren't at work, I was compelled to tell him every detail of her status. I needed someone to understand where I was coming from, and Trent always understood. Admittedly, I also needed to have someone comfort and encourage me.

"It sounds like you're doing a good job, Trish," smiled my childhood friend, not letting me down. "There's really nothing to do but exactly what you're doing. Keep her comfortable and wait." He put Abigail down as we stood and talked in the kitchen, turning his full attention to me.

"That's just it, Trent," I said. "I'm just so unsure about this, and I don't want to give her too much medication, but I want her to be comfortable enough."

"If you're that unsure, I'm sure I could stay for a while," he offered. He looked at Melissa while she found room in the fridge for some of the food they'd brought.

Melissa nodded without hesitation. "Of course you can, Trent. She's my aunt, but I'd be no good to anyone here."

"That's not true," I said. "She wants to see you, Melissa. She asked for you guys to come."

Again Melissa teared up as I tried to keep my emotions in check by looking away.

"Where's Joe?" asked Trent, probably trying to change the subject so we wouldn't break down.

"He went for a walk," I managed, trying to turn my attention to Abigail, who had found a few of Kylie's toys in a wooden box in the corner. We had purposely left some for the next time she'd come to the cabin, and Abigail had seen them as soon as they'd arrived. She squealed in delight now as, without success, Melissa tried to keep her quieter.

Kylie and the boys had just gone to stay with my mom, who had welcomed Melissa's mom, Sue, into her home to help with them while we were saying goodbye to Sandy. Although we knew it really wouldn't be long now, I was still torn between my children and the need to be present with Grant at Sandy's side.

My mother had assured me the many times I'd called her over the last few days that they were all doing fine, and I shouldn't worry about them. I would come away from those conversations thankful for her and knowing I was in the right place.

"Trish," Grant said, close to my ear. I hadn't realized he'd come out of the bedroom until he was right beside me, and I jumped a little.

"Oh! You okay?" he asked, immediately concerned.

"Yes," I nodded. "Of course. I'm fine. Just thinking about the kids. How's Sandy?"

"Finally sleeping," he said as he swiped back the hair that had fallen over his forehead. I could hear relief in his voice as he greeted Trent and Melissa. Oh, how hard this was on the man I loved! I had cried for him more than anyone, I think, up until that point.

"You should rest too," I said, putting my hand on his shoulder as he turned to face me.

He shook his head as he kissed me on my forehead and asked quietly, "Me? What about you?"

"I'm fine," I answered sincerely.

"Maybe you should go and check on the kids," he started.

"I'll wait a little longer. Mom says she and the kids are fine. I don't want to leave yet, but Trent says he's okay to stay for a while if I do, so I'll think about it."

Grant smiled down at me, knowing how torn I was.

"Where's Joe?" That was my Grant—he couldn't stop thinking about everyone else.

"He went for a walk," I answered as I glanced outside at the waning sun. "It's been a while, though."

Before anyone could say anything else, Jack opened the bedroom door and stood there. As haggard as he looked from days without any solid sleep, his eyes were bright. He seemed to search the room before he spoke, and when he did, we all felt surprised. Instead of acknowledging anyone else, he looked toward the corner of the room.

"Sandy wants to see you," Jack said, looking down at the little girl playing on the floor. He looked at Trent and Melissa. "She's asking to see Abigail."

Chapter Forty

JOE FELT AS THOUGH HE WAS CRAWLING OUT OF HIS SKIN. HE'D TRAVELLED many places in the world, and he'd even seen a few deaths—one of them had been on a flight to South Africa. The guy had a heart attack or something and had been sitting a few seats over from him. When the woman next to him started screaming, the whole plane seemed to erupt. But the guy was dead. Gone. It had freaked him out a bit, but nothing like he felt now.

His mom had been so healthy, so happy, so … alive. Now she seemed to be almost a shell of herself. She'd never been big, but now she was only skin and bones. He shook his head as he stopped by a tree a distance from the cabin to put his hand on its large trunk. It almost felt like he needed its strength to hold him up. He'd watched his mother over the last few days seem to be slipping away from him faster and faster. She was the woman who had always shown him love and acceptance. Sure, she'd preached at him too much, he thought, but had she really? Or had it been his conscience that had bothered him more than what she'd say? When he thought about it, he couldn't remember anything but a few sentences she'd actually said. "God loves you, son." "You belong to Him, Joe." And the latest, "Remember who you belong to."

Joe shook his head to clear it, took his hand from the tree, and stood straighter. He took a few deeper breaths and turned. He thought he'd heard a vehicle but had dismissed it from his mind as he'd walked away from the cabin.

Now, staring at him from behind, was Stephanie.

"Wh … what are you doing here?" he stammered.

• • •

Stephanie had seen Joe walk away from the cabin when she'd pulled up to it. Jack had called her and asked if she'd come—that Sandy had asked for her—and she was getting weaker. Stephanie knew she should go into the cabin, but something stronger told her she should follow Joe instead. He hadn't walked too far into the woods when he'd stopped to lean on a tree. There seemed nothing profound in those few moments of silence, but all her heart could do was ache for him in a relentless way, and she just knew … she had to be there. Although she knew she was in the right place, her face still flushed in sudden embarrassment when he turned and spoke to her.

"Joe," she managed, "I just got here and saw you by the cabin. I thought …" Her mind went blank. What had she been thinking? She had no right to be here. Sandy had asked for her—not Joe. "I'm sorry," she started, stepping back.

"Don't," Joe interrupted. "Don't be sorry, Steph. I'm glad you're here."

They stared at each other for a few seconds before Joe moved closer to where she stood.

As he came toward her, Stephanie suddenly felt the urge to cry. She wanted to wrap her arms around him and take away all the pain she saw imprinted on his face, but at the same time she wanted to slap him to wake him up. He had a family who loved him no matter where he'd been or what he'd done, not to mention a God who was waiting for him.

When Joe came closer to her, he couldn't tell what her expression held. He stood a few feet away from her and sighed.

"Are you doing all right?" Stephanie asked, inwardly berating herself for the question as soon as she'd asked it. How did she think he'd be? Certainly "all right" wouldn't be one of the options.

"I'm okay," he answered vacantly, both of them knowing it wasn't true. "It's hard to watch," he added truthfully.

"I'm sure it is," she agreed, with a sudden twinge of nervousness over what she would see when she went inside. "Well … I'm here for you, Joe. You know …" She paused. "If you need me for anything."

Joe looked at her with a painful intensity she'd never before seen in his eyes, and she couldn't tear herself from his gaze. They both moved toward one another, and their hug was as innocent as it was sincere. Joe hung on to Stephanie, as if for his very life, and when she thought she should back away, she felt his shuddering cry. His shoulders shook as she held on to him, and she knew she couldn't let go. For a long while they stood together as the sun dipped lower in the sky.

The horizon darkened before his sobs subsided and he finally let her go. He didn't look at her again but turned and walked toward the tree where she had first found him.

"Can I have a few minutes, Steph?" he managed.

She nodded, saying nothing, as she quietly turned to walk back to the cabin.

Even before Stephanie's footsteps had completely faded, Joe couldn't help himself any longer. On that night, in that moment, Joe Evans fell to his knees and begged God to take him back. He prayed as he had when he was a small child those many years before that God would forgive him for everything he'd done. He prayed in earnest, confessing everything, and suddenly, with the chill of the evening in the air and the now dark night surrounding him, Joe felt it—the simple but completely encompassing love of God.

"Remember Who you belong to," suddenly sang through his mind again, and he couldn't help but smile. He felt it now, and he knew—without a doubt—Who he belonged to. His mom had known, even before Joe knew it, that he would belong to God.

He didn't know how long he'd been there, but his knees had started to hurt. Before he stood, however, Joe looked up into the starlit sky and whispered one more prayer from the deepest fathoms of his soul. "God … please send us a miracle."

As Joe stood up on wobbly knees, he looked up at the sky and sighed. A peace he couldn't remember feeling before infused his entire body. He stood for a long while then, thanking God for thinking him worthy enough to save.

Chapter Forty-One

AS CHILDREN DO, ABIGAIL LOOKED UP AT THE GREAT-GRANDFATHER SHE'D learned would play with her on the floor and let her have her way in almost any situation. She grinned, screeching with glee as she tried to run toward him, stumbling a few times on the way. His large, muscular figure didn't intimidate her and never would.

"Hey, little one," he greeted now with a smile of his own as he easily scooped her up, saving her from another topple. "We're going to see Nana," he said as he bounced her a little in his arms. "You have to be gentle, okay?"

Abigail smiled and touched Jack's cheek with her left hand. Although she didn't talk as much as Kylie, she seemed to have a three-year-old's understanding of most things.

Grant, Melissa, and Trent followed Jack and Abigail into the larger of the cabin's bedrooms, where Sandy lay. She opened her eyes as soon as she heard them enter and smiled up at Abigail. As Jack sat beside her on the bed, Abigail clambered next to her grandmother and nestled in beside her.

"Oh!" Melissa exclaimed, moving toward the bed to keep Abigail still. She didn't want her daughter causing any pain or discomfort to Sandy. "Maybe she shouldn't—"

"It's fine," smiled Sandy, with closed eyes. "She's perfect." She wrapped one thin arm around the little girl who called her Nana and then smiled again. When Sandy's eyes opened, Abigail was watching her with an innocent gaze.

With the ensuing night, the room had fallen quite dark, and only one warm, golden light shone from the small lamp on the table across the room. Everyone was silent as they watched Abigail and her grandmother, sitting quietly.

After arranging some food on the table in the kitchen area for everyone, I'd come into the room and could immediately sense Trent's alertness as he stood at the foot of the bed. Melissa had told me that, at times, the only warning of Abigail's coming seizure would be the vacant stare she seemed to be having now.

No one seemed to breathe as Sandy straightened her body to better gaze into Abigail's eyes. In a quiet, simple movement, she placed her hand over Abigail's left cheek—directly over the heart that had been made in secret just for her—and whispered words that all of us in the room guessed to be a prayer to Almighty God. Tears fell from Sandy's eyes as she mouthed words all of us couldn't hear and wouldn't understand anyway. The whole time she whispered her prayer, Abigail, as if frozen, didn't move or take her eyes off Sandy. The moment lasted not even a minute, but in those few seconds, something undetected moved in that small room. Suddenly, as if something unseen swept through, everything changed. Sandy's eyes closed as her hand dropped from Abigail's face. Her head was thrown back in another of the seizures the medication had previously abated. As Abigail started to cry, Melissa dove to pick up her daughter, and Trent joined them.

Grant had been sitting on the opposite side of the bed and, with tears falling from his eyes, leaned in closer to grab Sandy's convulsing hand. At the same time, Jack moved in to cradle his precious wife as she shook.

I glanced toward the medications that lay on the dresser across the room, trying to decide what I could give her. I debated drawing something up, but I stilled when I looked back at Jack. The great and strong man we had grown to love so deeply had begun to weep. Sobs wracked his body. As he'd held her, Sandy's body had stilled, and now, feeling her move no longer, the room filled with his anguished cry.

Trent and I looked at each other with the solemn, knowing look we both had seen too often. It only took a moment before I crossed the room and knelt to hug Grant, whose own tears covered his cheeks.

Trent and Melissa took a now smiling Abigail out of the room, unaware as children often are of any sadness that surrounds them. Oh, to be a child and oblivious to the seriousness of moments such as these. Before she was carried from the room by her daddy, however, I couldn't help but smile as she grinned at me, waving her goodbye from over her daddy's shoulder.

• • •

Long minutes later, Jack laid Sandy's lifeless body on the pillows behind her one more time. He sighed deeply as he moved her hair away from her face with gentle fingers. Then he looked at Grant.

I felt like my presence was somehow infringing on their silent communication, so I stood quietly to exit the bedroom and join Trent and Melissa, who were in the kitchen with their daughter. Abigail played happily again with the toys in the corner as we hugged each other and talked in low tones, saying the normal things that people say at times like these. Although we all knew Sandy was in much better place, and saying it may have helped, the rawness of our pain without her presence was overwhelming.

"You should eat something before you go," I said, hugging Melissa again. Although it was probably wrong timing, I suddenly heard my mother in my head as I said those words, and for the first time ever, I wasn't upset by it. In fact, suddenly I wanted to call her and tell her how wonderful she was.

Melissa shook her head as she moved away from me and said, "We had a late lunch. We'll be okay." Then she looked at Trent and, as if reading his mind, changed hers. "Maybe we'll take some snacks for the road instead."

I helped my friends quickly compile a few sandwiches in a plastic bag for the trip home, and soon we stood beside their SUV as Trent buckled Abigail in the backseat.

"We're here for you, Trish," Trent said, turning toward me when he was done.

As he enveloped me in a hug, my mind went back to the many moments he'd hugged to console me over the years. The familiarity of his hug gave me a peace only someone who has a friend like that can understand.

Melissa agreed as she got into the passenger's seat. "We are, Trish. We'll talk soon but call any time if you need anything at all."

I waved as they pulled away, and then I stood for a few moments looking up at the night sky. How bright the stars shone through the black canvas! I broke from my reverie after a minute or so and was going to head back to the cabin when I heard something. Stephanie was walking out from the woody area, not far from the lake. I took a steady breath, knowing I should say something to tell her, but as she neared, she must've guessed by the expression on my face. All I could do was nod as she moved into my arms.

• • •

After Stephanie and I had cried together outside for a long while, I told her that Sandy had probably died a fairly painless death, but that wasn't what comforted her. It was when I told her of how Sandy had held on to Abigail and prayed that made Stephanie smile.

"That's Sandy," Stephanie said. "Always praying for others and loving everybody so much." Then her tears fell fresh when she added, "I can't believe Abigail was the last person she prayed for. My Abigail."

I hugged her tight again, and tears filled my own eyes. Somehow the very preciousness of that hadn't escaped me either. What a wonderful thing to tell Abigail about as she grew, and I suspected Trent and Melissa would never forget it either.

Stephanie soon took a few cleansing breaths and stepped away from me, nodding. "Well, that's good," she said, wiping her eyes. "Now she's home. Like she always said, she was just going home."

I smiled at my niece, putting my arm around her before we walked back to the cabin together.

"Oh!" Stephanie said, remembering. "Joe's down by the lake."

"It's okay," I assured her. "I'll let Grant know."

• • •

Grant had just come out of the bedroom when Trish and Stephanie entered the cabin. When Steph told him where she'd left Joe, Grant hadn't said anything but immediately grabbed his jacket and left. He found Joe near the water, looking up to the starlit sky, facing away from him. Joe didn't notice his brother, and Grant paused, thinking of how to break the news to him. He suspected Joe would take their mother's death harder than his little brother even knew. Although they hadn't talked about it, as Grant had watched Joe during the last few days, he knew he hadn't been handling things so well. As things had gotten worse for their mother, Joe had stayed away from her a little more. Grant had empathized for his brother, though, because he himself had found her last days tough to watch.

Grant's heart ached for his brother now, but he knew it had to be done. With a deep breath he headed toward Joe. He hadn't moved much further down the slope toward the lake before Joe heard him and turned. As Grant came closer, although it was dark, he thought he saw his brother grinning. Grant groaned inwardly, thinking how much harder this was going to be if his brother was in a suddenly great mood.

"Hey, Grant!" Joe exclaimed.

Yep. Good mood.

"You're not gonna believe this, man!" Joe continued enthusiastically.

When Grant didn't say anything, but rather kept coming toward him, Joe ignored it.

"I get it!" Joe kept on. "I get it! I do! I just invited God into my life, Grant!" In his excitement, Joe had lifted his hands to heaven as he exclaimed the news that Grant and his family had waited so long for.

Just short of reaching Joe, Grant stopped. How could he tell him now? Inwardly, Grant had to admit that this was typical of his brother. Timing. Grant fought the urge to roll his eyes before he did the only thing he could possibly do—and the thing that he knew his mom would do—he grabbed Joe and hugged him. Hard.

"That's amazing, bro," he said, smiling in genuine praise as he hugged him and slapped him on his back.

Both Joe and Grant had tears in their eyes when they stepped away from each other, but Joe was still grinning. Joe swiped one hand across his face, looking a little embarrassed by his show of emotion.

Grant shook his head and glanced away but then took another deep breath and looked at Joe again. This time when he looked at him, Joe saw that his brother's eyes remained tear-filled, and a sadness had moved into his expression. As he watched his brother, Joe's joyous demeanour turned to one of aching pain.

"No," he whispered in a low groan, looking at Grant. "Mom?"

Grant's nod was barely perceptible, but Joe instantly knew. He left Grant standing alone by the lake as he ran toward the cabin.

Chapter Forty-Two

ALTHOUGH I DON'T LIKE BEING GIVEN FLOWERS WHEN SOMEONE I LOVE DIES, food is another matter. Whoever was the first to think of that kind gesture was a genius. Of course, I might've felt differently if my cooking had improved in any way.

Over the next days, our home was inundated with not only people who brought condolences by way of copious amounts of food, but also flowers and many cards as well. Between the busyness of small children, who really don't understand the grieving of adults, and final preparations for Sandy's funeral, the days sped by, and before we all knew it, the funeral was over. Of course, the grieving was not.

"Jack," I asked a few weeks after her funeral, "can I get you anything?"

He'd again agreed to come over to help eat more of the food we'd been gifted with and that I'd still been pulling out of the freezer, but he hadn't eaten much, and neither had I. After Kylie ate and we had tried, we sat on the floor with her and the boys, staring at them more than playing. At almost eight months, the boys were too young to notice, but Kylie tried valiantly to try to keep Jack's attention on her.

He shook his head but thanked me, and I smiled back at him, wishing I could speed up his grief … and the rest of ours as well.

"Nap time, little girl." I turned my attention to Kylie, sure that Jack would be as relieved as I for a reprieve from her constant chatter.

"No," she stated, not taking her eyes off her grandfather.

"Oh, yes," I answered her, in no uncertain terms. "Even if it's a short one, you've had a busy day, and you're getting grumpy. It's okay to nap once in a while."

She would have none of it, however, but stood her ground by completely ignoring me as she kept her attention fully on her grandfather, showing him the doll in her hands.

"The boys are going to have a sleep too, Kylie. All of you are having a nap," I said more firmly as I gathered one son, and then the other, into my arms.

"No!" she yelled, glancing at me in open defiance.

I said nothing more but carried the twins upstairs, preparing myself to deal with her after I got the boys tucked in. Two soothers and a short back rub for one of them, and I quietly shut their door.

Grant and I knew that Kylie had been going through her own grief, and although she knew her grandma was in heaven, it didn't change the sadness she felt either. We'd been patient with her, and were prepared to be, but today my own exhaustion was catching up with me, and I felt I had no patience left to fight over one nap, but I'd do it to keep my own sanity.

I had just started my descent and was still near the top of the stairs when I heard Jack speaking in the low tone that almost made the stair I had just sat down on, vibrate.

"She's your mom, Kylie. You must listen to her."

"No," returned the small but determined voice of my stubborn daughter. I wished Grant was there, and I felt a little perturbed that he'd gotten to go to work today. Lately, work seemed like a pleasant dream that I often looked forward to returning to. At least on most days I'd get a coffee break there.

I shook my head as I refocused on the conversation I heard coming from below.

"Well," Jack said, "your mom and dad know what's best for you, Kylie, even if you don't think so."

"I don't think so," said the three-year-old who usually had listened to us fairly well, until more recently.

"Oh ... I know so," interjected Jack. "Your parents are kind of like God, you know."

Being a person who so often felt the furthest away from being anything near godly, I snapped to attention.

"They aren't God, Grandpa," she answered, in what sounded to me like a scoff.

"Of course they aren't God, Kylie." I could hear an almost laughing tone in the timbre of his voice before he continued, more seriously. "But when we belong to God, it's kind of like belonging to your mom and dad. When you belong to someone, they love you no matter what happens, and they want only the best for you. So your mom knows what's best for you, Kylie, even if you don't think so."

I could almost hear her shrug of indifference in the silence that followed.

I heard Jack sigh. "Kylie, you have no idea how much they love you."

"No," she disagreed. I crept lower on the stairs, hoping to peer at them without being noticed. "And God doesn't love me either, or He wouldn't have killed Grandma."

I stopped moving so suddenly I almost went head over heels down the rest of the stairs but caught myself just in time. Although my breath was taken away, Jack's wasn't. He continued as if in any easy conversation.

"Now, Kylie," he started, "God didn't kill your grandma. He took her to be with Him because He needed her there now. I miss her too, and I know it feels bad that grandma is gone from us, but in heaven, your grandma is happy and dancing and seeing your Grandpa Ted, and she has no more owies and ..."

I carefully inched further down the stairs as my eyes blurred, hoping I wouldn't be spotted as I watched them both. Kylie was snuggled in Jack's lap, and she looked up at her grandpa.

"Daddy says God is good all the time," she stated, almost questioningly, as if within her grandfather's answer would be an authentic truth she could really believe.

I didn't realize I'd held my breath until I let it go when Jack spoke again. "Yes, Kylie. It doesn't always feel that way, but God is *always good*." His voice caught as my tears fell.

"It's okay, Grandpa," Kylie said, almost in a whisper. Then, in an act of pure, innocent empathy, and in one of the sweetest moments I've ever seen, she reached up with one small finger and wiped a tear off his scarred cheek. "I'm here for you."

Jack smiled down at her and quickly swiped a few other tears away with his hand before clearing his throat and adjusting his bandanna.

Kylie grinned up at him. "Maybe you should have a nap too," she suggested.

Jack laughed, hugging her tightly.

When I entered the living room, they both looked up, and before I could say anything, Kylie ran past me. "I'm going for a nap, Momma," she sang out as she bounded upstairs.

One more trip up the stairs to tuck her in and another down again and I flopped onto the couch across from Jack, who had gotten up to sit in the recliner across from me.

"Thank you, Jack," I said, smiling with deep sincerity at him. The ache in my heart when I looked at him still hadn't abated, and I wondered how long it would take before the pain in all our hearts would be lessened.

Chapter Forty-Three

OVER THE NEXT WEEKS AND MONTHS, KYLIE OFTEN ASKED FOR HER GRANDPA, and Jack was more than willing to not only come over but babysit as well. The busyness of a preschooler, along with almost year-old twins, which seemed overwhelming to me every day, didn't seem to faze Jack. He seemed to take their antics in stride but could only be pushed so far before his soft but commanding voice would stop them in their tracks. I could rant over and over about something I wanted them to stop doing, but he just had to say one quiet word, or throw them a pointed look, and they'd all immediately respond, most often doing whatever he asked. I have to admit that sometimes that would irk me, but then Grant would come home and have the same result, and I'd just throw my hands up in the air, rolling my eyes and leaving the room to have my much-deserved mommy time-out.

I'd often wondered about some things in Jack's past, but he never seemed interested in speaking much about his life before meeting Sandy. Looking at him now, I still suspected that at some point he must've been a professional wrestler, and how easily he handled our three children convinced me further. He didn't admit to this, but he'd watch the WWE with me on occasion, as my father had.

"Oh!" I grimaced, looking away as my favourite wrestler got thrown down for the last time. When I looked back at the TV screen, I saw Jack smiling at me from the corner of my eye. "What?" I asked, looking at him.

"You know this isn't real, right?" he chided.

I shrugged. "Maybe," I said, admitting only that.

"Reminds you of your dad?" he observed, still smiling.

I nodded and returned his smile. "Yeah, he loved this. I don't really know why, but I think that's why I still watch it sometimes—to remember him, I guess." I felt a little self-conscious and added, "Weird, huh?"

"No," he disagreed immediately. "Not weird, Trish ... kinda sweet."

I looked back at the TV. The program was ending, and since my favourite guy hadn't won, I turned the volume down and looked at Jack. "Can I ask you a question?"

Jack nodded once. "Anything."

Something my mother had said one day had me wondering, and now that Jack and I were alone, I thought I'd venture out. "I was just wondering ... about your sister, Annie. You don't talk much about her, but my mom mentioned her the other day."

"That right?" nodded Jack, sounding nonchalant but looking more interested.

"Yes." I paused, waiting to see if he'd continue. When he didn't, I did. "Well ... I was just wondering how she's doing?"

Jack looked directly at me before speaking. "Annie or your mom?"

I paused then. "Wh ... what?" I managed.

"Do you want to know how Annie is doing, or how your mom is?" smiled Jack, looking completely at ease as he gazed at my confused expression.

"Why would I ask you about my mom?" I stopped. So many times I'd felt I'd been missing something when I'd watched my mother and Jack. Lately, because of different people's birthdays and other small events that required family gathering together, they'd both attended, but everything seemed normal.

Jack now looked at me with the smallest of smiles.

I suddenly berated myself for possibly missing what perhaps should have been clear to me. Thoughts raced through my mind as I tried to remember what had occurred when I'd seen Jack with my mother. Had there been blatant gestures of a relationship I hadn't expected? No. Had there been any nuances of a romance? No. But now he was basically asking me to ask about him and my mother, like he wanted to tell me something.

What kind of assessment skills did I even have? Had being away from work and staying home with the kids make my mind shrivel? Or could this be remnants of the "pregnancy brain" I was sure had stayed with me? What was happening?

I shook my head to clear it and looked directly at Jack with a more serious expression. "I meant your sister, Annie, but now I want to know what you have to say about my mother."

That may have sounded more forceful than I'd meant it, but it didn't seem to faze Jack.

He smiled more broadly before answering. "Trish," he said, leaning even more forward in his chair and clearing his throat, as if a great reveal was about to be announced.

"Wait!" I interrupted, holding my hand up to stop him. "If you're going to tell me that you and my mother are … going out or romantically involved … well, I'll just tell you that—"

"Trish," Jack interrupted, more loudly than I expected. "Nothing like that's going on. You can breathe."

And I did. As my voice's pitch had escalated, I didn't know I'd been holding my breath until he told me to breathe, and I let it out in one big gush.

"We talk sometimes, but we aren't dating or anything. I'm not ready for that, and I don't think Helen is either, but …" His voice trailed off as we continued to watch each other. "As far as Annie is concerned," he continued, "well, Helen and I have both been really praying for her. She struggles, even though she thinks she's got it all together. I'm really glad she has your mom for a friend, though. From what Annie tells me, she doesn't seem to have many people of any kind of substance in her life, so I'm glad your mom's there for her."

I nodded again, thinking of the little my mother had told me about her conversations with Annie. I had to admit that when she told me the story of the necklace, I was amazed. A lot over the last few years had amazed me about my mother, actually. She'd been through so much when she was young and also through her adult life, but she'd risen above it all, a stronger and more faithful woman of God—the kind I wanted to be but so often failed at.

"Someday I hope Annie will understand how much God loves her," he added, looking down at his lap.

"I do too, Jack," I agreed, empathizing with him and the burden he carried for her. As I watched him lift his long hair away from one side of his face and place it back, he looked at me again.

I couldn't help myself. "I'd be okay if you and my mom ... well ... you know." I blushed, shrugging. When he didn't say anything in return, I grabbed the remote that lay next to me and snapped the TV off. And with that, our conversation ended as well. Part of me wanted to know how Jack would reply to me, but for the first time in my life perhaps, I felt that I'd be fine leaving it in God's hands.

Just as the screen went dark, Grant came into the family room. Jack had joined me earlier after reading to Kylie, but Grant had put the boys to bed while my program was on. He didn't get the whole WWE thing.

"Boys go down okay?" I asked as he came to sit next to me on the couch.

"Pretty good," he sighed, putting his arm around me. "The bathroom's still a mess, but I didn't clean it. I'm too tired."

Jack stood up then. "That's my cue," he started. "Thanks for having me over again. I know I hang out here a lot."

Grant and I both jumped up as he spoke, and with all the sincerity we both felt, Grant said, "We'd have it no other way, Jack. We like having you here, and the kids love you so much."

"Well," Jack smiled, "I love them too."

I moved to hug him. "I think they prefer you over me, Jack."

He laughed as he returned my embrace. "You're the momma. You have to do the hard stuff."

"Don't forget the birthday party for the boys," I reminded him as he turned to leave.

"I won't," he smiled before he let himself out.

Jack got on his Harley, and I couldn't help but sigh as I watched him from the window. Grant came alongside me, placing his hand at my waist as we watched him drive away.

As I put my head on his shoulder, he whispered, "What?"

I smiled, not moving my head, and shrugged. "I just feel sorry for him."

"You've been saying that ever since Mom died, Trish," he said, holding me even closer. "He's doing all right. The last time we went for coffee, he told me he's been hanging out with a few guys from church and, believe it or not, he's been going out to the cabin and hangin' with Joe."

This was news to me, and as I looked up with a quizzical expression, he continued. "I didn't get it either, at the start. Jack didn't have much use for Joe, but ... things are different now."

We turned away from the window, and I grabbed the glasses that were sitting on the tables in the living room. As I started toward the kitchen, I said, "I can see it. Joe sure has changed—probably similar to how Jack did—and they both go to AA. I think it's a good thing."

Later, as we made our way upstairs for the night, I couldn't help but ask, "What do you think they do out there?" I could picture my brother-in-law and Jack sitting by a campfire at the lake. In my imagination, however, all I could muster up was Joe nattering on about nothing important while Jack occasionally grunted. For the life of me I couldn't imagine what their conversations would consist of. Joe had always seemed intimidated by Jack, but with this news, obviously that must've changed. I'd have to ask Stephanie about it when I saw her next.

As we readied ourselves for bed, I thought about my mother and all the planning she was doing for our boys' birthday bash. As with Kylie's first birthday, it had grown into a larger affair than we had originally planned. My mom and I had gone over a few last-minute details, and I told Grant about them as I climbed into bed next to him.

"Uh huh," he said, yawning after I turned out the light.

"You're not even paying attention to me," I said as I placed my cold hand on the warmth of his back. With one quick movement, Grant rolled over to face me, and I could feel him whisper near my ear, "They pray."

"What?" I asked, feeling him kiss my ear.

"You asked what they do out there at the cabin. I'm telling you ... among other things ... they pray."

I couldn't say anything as I let that sink in. Stephanie and I had been praying more together also. It had brought us closer than we'd ever been before. Suddenly I felt I needed to know more, but as I turned to face Grant in our dark room, I heard his soft snore and knew I'd have to wait.

Chapter Forty-Four

STEPHANIE SIGHED. SHE COULDN'T KEEP HER MIND ON HER WORK, AND because that hadn't often happened before, her frustration grew. She glanced at the time on the bottom of her computer screen. Only five minutes since she'd last checked. She sighed again and leaned back in her chair. Looking up at the ceiling, she closed her eyes. She couldn't get the memory out of her mind. It had been months, but still it plagued her.

"That's it!" she whispered to herself, making the decision and standing abruptly.

"Where are you off to?" inquired Alicia as Stephanie breezed past her desk toward the exit. "I don't think you have a meeting." She scrambled, looking at her computer screen and tapping some buttons to again review the schedule for the day.

"Not a business meeting," stated Stephanie. "Something else." She looked back at the secretary before departing and added, "Please tell Grant I won't be in for the rest of the day."

Stephanie was gone before Alicia had time to ask for details.

• • •

It had seemed like a good idea at the time, and she knew it was the only option, but as soon as she left the city, Stephanie became more and more nervous. She hadn't been able to turn around because the traffic was ridiculous, and the one time she had tried, a horn from the semi she almost turned in front of blasted, waking her back to reality. *This must be that still, small voice Trish talks about*, Stephanie thought. *Along with God's protection*, she added, after her heart had calmed to a normal rate. Strangely, as she'd driven closer and then turned off onto the dirt road that would take her to the cabin, Stephanie felt more peace than she had in days.

As she pulled closer to it, she parked her car and sat, staring at the beautiful work Joe had done. It looked like he'd stained the cabin logs recently, and they were a darker shade than she remembered. She smiled at the heavy wooden chairs she saw on the cabin's veranda. They hadn't been there before, and she suspected Joe had made them.

It had been close to six months since Sandy's death. Stephanie had talked to Joe since, quite a few times actually, and had seen him a few weeks before. When he drove in for church on Sundays, and when they were both at Trish and Grant's at the same time, they'd occasionally visit. It always seemed nice, and they were both polite with each other, but that was about it. They hadn't had a deeper conversation about anything, except for a few months ago when he'd looked at her and apologized, again, for his previous behaviour. She knew he was going through his twelve steps in the program and was probably saying it to check it off his list, but he'd seemed more genuine that time. Of course she'd told him he was forgiven. She had done that long ago and had meant it. She wasn't angry with Joe anymore, but there was still something she needed to address. That's why she was here, but looking around now, she became more anxious again. If only she could be brave enough to talk about what he'd said that night, she could finally go on with her life in peace. She knew he'd given his life to God but they hadn't really talked about that either. There were just some things she needed to say and ... it was time.

Stephanie knew her grandfather had been coming out to the cabin to fish and whatever he and Joe did while they were together. He'd asked her to come with him a few times, but she'd always declined. Stephanie wished now that she had asked her grandpa to come along with her, but knowing that she was being childish, she opened the door and climbed out of her car. As she walked closer to the cabin, she paused to close her eyes and take a breath of the fresh air you don't get in the city.

"Nice, huh?" came a masculine voice from behind her.

Stephanie jumped as she whipped around to find Joe smiling at her.

"Geez! You scared me!" she accused, taking in his longer hair and unshaven face.

Joe's grin grew as he looked at the ground and then up at her again. "Sorry. Didn't mean to."

"I know," Stephanie replied in a defensive tone. She was uncomfortable now and wasn't sure why.

"To what do I owe the pleasure of your company?" he asked, a smile still playing on his lips as he watched her.

Stephanie couldn't help but laugh. "Really, Joe?" she grinned. "That's pretty proper, even for you."

"Well," he smiled, "I'm trying to better myself."

"Well … I don't know about that," she quickly returned.

Stephanie was instantly sorry she'd said it. What was she thinking? He shouldn't better himself? Would he think she was mocking him, thinking she thought it would be impossible for him? Even to herself she'd sounded pretty "better than thou." Suddenly she didn't want him to think of her that way.

His eyes had turned serious as her face reddened, and Stephanie looked away. She couldn't have been more relieved when he then asked, "Wanna coffee or something?"

"Sure," she agreed, relief filling her. Maybe they'd just chat again, about weather or whatever surface talk they'd fall into, and maybe that would be their relationship, and it would all be … okay.

"I love the porch furniture," Stephanie said as they walked by it before entering the cabin.

"Yeah?" he asked, glancing over his shoulder before going to the counter to ready the coffee maker. "It's pretty rustic, but I like that. I have to make furniture everyone else seems to like more at work, but out here I get to make it the way I like it."

Stephanie sat down at the large table in the middle of the room and admired the craftsmanship, running her hand over a knot in the top. "Oh," she breathed, "I like it too. This table was here before …"

She looked up at Joe, feeling foolish for what she'd almost said, but Joe caught her eye and held it with his nod. "Before my mom came here to die," he ended.

Stephanie couldn't help but glance toward the bedroom where, only short but still long months before, his mom had slipped from the earth. The memory of that night was still fresh in their memories as they sat in silence.

The coffee was done quickly, and as Joe handed her a full mug, with the splash of milk he remembered she took, Stephanie looked up at him. "I'm still so sorry about your mom, Joe."

It wasn't just Sandy's death that Stephanie was empathizing with, but she had thought, many times over, that Joe must have been incredibly upset when Grant went to tell him of her passing and that Joe had missed it.

Stephanie looked down at the mug she'd taken from him. When he remained silent, she took a sip but then slowly looked up again. He had sat across the table from her, with his own coffee, and was staring intently at her.

"There's nothing to be sorry for, Stephanie," Joe said softly. The sincerity in his voice was clear as he continued. "It was totally how God planned it. I mean, there I was, finally giving my life to Christ at the same time as she went to be with Him. I don't see how I could ever be sorry for that."

"But," Stephanie started, "you never got to tell her."

Joe laughed, and Stephanie, surprised, couldn't help the small smile that came to her own lips from the look of joy on his face.

"When Grant told me that Mom died, I tore into here like a bat outta you-know-where, but when I came to the side of her bed and looked down at her ..." Joe's voice trailed off as he stared toward the bedroom. As if he could see himself hugging his mother again, he smiled before turning his eyes back to Stephanie. "She knew, Stephanie. I just know ... she knew."

Joe then explained that he and Jack had been studying together—about heaven and what the Bible says about it. As Joe, with great animation in his voice and actions, told Stephanie about the great rejoicing that happens in heaven when one person believes, her eyes teared. "She went to heaven in the middle of that party, Steph. My mom absolutely knew—everything about me that night—and she knew it would happen. She never doubted God for a minute. And she was right about more than just that, I think."

Joe's voice had gotten quieter, and he suddenly looked more serious than Stephanie could ever remember him being. As he looked deeper into her eyes, she couldn't take hers away from him. "I believe," he started, as he placed one of his hands over hers, "she meant 'remember Who you belong to' in more than one way."

In that moment, a pin could've dropped in the entire forest surrounding that cabin. In the silence, Stephanie's eyes teared even more, and she couldn't move. How many times had she thought that same thing but then would battle over and over with the thoughts she couldn't comprehend? Now, as she felt the warmth of Joe's hand surrounding hers, she couldn't help the small nod she gave him.

As if Joe didn't think he was being clear, he started to explain. "My mom knew I needed to remember I belonged to God first, and she knew I needed to remember how much I love belonging to this family, but"—he looked at Stephanie with a more unsure smile before he continued—"I don't want you to get mad or anything, but I really do believe that—"

"We belong to each other." Stephanie's breath escaped in a rush she hadn't expected.

Joe looked a little surprised before his small smile grew. As they stared at one another, neither moved. They were both lost for words, their minds reeling with what they'd just admitted.

Suddenly, almost as if on fire, Stephanie took her hand from under his and stood up. "Thank you for the coffee, Joe."

He looked up, the smile gone from his face and replaced with concern, as he searched her unreadable expression. She was out the door before he could stand up, but as soon as he did, he tore after her.

"Stephanie!" Joe called, running toward her. "Stop! Please! I didn't mean to freak you out."

She was almost to her car when she turned to face him again. "You didn't freak me out, Joe. I freaked myself out."

Joe's look of confusion made Stephanie pause to take in the wild look in his eyes. "I just… I can't do this."

"I love you, Steph."

The forest seemed to still again as Stephanie stared at the man she knew she loved, even though their history wouldn't think it ever could be so.

"And I'm not drunk this time," he added with quiet earnestness as his cheeks reddened a little.

Stephanie didn't know what to do so she stood, waiting.

It was all Joe could do not to run to her—to grab her or do something to make her understand—but instead he looked at her and owned up to the truth. "I remember telling you that—the night I came over—but I should've never said it then, and I didn't want ... I mean ... I don't want you to remember that as the first time I told you something this important. I want—right now—to be what you remember. Here and now. I'm a new person, Stephanie, and I know, without a doubt, that I love you. I really—"

"I love you too," Stephanie gasped. Suddenly, with the cool breeze felt vividly on her now wet cheeks, she had to admit it. She did love him, and there was no use in lying to herself any longer.

As Joe's head tilted back and his face turned toward the heavens in a prayer of thanks, Stephanie knew without a doubt that Sandy had been right. They belonged to God, their family and—to one another.

Joe walked toward Stephanie, but as he came closer, he slowed, putting his hands in his jean pockets. He looked at her with a small smile until she became uncomfortable with his scrutiny.

"What?" she whispered, after he'd stared at her for what she felt was too long.

His expression changed to an intensity she hadn't seen before. "I don't want a big wedding," he stated quietly.

Stephanie laughed but didn't feel as shocked as she thought she should, because in that simple statement, there was nothing surprising.

"Okay," she smiled.

He didn't kiss her then, like she expected, but rather caught her in a hug that brought her memory back to that night, months before, when he had embraced her under the trees.

Chapter Forty-Five

ABIGAIL PLAYED WITH THE FAMILIAR TOYS IN THE CORNER OF THE SPECIALIST'S office, oblivious to the adult conversation around her. She clapped her hands in delight after she successfully found the perfect fit for the wooden triangle she'd placed correctly into the puzzle. Melissa glanced to where her daughter played, and tears formed in her eyes. It hadn't been their imagination after all.

Shortly after Sandy's death, both she and Trent had thought they'd seen a rather marked improvement in Abigail's strength. She started to fall less, to work more with her right arm, and even to speak more clearly. They'd both commented one evening on how the newer medications and physiotherapy exercises were helping their daughter improve more than in previous months, and they'd been so thankful for that.

It wasn't until more recently, however, when Abby had been very angry about a toy Melissa had taken away from her, that she had really stopped to look at her daughter. As she watched Abby throw what could only be classified as a toddler's tantrum, something made Melissa pause. Abby stomped her feet and waved both arms in clear defiance of her mother. Melissa knew she should try to stop her behaviour, but all she could do was stand and stare. Then, as the tantrum subsided and she stepped closer to gather Abby into her arms, she tried to remember. When was the last time she'd had a seizure? At the cabin when she'd stared blankly at her grandmother ... but no. They thought she was going to, but then Sandy ... Had it really been that many months ago? Hadn't they just thought it was the new medication's success?

Melissa returned her attention to the doctor, who had continued speaking, but after what she'd just said, she had lost Melissa's attention. The doctor was showing Trent the report of Abigail's last CT, and as Melissa watched him, she saw him stare at it, as if fixated. Slowly, Trent reached for her hand, and together they listened as the doctor finished. Along with physiotherapists and neurologists, this paediatrician had known Abigail for years. All those appointments for Abby, to help her in any way possible, and now ... this.

As Melissa looked at Trent, who was still staring at the doctor, his colour paled as he haltingly said, "You can't be serious. I mean ... she's been getting stronger, but we thought it was the meds, and—"

The doctor smiled, nodding her head as if she too was dumbfounded. "I can't believe it either, Trent, Melissa ... but I and at least three other colleagues have reviewed Abby's tests. It's absolutely true. The calcifications are gone. Her CT is ... normal."

Melissa turned her head once again to look at their daughter. Her now longer auburn hair was a mess, coming out of the ponytail Melissa had put it in just that morning. She watched as Abby pushed some of the stray strands off her face with her right hand and then continued playing.

The doctor, still unable to grasp the full weight of what she'd just told Abigail's parents, rose from her seat and walked over to her young patient. As if to convince herself one more time, she smiled. "Hi, Abby," she greeted, kneeling in front of her and taking her two hands in her own. "Can you squeeze my hands?"

Abigail looked at the doctor she knew so well and did as she was told, first squeezing and then pulling, as directed, along with the doctor. Then she walked for her, and Abby giggled as she mimicked the doctor as they each took turns standing on one foot and then jumping on both. These seemingly small movements had never been successfully achieved by Abigail before, and as her parents watched, they were in awe of what their daughter could suddenly do.

After checking her reflexes again, the physician turned toward Trent and Melissa, and this time she had tears in her eyes. "Well," she began with a shrug, "I guess that's it, folks. I can't believe I'm saying this either, but you may never have to see me again."

Melissa still hadn't said anything, but with that she got up, crossed the small space between them, and hugged Abby's doctor with all her might.

"We've prayed for this," Melissa whispered, her eyes tearing as well. "I don't know why it's such a surprise, because we did ask for it. Did we think He really couldn't do it?" She looked at Trent, and although tears had fallen from his face as well, his smile could not be contained.

"He did it," he agreed, getting up to hug his wife, lifting her up in his enthusiasm. "He did it!" he exclaimed.

They both turned to face the doctor, who had been nothing but supportive to them and had seen them through so many ups and downs with Abigail that they couldn't possibly have counted them all.

"Thank you," they said in unison before gathering the little girl they loved into their arms. The doctor could only nod and smile at them as she gazed, one last time, at the little girl who had truly experienced a miracle that would be spoken of at medical conferences for many years to come.

Chapter Forty-Six

"HMM," I HUMMED IN THE DIRECTION OF MY MOTHER, GAZING JUST PAST HER TO the balloon falling down from its place near the wall. "I don't know why," I started in frustration, moving past her to catch it for the third time, "this one won't stay where it's supposed to be!"

"Trish," started my mother, "it's just one balloon. There are enough of them up there. No one will notice. Just bust it and forget about it."

I grabbed at the stray blue balloon but then forgot it was in my hand as I turned to stare at her. "Do my ears deceive me, or is my perfectionist mother telling me to relax? About decorations, no less?"

This was very uncharacteristic, coming from one of the event-planners of the century. She looked at me and shrugged with a nonchalance I'd never seen before. I didn't have time to wonder further, however, because the doorbell rang, signalling the first of our party guests.

I looked at Theo and Charlie, both of whom were sitting in the living room, watching me struggle to get the balloon to stay next to the rest. Satisfied it might stay, I then glanced around quickly, looking for Kylie, who had become bored with keeping her brothers entertained and who, I suspected, had slipped away with Grant.

"You guys!" I yelled from the bottom of the stairs. "People are here!"

I heard Grant laugh at something I was sure Kylie had done, and I couldn't help smiling. He had such a soft spot for that girl, and she was at a hilarious age.

"Hello," I heard my mother greet someone at the door. When I watched her turn toward me, her face looked a little flushed. When I saw Jack walk in after her, I smiled.

"I brought the cake," mentioned Jack, more to my mother than to me. She took it from him before he walked in the direction of the boys.

I walked toward Jack and hugged him in welcome. "You know you don't have to ring the bell when you come here." He smiled at me and nodded.

The boys both tried their best to stand in the excitement of seeing their grandpa. Theo had taken a few steps, but Charlie still preferred crawling, which was fine with Grant and I. I followed my mother into the kitchen and asked about the cake, which I thought she'd planned to make.

"I've been so busy with the other two events this weekend, Trish, and Melissa has been more than a bit distracted with what seems like way too many medical tests for Abigail this week. I'm afraid they may not have the best news to share with us, actually, so let's not make the cake be a big thing."

I knew about Abigail. Trent and Melissa had called last week and told us that the doctors needed to run more extensive tests on their daughter, but they didn't say much else except that Abby had been doing better. Grant and I hadn't seen Trent, Melissa, or Abigail for months. Although we'd tried to make arrangements many times, between Grant's work demands, Trent's shifts, and Melissa's very demanding business, it just hadn't worked out. Grant and I had recently spoken about how to remedy that, but at least they'd be able to attend the celebration tonight.

"I'm sorry, but I just couldn't get the cake made, and Jack offered to pick this up. It's a lovely cake, Trish. The same baker who made your wedding cake made it. You'll love it, and so will the boys."

When she finally took a breath, I tried to get her to look at me.

"Okay," I stated.

My mother began working in the kitchen with a pent-up nervous energy I had never witnessed before. She was never too busy to make a cake, especially, one would think, for her grandsons, and now she looked unnerved as she worked. I thought about the conversation I'd had with Jack recently and smiled. My mother probably hadn't learned of that, and now she looked almost as if she was purposely evading speaking about anything regarding Jack. As I watched my mother, she lifted her head, as if in defiance of something, but then she smiled at me.

I could hear the front door open and heard the forthcoming "Hi," which made me close my mouth and stop the questions I wanted to ask.

"Saved by the bell," I said to my mother under my breath, moving toward the living room again.

Grant had reached the front door before me and slapped Joe on his back. "Hey! Where's Steph?" he asked, looking past his brother.

"She's coming in her car," Joe answered. "Should be here right away."

"Well, she's not working late. That I know," stated Grant, glancing at his watch.

"She said she just wanted to go back to her place after work and change or something," answered Joe with a shrug.

He caught my eye then and grinned as he took in all the blue decorations that filled the room. Coming close to me he whispered, "No unicorn puke this time, Trish," he whispered. "I'd say that's a step up, but … man! Is this blue!"

I slapped him on the arm and then hugged him hard. "Brat," I whispered back.

I smiled as I watched Joe talk to others in the room. Even Doug and Vi appeared to be more comfortable with him. The change in Joe had been nothing short of miraculous. His burden had definitely been lifted, and although he'd been through some tough things, working his way through the steps of the program he and Jack still attended, he'd changed by leaps and bounds from who he'd been.

Stephanie had called me recently to tell me that they had come to an understanding, but although I felt she was keeping other details to herself, she said she was at peace with how things stood between them. She had sounded almost excited as well, which made me feel more relief than I'd expected. It was good to know that at least they'd be more comfortable in the same room together, which would make it a whole lot easier for the rest of us when the family gathered.

I turned to go back to the kitchen when the doorbell rang again and Shauna, along with a few church friends, entered, laughing as they wished our boys a very happy birthday.

The noise level had grown as more people arrived, and my mother and a few friends who had come to help her began serving the appetizers. I thought it unusual when the clock told us it was after six, and Stephanie hadn't shown up. She was never late, and the one time she had been she'd texted her apology because she'd been in a fender-bender. As I looked at the clock and was just about to text her, I heard the front door open, and there she stood. As I stared at her, I suddenly couldn't remember the last time I'd been free of baby drool or spit-up. I looked down at the jeans and T-shirt I was sporting and then took a quick look around the room. Yep. Everyone else was dressed more like me—casual and comfortable. I guessed Stephanie hadn't gotten the memo. After all, this was a party in honour of one-year-olds.

Relieved to see no signs of baby vomit on my shirt, I looked toward the front door again. I couldn't help but smile as I saw her standing there. In fact, everyone in the room seemed to be smiling. Stephanie looked more stunning than I'd ever seen her, and as she entered our living room, it was if we were watching a runway fashion model. Everyone held their breath as she moved toward the twins to smile at them and wish them a happy birthday.

I took my eyes off my niece long enough to look at Grant, who wasn't watching her but was looking at his brother. If I hadn't known what the word gawking meant before, I certainly knew it then. As if struck by a suddenly brilliant idea at just that moment, Stephanie turned toward Joe. She smiled at him then, as if hiding a special secret. The room held an almost electric current as she neared him. Everyone in the room had stopped talking, not knowing what to expect but not wanting to miss a minute of the possible drama to come.

I couldn't blame Joe. Even I couldn't help but look at all of her. The dark green dress she wore was amazing, and suddenly I was even more proud of the beautiful red-head in it. Admittedly, I was a little envious of the heels, which I've never mastered, but I had to smile when she looked him square in the eye.

"Joseph Evans," she stated, as if staring him down, "I *do* want a big wedding."

My mouth gaped as my head whipped in Grant's direction, who looked to be in the same shock I'd been hit square in the eyes with.

Joe didn't look away but answered her in almost a low growl, "That's not what we agreed on."

Stephanie smiled. "Well, I hadn't thought it through then, and I see no ring on this finger, so I've decided something else." As she held up her left hand to wiggle her ring finger in front of his face, Joe broke into a grin while smoothly reaching into the pocket of his jeans, but as if thinking better of it, he looked at Jack. "This okay with you?"

Everyone's face moved to stare at Jack, who was standing near my mother at the entrance to our kitchen. When I saw his small smile and the quick nod, I suspected that this was not coming as a surprise to him at all. We all gasped as Joe fell to one knee and opened the small box, holding it up to the beautiful woman standing tall in front of him. It was then that the Stephanie I knew blushed and suddenly nodded, unable to speak.

Joe's face became serious as he looked up at her. "I guess I should really ask you—will you marry me, Stephanie? I want to belong to you, and I want you to belong to me, and I want us to belong to God together."

It was like the rest of us didn't exist in those few minutes. Trent and Melissa had come in at some point, and even Abigail was now staring at what was happening in our living room.

"I want that too, Joe," Stephanie answered with tears in her eyes.

Joe jumped up, put the ring on her finger, and gave her a quick kiss before pulling away and whooping. There was nothing more to do except cheer and congratulate them both.

• • •

The birthday party was a great success, even more so because no one had suffered any injuries. Near the end of the evening, after the boys had eaten what seemed like enormous amounts of cake and had gotten just as much, if not more, all over themselves and their highchairs, Grant and I came down the stairs after bathing them and putting them both to bed. Kylie and Abigail, being a bit older now, were having such a good time that we'd allowed them to stay up later. Most of the guests, except for our more immediate family, had gone, and although I saw the state of our home, I flopped myself on the couch beside Grant. Tomorrow was another day, and we'd clean it up then.

Knowing my mother was still busy in the kitchen, I spoke loudly from the living room. "Mom, come and relax. We'll clean it up tomorrow. You rocked this party, by the way."

Joe and Stephanie had sat down near us and were discussing possible wedding plans in what was growing into a near-argument.

"Seriously, Joe," Steph said, "there are two wedding planners in this family. Do you really think a small wedding is an option?"

"Hey," he reasoned, "they can still plan the wedding if they want to. It just doesn't have to be so big."

"You haven't even met nearly all my relatives, Joe. My parents will want to invite them."

"Can we talk about this when we're alone?" asked Joe, suddenly looking a little embarrassed by their discussion.

Stephanie glanced at the rest of us and then rested her eyes back on Joe. He seemed to melt a little as she smiled at him, and I guessed that we'd be planning whatever size wedding she wanted in no time.

"Grandpa says we can't have anymore cake," said Abigail suddenly, rounding the corner from the kitchen and running toward Trent and Melissa.

"I don't want cake," added Kylie to the conversation, "but Grandma says the kitchen's closed. What does that mean, Momma?"

My mother and Jack had come to join us, and my mother cleared her throat. I smiled, remembering my mother saying that to me when I was a young child who constantly wanted snacks.

"That means," I replied, letting her crawl into my lap, "that it's time for bed. You and Abigail should get your jammies on soon."

"Sleepover?" Kylie asked excitedly, unaware that her friend and her parents were staying for the night.

"Yes," I said, bopping her on the nose with my finger. She bopped me back and I smiled at the bright blue eyes that reminded me so much of Grant.

Trent and Melissa had been quiet during the evening, but I'd been too busy to really think about that until now. Abigail had climbed onto Trent's lap and was facing him. I couldn't help but stare at all three of them as Melissa smiled at her husband and their little girl. Trent looked at Melissa and then back to Abigail, and in those few moments it was as if the rest of us didn't exist. Abigail and Trent were playing patty-cake, and although a simple child's game, it suddenly seemed like so much ... more.

As I watched them, a dawning realization came over me. Abby was lifting both arms as if it took no effort. Something in a more distant memory suddenly came to me, and I couldn't help but hold my breath as the vivid scene played over in my mind, as if I was there again. We were in the cabin, and Trent had just taken Abigail from Sandy's side as she was thrown back in the last seizure she'd ever have. He had carried Abigail from the room, but in those fleeting few seconds before they were gone, Abby had smiled and ... waved. My mind raced and my heart beat faster as I tried to remember which hand she'd lifted. Right! It was the right one! The weak arm that had hung by her side, getting weaker as she grew, had lifted, and that small hand had waved at me!

My eyes shot to Trent, and as I stared in awe while he played a simple game of patty-cake with his daughter, I knew. Trent's eyes lifted to mine and he smiled. His small nod told me everything, and as we held on to that moment for only a fraction of time, my eyes filled and spilled over. Melissa, as if suddenly aware of all the people watching them, burst with the story they'd been waiting to tell us.

• • •

Later that evening after even more celebration and happy tears, Grant spoke. "Before our mom passed away," he started, looking directly at Joe, "she said some things that are clear to me now."

I placed my hand on his shoulder as he looked around the room at all of us.

"She told me that she believed this family would see miracles ... and it wasn't like she had some sort of gift that could see into the future or anything like that, but she was a woman with an incredible faith. Even when I doubted a lot of things, she always stood firm in her belief that God is good and has a plan for each of us."

Everyone nodded as we waited for Grant to continue. He cleared his throat and brushed the hair that had fallen over his forehead back with one hand before going forward in the telling of his time together with his mom just days before she'd left us. "She told me she would be healed, but she didn't think it would happen here—with us. And she was right about that. She did get her miracle, and although it hurts so much that she's gone from us, she is healed and happy and in such a better place." Grant looked down before taking a deep breath. When he looked up again, he smiled as he gazed around the room. "She believed miracles would happen, and she was absolutely right. Joe ... Abby ... and Jack."

As Grant looked at Jack, tears filled his own eyes. Everyone fell silent—even Kylie, who had gone to sit on my mother's lap, and Abigail, who had nestled into Trent, were watching Grant.

"I think my mom was wrong about you, Jack." Grant stared at him then.

Jack's expression was unreadable, but he adjusted his bandanna, and I wondered if he was as nervous as I'd become.

"My mom was worried that you'd doubt God after she died, but if anything, you've become stronger in your faith. Maybe more than any of us."

Jack's slow smile deepened the scar on his cheek as he quietly said, "Many things your mom told me will stay with me, Grant, but when I catch myself doubting, I come back to just one thing." He looked down at his lap but then continued after looking up again. "Jesus said He'd die and then come back to life. People can refute that all they want, but it's a fact, and all *my* sin died with Him." We were quiet as Jack looked around the room. "Sandy was right. Even after her diagnosis, she told me God had her life planned out perfectly." A sad smile came over his face before continuing. "I didn't get it then. I even got mad at her." His smile grew a little as he remembered. "But she got so angry back at me and said, in the way that held no room for argument, that if we belong to God, He knows the perfect plan, and we should just follow it." Now Jack's eyes teared as he raised his hand to the bandanna that needed no adjustment.

"She always told us that too," said Joe, looking at Jack and nodding. "It was just truth to her, and no one could say differently or you'd have a fight on your hands."

I looked at Grant, who was nodding and smiling as well. My eyes suddenly teared, remembering my mother-in-law and the many things she'd taught me. Grant took my hand as he looked toward me, but I wasn't looking at him. Instead, I gazed toward my mother, whose own tears fell down her cheeks. As I stared at the woman who had raised me, I saw only a person of great worth. She'd gone through so many struggles and freely admitted that she'd failed many times, but then came grace ... the same grace God has given me.

"I didn't know Sandy well, but I believe she was a woman of great faith," my mother whispered then. "I pray every day that I'll have that same faith."

I stood up and crossed the room to where my mother sat with Kylie. As I knelt close, I reached to embrace them in the warmest of hugs. In that brief, sweet moment a feeling that cannot be fully expressed in spoken or written word came over all of us. The closest word would be a complete and finite ... belonging.

Epilogue

JACK HELD THE TWO BOUQUETS OF FRAGRANT FLOWERS IN HIS HAND AND stood looking down at the gravesides he'd frequented many times. Stacy … his Stacy. A girl he'd never known was waiting for him somewhere in a place called heaven. Someday he'd join her there and then he'd get to know all about her. He turned his head to stare at the other headstone that lay not far away, and his heart hurt even more. No matter what, he had loved Sandy with all his being and knew that she also was dancing in heaven with Stacy and Trevor, the grandson none of them had known. His tears spilled over as he placed the flowers, thinking of the glorious day when they would all meet again.

He had walked a very broken road, but as he stood there thinking of God's faithfulness to him, he could only be thankful for what he'd been blessed with, through all of it. He'd often made poor choices, battled with himself and others, and relentlessly fought within his spirit, but still God had pulled at him. God still fought for him, and Jack was humbled by that and thankful that his Saviour had never and would never give him up. He belonged to Him, and in that belonging came completion, peace, and rest.

Jack read the verses again as he stared at Sandy's weathered gravestone. She had said them so often to him that he had them memorized too. They were truth, but when he was about to say them again, he heard her.

"Ready to go?" she asked quietly.

He hadn't realized she'd come alongside him until her hand was nestled within his. He turned to look at her then, his eyes shiny, and he nodded.

"Just saying goodbye," he whispered. "Are you done?"

She smiled up at him and nodded before staring silently at the resting places of the people she had never really known. She prayed silently then, somehow knowing that God had meant for it all to happen—just the way He had planned.

"It's getting cold," said Jack, hugging her. "We should go."

As they walked from the gravesides, both felt overwhelmed—not only by the unending goodness and faithfulness of their Father, but in a renewed feeling of belonging to Him and each other.

Trish's Last Thoughts

IT'S TRUE THAT WE'RE NOT MEANT TO KNOW WHAT WILL HAPPEN IN ALL THE days and seasons of our lives, although since I'm raising three small children, I wish I could look ahead some days and see if they survive my parenting—or if I survive them. Balancing our work and home life can, at times, be an overwhelming challenge. Some days it feels like, quite honestly, drudgery. But then I'll watch another baby come into the world, or it will be late at night and I'll peek in at our sleeping children, and I see the miracle all over again.

I have more peace when I remember that it is God who numbers my every moment. He knew me as I was being formed, and He knows me now. Many times I don't listen to His still, small voice, yet He remains good and forgives me, unconditionally, when I miss it. I can hardly wrap my mind around that. I'm not sure, in my human condition, that I fully understand unconditional love.

I think Grant is right. No human being can understand how deep His love is for us—because we're not God. We wouldn't give up our children for the sin of anyone else, never mind a whole world. Would we? Could we? Yet God did. He gave His only Son—for every one of us—proving He is faithful and loves us more than we can fathom.

I watch my mother and think of all the love she showed me, even when I didn't recognize it. She is the woman of substance I strive to be. Her quiet strength, through the many hardships she's experienced, remains. She doesn't deny the mistakes she's made, but that endears her to me even more because it proves that there's hope for me. I know ... I have too many feelings. She still reminds me about that at times, but then we smile at each other and know that we really aren't so different. I'm just louder.

I'm such a work in progress—every day. As I've told Grant many times, I fall short and then I feel so bad about it sometimes I'd like to just give up. Becoming a mother hasn't quelled the many feelings of guilt I have about everything, but the kids seem to forgive me, as little children seem to easily do. They know they belong to me and I to them, I suppose, and they feel safe in that belonging. I guess that explains God, really. If we take Him in, we belong to Him—no matter what.

Some days are easier, and it's in those days when the goodness of God seems completely obvious and true. There are many other days, however, when His goodness doesn't seem to be there at all, but I still know it must be because He promised He'd never leave me, and I know I belong to Him.

As I sit and ponder that, I think of Sandy's favourite verses. They are etched on her gravestone now, and because of that they also make me sad—but she wouldn't want that. She would cling to the promise in those verses and tell me to think only of that.

> *For none of us lives for ourselves alone, and none of us dies for ourselves alone. If we live, we live for the Lord; and if we die, we die for the Lord. So, whether we live or die, we belong to the Lord.* (Romans 14:7–8)

I hope that after reading a little about my life and the people in it—imperfect as we are—you too have accepted Jesus and know, beyond the shadow of a doubt, that you belong to Him!

The End

The Music of the Trilogy

SOMEONE OF SUBSTANCE

IT'S NO SECRET TO THOSE WHO KNOW ME THAT I LOVE MUSIC. I'M AN AVID FAN of many worship artists, and my radio is set to one Christian music station on Sirius XM: The Message. Sirius XM 63, you rock!

I mention several songs in this trilogy, which I'll list here with a personal note of how they've impacted my life. This is in no way an exhaustive list of the many songs (both hymns and other worship music) that lift me up when I'm down and give me great encouragement. There are many more that I've danced to in the kitchen and played and sung in church. This is just a little taste of a few …

FROM BOOK ONE—*The Goodness*

"He Knows," by Jeremy Camp. What an amazing blessing it is to know that Jesus walked this earth and knows everything we could possibly experience—the good, the bad, and all the ugly. What peace and encouragement I get from this!

"Something Beautiful," by the Newsboys. This joyous song makes me want to dance every time I hear it! It was also the song that our daughter Kaylee and her new husband, Ben, walked down the aisle to after they were announced "man and wife."

FROM BOOK TWO—*The Forgiveness*

"Slow Fade," by Casting Crowns. It's true: people don't crumble in just one day. It is, indeed, a slower fade, but in a world that's moving faster and faster, we need to guard our hearts more and more. This song hadn't been written yet when I experienced the danger of the fade, but it resounds with me on a very personal level.

"Fix My Eyes," by For King and Country. A song I've often sung when my mind is battling with anxiety and I become fixated on my struggles. After I get out of my own head and my narcissistic thoughts, I try to refocus on my Saviour and the mission He has for me on this earth. I fail often, but this song is a great reminder!

FROM BOOK THREE—*The Belonging*

"If We're Honest," by Francesca Battistelli. So often I've felt like a complete mess, but it's in the middle of those times that God has proven Himself to me even more. It's never fun—the valleys of pain and sorrow—but His mercy is on the other side *every* time.

"Mended," by Matthew West. I think we've all been here—when we feel so broken we think there's no coming back from it. But then God shows us His mercy even in our greatest devastation because He's not finished with us yet!

"Chainbreaker," by Zach Williams. This powerful song spoke to me the first time I heard it. Perhaps it means even more because of the testimony given by the artist who sings it, but I believe it doesn't matter who we are or what our personal experiences have been—we all have or have had chains. Only Jesus can truly break these and bring us out—saved and joyous on the other side. I praise God for being my chain breaker!

Special Acknowledgements

IN CASE I NEVER PUBLISH ANOTHER BOOK, I FEEL THE NEED TO ACKNOWLEDGE some very special people who have been a never-ending source of encouragement to me as I've travelled the road of my life thus far. Also, I am thankful to the people who have helped me with writing and publishing this trilogy—Someone of Substance. There aren't enough words in this language to express my thanks to these people …

Brian—best husband ever!

Jayda—our eldest child, who I think might be my biggest "fan." She also gave me the great idea for one of the twists in Book One, so she gets huge credit for that!

Kaylee and Troy—our other children, whose support and love through all my imperfection does not go unnoticed.

Matthew, Ben, and Joy—the other children I prayed for long before they were in our family. Thank you for being awesome spouses to our kids and great parents to our beautiful grandchildren!

At the time of this writing, we have ten grandchildren, whom we adore. Big breath and here goes (in order from oldest to youngest in each family): Dawson, Mikah, Sullivan and Saylor; Lincoln, Elisabeth, Casey and Judah; David and Ari. My heart is full with the love I have for each of you.

And a few more very special people …

Laura Wiley—your encouragement was amazing, and I'll never be able to thank you enough for everything you've done.

Laurel Teichroeb—you have no idea just how much our "theological" visits have meant to me. I learn something that I carry with me every time we get together. Please never stop studying and sharing your wisdom with me.

To Ariana at WAP—I like you for so many reasons, and I've never even met you. Thank you for communicating with me frequently and for keeping me organized.

To Kerry Wilson—the editor whose encouragement and enthusiasm for my writing has been overwhelming. Thank you from the bottom of my heart. I hope we can work together again very soon.

To Cindy Thompson—one of the most creative souls on earth. Thank you for making these three books look so great—inside and out.

Calvin Daniels—the editor who first published my meagre thoughts in the newspaper over twenty years ago. You gave me more hope than you'll ever know, and because of you, I could cross "get something published" off my bucket list!

Lindsey Kautz—the photographer who made me feel as at ease as someone who hates having her picture taken can feel. You are very gifted, and I'm so glad God brought you into my life.

To the many, many colleagues, friends, and family I've had the privilege of knowing and loving. I wish I could list all of you, but it truly would take up a book. This will have to suffice—THANK YOU for blessing me! God has shown His goodness to me by placing all of you in my life. May He bless you in every way!

Read the rest of the

Someone of Substance

series...

the Goodness
Someone of Substance
BOOK ONE
PD JANZEN

Is God truly good always and in all ways?

Trish is a nurse working in a busy Labour and Delivery unit in a large city hospital. One night shift will change her life forever, but will she see any of it as "good"?

Grant and Stacy have suffered loss before and now live in the hope that their dreams will come true. The arrival of their baby girl is an answer to their prayers, but the joyous celebration soon turns tragic.

An unexpected love, challenging family relationships, a mysterious relative, and other surprises infuse *The Goodness* as these families come to understand that sometimes "good" isn't always recognizable.

Readers will love this novel about the great and bountiful goodness of God—even when we don't see it.

the
Forgiveness
Someone of Substance
BOOK TWO
PD JANZEN

God can forgive anything, but can we truly forgive others and ourselves?

In the continuing story of Trish and Grant Evans, Helen's past catches up with her, and a poor decision threatens the future for her and those she loves. Stephanie is sure she made the right decision for her baby, but will that change when the father re-enters her life? Grant's dream about Stacy continues to haunt him. Will he be able to fulfill his promise to her?

When the past becomes the present and suddenly stands before them, will this family experience the power of forgiveness not only from God but for themselves and each other? Readers will be riveted as they watch the story, and God's grace, unfold on every page.